ii   •   Arthur J. Hughes

Crispus

Attucks

iv • *Arthur J. Hughes*

Crispus Attucks

By

Arthur J. Hughes, Ph.D

Lion & Lamb Press
Manhasset, New York

Copyright 2002

Arthur J. Hughes

ISBN 0-9678286-4-3

Dedicated

To

The "Six J's"

Acknowledgements

The author wishes to thank Jerome Hughes, Julie Hughes, Irene Hughes, Jennifer Plaisir, Patricia Deasey, Katherine Arena, Brian Galligan, Gina DaSilva, Allen Burdowski, Ali Moini, and Kathleen Di Trento for their help in the production of this work. The tombstone art is the work of Brian Johnson, to whom the author is most grateful.

This book is a work of fiction. Although the names of actual persons have been used, they only served to establish an environment for the story, which is all together a work of fiction.

The Remains of

CRISPVS ATTVCKS

Victim of the

Boston Massacre,

March 5th, 1770,

were here interred

by order of the

Town of Boston

Chapter 1

Minny's teeth ground stoically, rhythmically, in keeping with the fierce waves of child pang sweeping over her. As her body involuntarily twisted from the agony, the heavy quilt covering slipped off her shoulders. Her black hands quickly grasped the edge and pulled it back up to her chin. Her inborn dignity forbade the revelation of nakedness, even before her beloved mistress.

Under the quilt, the slave's nude body writhed at the peak of each now frequent labor pain. Lean and sleek from her farm duties, no trace of fat spoiled her mature body. Only the near bursting dome which housed her second child marred the beauty of her strong form.

No gasp, no complaint, no word. Only quick breaths taken almost slyly while her wide eyes sought strength from the frail farm wife sitting by her side.

The final pang forced an unasked cry from her: "Miz Brown!"

Mrs. Brown stood up quickly, grasping her dear slave's hand, trying to draw some of the agony into her own body.

"It's coming, Minny, coming, my dear."

It was time. She swept back the quilt but tried to avoid embarrassing her slave by looking away even as she pressed down upon the swollen belly.

A black head, draped in mucous sheath, pushed methodically out. Once free, the rest of the body rushed forth onto the bed. The mistress clipped the cord and deftly fixed the knot. She lifted the infant and slapped it sharply to life.

Minny raised her head dumbly to see that the baby was gone, then lay back panting, her body rising and falling in the ecstasy of pain relieved. She rolled slowly over to one side, rejoicing in the liberation of her body from its hardy passenger.

Holding the infant as tenderly as she had her own, Mrs. Brown brought it to a bureau and laid it on a clean cloth. She began wiping off the slimy afterbirth which clung to it. The bathing over, she wrapped the baby warmly and brought it back to her slave. Minny took the baby eagerly, then glanced at her mistress gratefully. For a moment, the two women were equal partners in the engineering of life, smiling at each other over their triumph.

Minny's body slowly relaxed as the mistress gently washed her.

Mrs. Brown pulled a dry blanket over her as she sank into an exhausted sleep.

Before leaving the one room hut, the mistress checked little Tom. The two year old slept peacefully in a rough hewn cradle under an open window. He was an ugly baby, she thought, one of the few really ugly ones she had ever seen. And it was not the blackness of his skin that made him so mean and plain looking. There was a puffiness about the eyes that gave young Tom a cruel appearance.

"Poor baby," she sighed in a low voice, "how will you grow up? Will you be a rogue like your father?" To herself, she said: I must not think such thoughts. He's just a baby. Turning to the bed where Minny and her new son slept, she added: Oh Minny, why do you do this? Why bring them into a life of bondage?

She left the hut, not prepared for the chill November air that swept over her. It was pleasant, though, bringing the cold odor of ripe apples from the orchard upwind. She pulled her homespun cloak about her and walked rapidly toward the cheery glow that burned from her own kitchen window.

The house looked stark and yet inviting against the cold fall moon. It was a good house, one of the few with two stories in Framingham. In design a salt box, its new clapboard siding was topped by a brightly shingled roof. It was the newest house in Framingham, too, she added to herself appreciatively. Only nine years old, built for her by her husband in 1711.

Anna Brown thought of her husband as she glided across the slate stones he had put down to make a walk way for her. He was a good man, even if a bit hard and not given to much piety, she thought. He gave me six children in our nine years together, she mused, and it was no fault of his that only the boy and girl lived. The Lord often gave many more than that before he let you keep one. Why, Susan Wall buried eleven before her house heard a child's footsteps.

The warm kitchen reached out to her as soon as she swung open the door. Its bright glow momentarily washed the moonlight off the porch. Her husband, seated at his corner near the huge open fireplace, made no sign of recognition. Stiff and stocky on a bare wooden bench, his dour face contorted with the effort to drive an awl through badly tanned leather.

Anna Brown came and stood next to him in front of the fire, warming her hands. For the first time in many hours she felt the pangs of hunger as the smell from the kettle dangling over the fire wafted up to her. She dipped a wooden spoon into the stew and tasted the strong venison flavor. He must have liked it, she thought, he ate near half the kettle-full.

Brown now made as if to notice her. "Woman, you're here at last. I thought you'd spend the night and the next morning midwifing and ruin another day. There'll be no work done around here as it is. No wood for the fire, the stew half-scorched, it's been near two days you were there 'till I heard an infant wail. What did the black wench drop this time?"

"A likely lad." Mrs. Brown replied calmly, sipping another spoonful of venison stew.

"Agh! Another mouth to labor for and feed." Brown pushed harder at the leather, skimming the awl through. "Why does that wench do this to me? I bought her for a kindness and now she whelps little ones for any stranger in Middlesex County."

Anna Brown's mild face sharpened, her Puritanism stiffening voice and body. "Minny was duly wed to both her husbands. The marriages are on record at the parsonage as you well know."

"It's not right, that's all. First Walter, then Attucks, and now both gone."

"'Twas you who wounded Amos Walter mortally, as I recall," Mrs. Brown said, watching her husband carefully. She knew the pattern of their disputes. He had but one lunge in him, if he failed to carry the field at once, he never regained the offensive. And she had long ago learned to parry that first onslaught, sometimes quite formidable, and then follow through with a series of short but sharp attacks until he crept humiliated from the lists.

"Amos Walter was faithless," Brown answered, strongly defensive, "running away as he did. He turned on me as I pursued him. I had to use my piece."

"Yes, he was as faithless as John Attucks was faithful. He died not six months ago, pulling you free from the slag you'd fallen under."

Brown put away his awl and leather. "Well, those young ones are still trouble for years to come." As he slammed shut the drawer of his rough board bench he added vehemently: "And by God I'll make one of them a cordwainer and never touch an awl again!"

"There will be no calling upon the Almighty in this house except for mercy, Mr. Brown," Anna Brown scolded him. "And I'll hold you to the promise you made Minny the night poor John Attucks died. The boy born today goes free at his majority."

"I make no promises lightly, woman. I'll honor my word. Come to bed."

xxxxxx

Crispus cried in horror: "You killed him, you killed my frog!"

The frog tried to creep away on its one remaining leg. Out of the stump of the other its life juices dribbled slowly upon the gravel.

Big Tom stood defiantly, a rough stone knife in one hand and the dripping leg in the other. Crispus still shouted.

"You shouldn'ta killed him! Why'd you do it, you Tom Walter?" Crispus clenched his fists with all the strength ten years could muster.

Tom answered angrily: "You shouldn'ta brang him in the house. I told ya what I'd do. You shouldn'ta brang him."

"I'm the eldest," Tom said, holding his two more years of life over his half-brother's head. "You gotta mind me, 'cause I'm almost a man."

Crispus sized him up as he had a dozen times before. Not small himself, he was no match for Tom, who at twelve was four inches shy of six feet tall and weighed over 150 pounds. Crispus' body remembered the aches of earlier encounters, but he stiffened himself with a last look at the expiring frog and dove head first at Tom's midsection.

Inside the house, Brown and a visitor watched idly at the window.

"Two likely boys you've got there, P. B.," the neighbor remarked. Along with everyone else in Framingham, he used Brown's initials only, since the farmer was sensitive of his Christian names. An older relative had prevailed upon his parents to name him Praisegod Barebones Brown, after a minor figure in the Cromwell era.

"Yes, they'd bring a good few shillings at Boston or Newport in a few years, I calculate," Brown replied.

"Or you could 'prentice them out right now, for that matter," the neighbor said, adding: "I'd take one off your hands."

"No, I'll find a use for them right here. We're shorthanded as it is." He turned to his neighbor and added: "I swore the night that little one out there was born, I'd make a shoemaker out of one of them."

The visitor smiled. "If you don't stop that, neither of them will be fit to shell nuts."

The boys rolled in the summer dust, punching and kicking ferociously. No matter where he began, Crispus invariably wound up on the bottom, his blows bouncing off Tom's hardy body with little effect. Tom, meanwhile, rained a storm of fists on Crispus' slighter body, numbing every part they struck.

"No need," Brown observed laconically, "watch that cabin."

In a moment, a black figure bounded out of the slave hut, skirts flying, a heavy stick in her hand. Minny caught Tom's collar with her left hand and switched his back a dozen times. Finally, he broke away, running at a limp toward the open fields.

Crispus lay in the dust, his chest heaving, the dirt-caked tears and sweat mingling with some blood from his nose to make him seem more damaged than he was. Minny pulled him up gruffly, dragging him over to a bucket for a good dousing.

Brown looked at his guest: "Rum, Edwin?" he asked quietly, his ears attentive for the approach of his wife.

"A drop, P. B., for the liver, thank you."

Brown removed the small jug from its hiding place and they drank.

xxxxxx

The greatest building in Crispus' memory was the tall white church he attended all his life. As an infant he had frolicked alongside Mrs. Brown, occasionally but only rarely hushed into silence by her indulgent shushes. Prayer time had always been a glad time for him. A buggy ride over exciting country roads, a few minutes of restless and noisy playing in the pew, a delightful nap brought on by the droning words of the minister, and then the return along the adventurous road filled with chipmunks, skunks, rabbits, and deer. As he grew older, Crispus could no longer sleep nestled on Mrs. Brown's sturdy grey cloak. He remained awake to hear the minister's sermon so that he might be able to answer his mistress' questions on the way home. He had also been charged by her with the task of setting a good example for Hettie and Paulie so that they might learn to behave in church, too.

As a boy, Crispus liked to walk up the church's wide staircase. In his heart he felt the quickening that all who came to Christ did. And his body enjoyed the coolness flowing through the open double doors. His feet liked the give of the stairs as he mounted them. In his innocence, he was only barely aware that there was some question whether he - or any person of color - might be allowed to enter church by the main doors or be permitted to sit with the white congregation.

A furious controversy had arisen among the Godly folk of the parish. Nor was it simply a question of there being only two sides. The struggle produced all the splinters of a newly sided house. Some believed coloreds should enter by the side door, then sit with the entire congregation. Some allowed for entrance through the center aisle doors but preferred an African corner to which the colored folk could be routed. A fragment of this faction agreed in all details but called the retreat a nigger pew.

Some held out for no restrictions as of yore, a few chose total exclusion. Some wondered what the furor was all about over segregation. They saw the white faithful divided by sex and wealth and position in society; they knew that even the graveyard was segregated, why not break down the congregation by color, too?

Crispus paid no attention to the controversy, since he had not yet learned that he was not white. In all particulars save his hut, he was one with Paulie and Hettie. Mrs. Brown was as discriminating as Almighty God in her love for all her fellow humans.

Brown worked his family and servants harshly, squeezing from them all the juices he needed to make his farm run smoothly. In this, however, he was no more the driver than any other pioneer New England man. And he was no less demanding of himself than he was of those he governed.

But Sunday was the one day ruled by Mrs. Brown. She it was who brought the family to church and she it was who forbade all but the most indispensable work on the Lord's day.

In the leisure time of the Sabbath, she held Dame school for Paulie, Hettie, and Crispus. The other servants around the place, including Crispus' half-brother Tom Walter, were considered unteachable. She had tried with them, offering sweets and gentle promises, but her soft urgings were unheeded by servants unused to persuasion and accustomed to peremptory decrees. The uneducated went their own way, obeying orders when under observation, and scrupulously adhering to the Browns' moral standards only when to do otherwise would invite a flogging.

The dozen servants on the place were a mixed lot. Two were older blacks brought directly from Africa by Newport slave traders. Both limped and had therefore been refused by the more selective Carolina and Caribbean buyers. Brown had bought them for a fine low sum from a cattle dealer about to retire. The pair knew something of stock raising and were not reluctant to share their knowledge with Crispus, whom they came to accept because of his unpretentious nature and innocent eagerness to learn.

Six Indian women and girls served the Browns also. Captured on raids or bought by Brown over the years, they did domestic tasks stolidly and unimaginatively, offering no clue as to their true feelings either to other servants or masters. Perhaps some were remembering the brutality of Brown and his fellow militiamen on their retaliatory expeditions against the Indians. The stench of gunpowder and blood and sweated bodies and death lasted longer in the nostrils of the defeated than the victorious.

Only one Indian - a young girl named Nora - manifested any willingness to recognize the world she lived in and the residents whose lives she shared.

Rounding out the complement of servants were two young Rhinelanders, indentured servants purchased by Brown for five pounds a head from a Boston shipmaster. They were dull, moonfaced fellows, somewhat bewildered by their surroundings. No one could ascertain whether they had left Antwerp voluntarily or whether they had suffered from the talents of one of the many spirits or soul-sellers who abounded in every port.

Brown cared not at all. He had them for the maximum of seven years and intended to use them to the fullest. Best for him, too, their Articles of Indenture neither required him to teach them a special skill nor restrained him from putting them to work in any way not sinful. Brown used his Rhinelanders mercilessly, holding back Crispus, Tom, and the two Africans for fear of injuring them.

The Rhinelanders were expendable rentals, the blacks were a permanent investment.

The only time the Rhinelanders showed their character was in the matter of religion. Devout Anabaptists, they resisted all Mrs. Brown's efforts to sway them from their grasp of Bible truth. They even resisted learning English, fearful that the use of this tongue might somehow corrupt their traditional faith.

Their fears were justified. The school Mrs. Brown held for her three willing charges was created for religious purposes and operated through religious mechanics. Hettie and Paulie and Crispus learned their alphabet from the New England *Primer*, which spooned Scripture into their minds with every letter:

A   "In Adam's Sin, we sinned All."

H   "Heaven to Find, the Bible Mind."

What history they studied was essentially Bible history or the recent history of the triumph of the True Faith over popery (and the popish practices of Stuart despots) in England.

In the seventeenth century, men had sold their souls for peace.

They bargained away their many "true faiths" to win a truce which allowed the local ruler to impose his sect's tenets upon them. This opportunistic system had nothing to recommend it except its common sense success. It replaced fanatical religious persecution with ordinarily nonviolent bigotry and discrimination.

The eighteenth century inherited this condition and, with no soul to sell, had to offer what remained - its body. Traffic in human slavery became the rule. It was permanent or temporary, female or male, child or adult, involuntary or freely entered into. Its geographical spread carried it from the fields of Portugal, where blacks labored for their relatively tolerant masters to cold New England, where Indians, Africans, and whites faced stern wind and whip with equal terror. On Brown's farm, as on hundreds of others, the only bond of unity was the knowledge that the sweat of three continents salted the poor soil of Massachusetts.

xxxxxx

Tom lounged in front of Crispus' bench and beseeched him: "Lemme have two shillin', Crispus. C'mon, lemme have it. You got the money, I know you has."

"Every time you get into the cider still you got to have money," Crispus said, "an' it's always me. I got leather to skive if ever I'm to get these shoes started. Didn't I give you a shillin' last week?"

"I know, Crispus, I know," Tom begged, "but I need two now, I really do. There's a gal over at the Barret's - Lottie - you seen her. An' she tol' me if I brang over some rum...."

"No," Crispus answered firmly, "no more. Missus give you wages."

Tom's face grew angry: "An' don't you get wages? Don't you? You knows you gets more than I do."

"Don't start that all over again. You know what I get. Mr. Brown pay me half of what he used to give the journeyman when he come by to make the shoes."

"Yeah, you get four shillin' a week for sittin' on your rear all day in this cool room and I gets half a' that for totin' hay from sunup to sunset."

Crispus wiped his knife on his leather trousers and replaced it in its compartment at the end of his work bench. He sighed: "You coulda' been the cordwainer, Tom, you know that. Mr. Brown let you pick first since you the eldest."

"That don't matter nothin'," Tom said fiercely, "I want two shillin' now or I'll go to your box and get it if I have to!"

Crispus' eyes narrowed. He slid his hand across the bench and grasped a heavy rasp. Standing slowly, his muscular frame reached two inches above six feet, yet Tom still towered over him.

"Tom Walter, you touch my box I'll break your head. Nobody touches my freedom money."

Tom saw the meaning in his eyes. He broke into a mischievous smile. "Don't go on like that, little brother. I wouldn't do that ta you. I know you're countin' on that money to take you 'way from here."

The obsequious tone changed to one of friendly familiarity. "An' by the way, how long 'til you be free?"

Crispus sat down and scanned the beam just inside the door. On it were rows of neat marks made in his own code to count the days until his twenty-first birthday. "I got six months and ten days to go."

"Wher'ya goin' then, Crispus?" Tom continued pleasantly.

"Mr. Brown says I can stay on here for regular journeyman's wages, but maybe I won't. Maybe I'll go over to Boston or even to Lynn to get me a job."

"Lynn? Where's Lynn? Is it farer than Boston?"

"About ten miles east a' Boston," Crispus said. "And there's men there make shoes real good. I could learn a lot from them."

"You're a good boy, Crispus, always was," Tom said, somewhat sadly. "You'll go free in six months and ten days and poor Tom will be here 'til they plant him, totin' hay all the time."

"Mr. Brown will free you. I heard him promise you'd go free on his death bed."

"With my luck," Tom said, "he'll fall off his horse and die right off. Who am I goin' ta tell then? Think Paulie and Hettie would let me go? They'd sell me to the Indians in a minute, they hate me so."

"Well, you been awful mean to them, Tom, you know that. You linger in the loft and Paulie has to do all the hayin' or Hettie send you for somethin' and you just curl up somewhere sleepin'. You gotta work to be noticed, Tom, you gotta work."

"I know, Crispus, I know. An' I will from now on."

Crispus searched his half-brother's eyes, looking for any glimmer of sincerity. As he did, he felt in his pocket for the two coins he had gotten that day for finishing a pair of boots for Mrs. Brown.

"Here, Tom, take it, it's yours."

"Thank you, Crispus, thank you."

"Mind you don't get caught after nine o'clock."

"Don't fear, Crispus, my back still aches from the ten kisses I got from the cat last month."

Crispus smiled sadly at the departing figure. Tom had more than his share of misery, he thought. He deserved something.

Before Crispus could think much further, his reverie was interrupted by the appearance of lithe-footed Nora. Nora had been captured as a little girl by Brown on a short raid undertaken during the late 1720's. She was now nearly a full-grown woman, small, it was true, but possessed of fine breeding hips which spoke of a houseful of children.

Indians did not breed well in captivity, though, so Brown never bothered to seek bucks to service his Indian females. Besides, Mrs. Brown insisted on treating the Indians and especially Nora as servants, not slaves, a concept Brown resented mightily.

Nora, on a farm errand, came deliberately close to Crispus' shop. He kept skiving energetically but watched carefully for an opening to speak to her. The almond-skinned girl held a broad berry basket on her hip, a thin but shapely arm resting lightly on its outer edge. Nora's long lashes gave her at once an allure and a reserve which distinguished her throughout Framingham for beauty.

Crispus stopped working as she came near his open door.

"Mornin' Nora," he called gently.

With a blush and a smile the girl returned his greeting. Crispus was grateful she'd stopped. Now, if only he could think of something to say.

Yes, that was it. Nora's lessons!

"How your lessons comin'?" he asked.

The girl looked surprised. "You know 'bout them?"

"Don't worry, you won't get into no trouble. Mrs. Brown told me. I take lessons, too. And Mr. Brown knows all about it."

Nora looked sideways at the big house. "If Mr. Brown knew about me, I'd be hided, mos' prob'ly."

"Not if Mrs. Brown was there," Crispus answered proudly. "She's always been a mos' kind lady. Like a mother, even, or a' aunt. She saw me born before anyone else, even my own Momma."

Nora watched the big black hands idly run a rasp across the leather. The sleeves of his red woolen shirt were rolled up to the elbow, revealing blackly glistening forearms with veins standing out so powerfully the blood seemed ready to burst from them. Nora wondered briefly - only for a moment - what it would be like to be inside those arms, crushed by their pulsing vigor. She admired the black man's lightly colored deerskin breeches, surprisingly neat and clean, perhaps because of the leather apron he always wore.

"You been learnin' from Mrs. Brown for a long time, haven't you?" Nora asked.

"Oh, yes," Crispus answered glowingly, "why, I been her prize pupil for years, she told me so herself. I read the whole Bible three times with her and the last time hardly needed any help at all."

Nora's eyes glowed as she watched Crispus' animation.

Somewhat abashed for running on, Crispus suddenly stopped, then asked: "How long you been studyin' Scripture?"

"Oh, only a week or so," the girl answered, "but I want to learn all I can."

"That's good," Crispus said, looking at her affectionately. She returned the gaze, then both became aware of themselves and turned away.

"Well, goodbye, Crispus."

"Goodbye, Nora," he said gently.

He watched the form glide on, then dreamed again a dream he dreamed often. He would gain his freedom and ask Mrs. Brown for the right to marry Nora. Mrs. Brown would agree and things would go as he planned. They would move to Boston or Lynn and he would alternate between farming and cordwaining. Sitting back at his bench, he watched the afternoon shadows lengthening across the well-tended farm. The odors of fowl, horses, sheep, and cattle mingled with scents of cured leather and took hold of his consciousness. Crispus breathed deeply. These smelled good. There was an innocent rankness about the smells of the farm, a kind of pure fertility.

xxxxxx

The black-garbed parson clucked to his horse and the small rig rattled out of the big yard. Crispus watched it form the tail of a procession of wagons, rigs, and single riders drawing away from the somber farmhouse.

It's over, he thought, poor Mrs. Brown is buried. And on my freedom day. There's no jubilee for me. She nursed me and Tom through many a winter and stood by Momma 'till the end two years ago. Glancing at the big house, Crispus turned away and headed toward his hut. I won't go up there today, he thought.

As he crossed the yard in the twilight, he heard Hettie call him.

"Crispus. Crispus, my father wants to see you."

Crispus turned back toward the house, his body struggling to hold down the mound of joy that began to form within him.

Hettie ushered him into the keeping room where Mr. Brown sat, head upon his hands. Crispus had never been in this room before, although his mother had once described its marvels to him. It was everything she had said it was. A long buffet loaded with the remnants of the mourning feast stretched along one wall, On it was the wreckage of a side of venison and the fat hog Tom had butchered for the occasion. A china closet stood against another wall, fronted by the largest piece of glass he had ever seen and housing a few lonely pieces of delicate china, the pride of the mistress. The room was dominated by an ornately carved mantelpiece over a huge fireplace. The opulence brought Crispus back to his master, who was staring at him sternly.

"Crispus, you were supposed to go free today."

"Yessir, I know, but I can wait. I know how sorrowed you are."

"Crispus, you're my slave. I raised you and taught you a trade. You can't go, you can't leave now."

"I can wait, Mr. Brown, I can wait," Crispus said, not understanding.

"No, Crispus, I mean you're my slave, my bondsman for life."

A numbness crept over the slave, giving him a floating sensation, a sense of disbelief. "But Master, you always said...."

"I know, I know, but that was to please your mistress. I never wrote down anything, did I?" Brown said the words fiercely, hoping they would end the argument.

Crispus had no cunning: "Well, no...but I... thought...Mistress always said...."

"That's all there is to it. You'll stay here and serve me 'til I let you go. Maybe in a year, two years, we'll talk again."

Still unbelieving, Crispus asked: "My freedom day, today's my freedom day, Mr. Brown." Crispus felt numb.

"Crispus, no more. Go back to your house and let me be."

Crispus reached the kitchen in a daze, noticing nothing until he felt a tug at his sleeve. He turned to see Hettie's tear-stained face looking up at him.

"Paw don't mean what he says, Crispus," she whispered. "He wouldn't, he couldn't do that. He's a good man. Wait a few days, I'm sure he'll recollect himself by then."

Crispus looked at the small figure before him, saddened further by her sorrow: "I'll wait, Missy, I'll wait."

Crispus waited a month, two months, doing his best work and still marking off the days on the beam over his bench. The summer trailed off into early fall and Indian summer came to Massachusetts. The wind from the east seemed freer than ever before, every breeze bringing him the message of freedom, of Boston, or of Lynn. There were many blacks in Boston, he knew. Almost one in ten were African in that great metropolis of 12,000. And many were craftsmen like himself, though most toted or dug for a living.

More than ever now he read the faded Bible Mrs. Brown had given him years before. He thought often of the hours she had sat with him, patiently helping him spell out the words. He was the only literate black on the farm and Mrs. Brown used often to remark that he read better than Paulie.

As he lay down in the hut he shared with Tom, the same one he had been born in, he fingered the worn pages of the King James version. He had always wondered who that king was, since he appeared nowhere else but on the title page of the book. He would never know, now, since there was no Mrs. Brown to ask.

Crispus turned to the Epistles of Paul. That was her favorite, he remembered, so much so, she had named her only living son for the Gentiles' Apostle. As he reached the letter to the Corinthians, he spied: "Let every man remain in the calling in which he was called. Wast thou a slave when called? Let it not trouble thee."

But how can I not let it trouble me, Lord, Crispus asked, when all I think of is my freedom? Sliding down to his knees, Crispus prayed for freedom. For freedom or strength, Lord, whichever you got to give. He prayed all the prayers he knew, bending over the rough bed with its thick quilt mattress. The fire burned low, only rarely casting a warm ray across the room.

A calmness came to him, and a need to rest. He lay down again and leafed idly through a few more pages, pausing at Galatians: "Stand fast, and do not be caught again under the yoke of slavery."

"That means me, Lord, right?" Crispus asked aloud. "He freed me once and can't go back on his word. It's all here in the book." He placed the book reverently on the window sill over his bed and lay back, excited yet relaxed, waiting for the early rays of morning.

"Good morning, Crispus," Hettie said shyly. The shame she felt for her father's actions had colored her dealings with Crispus. "Paw's not here, you know, he left early this morning for Natick to see about some stock."

"Missy," Crispus said quietly, "I gotta see him. I can't wait no more for my freedom."

"Just a little while, Crispus, only a little while. You can't run away now. It would spoil everything. Wait here a minute, I have something to show you."

Hettie ran back into the house and returned with the huge family Bible. She quickly found the blank pages which formed the diary for the family.

"Look, Crispus, read this."

On a page all by itself was a faded entry in Mrs. Brown's hand:

"This day was born to my bond servant Minny a son, Crispus Attucks, whom I pledge myself to free in 21 years or on my death, whichever comes first. May the Lord bear witness to this promise. Anna Brown"

"You're free, Crispus don't you see? Free! I'm going to show it to my father as soon as he returns and I know he'll let you go."

Crispus left the porch in triumph, thinking to himself : "Stand fast, and do not be caught again under the yoke of slavery."

Brown angrily slammed his hand down on the open book.

"What did you show him for, you mad woman. Am I not in enough trouble without you making more for me? Crispus is my best hand, he is worth more to me than any two others on this farm, including you and Paulie. The crops are blighted, the orchard has been wrecked by worms. Crispus is the only thing that I have around here that works. I'm going to let him out to the other farmers. His work is so good, I could get ten times what I'm paying him."

"But Momma promised, and even wrote it down. Doesn't that mean anything, Paw?" Paulie asked.

"You quiet down, Paulie," the father growled. "You got any idea what your Maw's funeral cost me, with the gloves and the scarves, and food and parson's fees?"

He looked out the back window at the row of small huts which made up the slave quarter. "It's just trouble, that's all. But I don't care, Crispus is mine and mine he'll stay as long as I need him." He returned to the table and tore the page out of the Bible. "This page means nothing. Minny was your Mother's, but Crispus is mine!"

He strode over to the fire and threw the crumpled paper in.

"There, he's mine and there's no argument about it." Brown stamped from the room, leaving his children looking at each other in confusion.

"It's not right," Hettie said, "and I'm going to do something about it. "

"What can you do?" Paulie asked.

"I'm going to help Crispus get away."

"I want to help, too, " Paulie said enthusiastically.

"No, you're too young. I can take a whipping better than you if Paw catches me. You can stay here and keep watch. I'll call out if I need you."

A few minutes later, Hettie stole out of the kitchen armed with a sack of food and some coins she had saved. Clad only in a nightgown and a flimsy wrapper, she glided quickly across the dark yard.

She entered the unfamiliar hut and moved quietly up to the nearest bed trying to recognize the sleeping form. Bending over, she shook the black shoulder.

Tom Walter stirred: "There ya' be, Lottie, you're a mite late, but welcome all the same." He pulled the girl down toward him.

"Wait! Wait!" she cried.

"Don't make me wait, Lottie," Tom said gruffly, pulling her closer.

Crispus stirred himself awake and sat up. "What's goin' on, Tom?"

Hettie struggled to free herself: "Crispus! It's Hettie, help me!"

Crispus flew across the dark room and tore the girl from Tom's grasp. Tom sat up, frozen with fright: "I didn't do nothin', I didn't mean...!" Crispus' fist crashed into his face, spinning him out of bed. He dove after him and landed a knee in the big man's abdomen.

Hettie continued to scream with fright until the yard was alive with people, slaves and free farm hands roused from their beds. The stirrings reached the big house, where a candle came on.

Tom struggled up, clawing Crispus away. He crashed a blow into Crispus' face which knocked him back onto the bed. In two bounds, Tom reached Crispus' bunk, snatched a small metal box from the shelf over it, then dove head first through the window.

When Crispus recovered form his daze, he saw a ring of candles around him, illuminating suspicious faces. Hettie still cowered on her knees near the bed.

"You! " Brown cried, stepping forward. "You ungrateful black swine." He held a heavy musket in his hand which he had not been able to load. He swung the stock around and smashed it into Crispus' face. Again and again he brought the butt down until Crispus lay moaning on the earthen floor, tangled masses of his flesh and cartilage soaking with blood beside him.

Chapter 2

Paulie stood flat-footed in the great flagstone kitchen of Brown's home. His jaw jutted firmly toward his father, eyes angry and piercing. Brown sat, slack-faced and moody, appearing indifferent to the young man's outrage. Outside, dusk settled without warning on the farm, blanketing it like a dark cloak. There was no moon.

"You will call Doctor Freidland," Paulie said, putting as much menacing feeling into the statement as he could.

"Costs good money for that," Brown replied laconically, shifting his weight on the kitchen bench. He sniffed defensively.

"Crispus will die if you don't," Paulie said, his fists clenched.

"He's a strong nigger and he's hardly hurt," Brown answered.

Both father and son stopped, listening to light footsteps on the gravel outside. The wooden latch lifted and Hettie entered, her face pinched and white with worry. Blood and other matter stained her apron. Her hands shook as she wiped them, almost wringing them as she slumped onto a bench. The fire leaped higher in the great hearth place, stirred by the cool wind Hettie brought with her.

Her whole body sagged with fatigue. Paulie crossed to the fire, where a cauldron simmered. He dipped a ladle into the thick liquid and brought out a rich brothy stew, pouring it carefully into a bowl. Hettie took it gratefully and spooned a little. The kitchen was quiet but tense.

The nourishment took effect and satisfied her hunger and exhaustion, bringing Hettie back to her principal problem.

"He needs help," she said to her father.

"No physician," Brown answered flatly. "Miz Brown had none when she came ill. Use her book."

Hettie and Paulie looked at each other. Her book! They brought a candle to the keeping room to the little desk Mrs. Brown had always used for her treasures. A horn bound book still rested undisturbed since her death. They returned to the kitchen's warmth, turning the faded pages carefully lest they tear against the string hinge.

"Here," said Paulie, pointing a finger at a carefully written page headed "Injuries." There followed descriptions of poultices, emetics and other nostrums, as well as directions for bloodletting. Much of it had been copied from sources they were unaware of, but a great deal of Mrs. Brown's lore came from her experience in a large farm household.

"We must be Crispus' doctors," Hettie said. "He's so hurt that he's fevered. Three teeth are broken and bleeding around the gums. His eyes are swollen closed and his cheek bone is broken."

Following the book's directions, they gathered the necessary tools and ingredients together and brought them to the rude hut Crispus lay in. Nora sat by his pallet, her rosy features gilded by the light from the meager fire. Crispus seemed shrunken as he lay under a faded ragged quilt.

Nora's eyes widened in hope as Hettie and Paulie came in, laying out their simple medical gear. Hettie mixed a poultice of bran mash. While it set, she washed the wounds out with a wet piece of flannel. When the wounds were clean, she applied the poultice to Crispus' broken face, covering the affected parts with wet flannel.

"We should bleed him and take out those broken teeth," Hettie said firmly. Paulie's face paled.

"I can't do it," he said.

Nora broke her silence for the first time since the attack a few hours previously. "You must do it," she said quietly.

Paulie reflected in desperation. He had all the farm boy's familiarity with knives and other deadly tools. He had gelded horses, butchered oxen and hogs and, of course, was as adept at killing and cleaning chickens and other fowl as anyone on the farm. But he had never cut or touched human flesh. But then, he remembered, he had once removed an abscessed tooth from an old plow horse.

He looked at Crispus, thinking of the many happy hours he had spent in the little cordwainer's shop Crispus had.

"I'll do it," he said, to the obvious relief of the women.

What the operation needed was an extractor specially made for the removal of teeth; but such an instrument, shaped like a corkscrew with a hook on its end, would only be found in a surgeon's kit. The Brown farm had hundreds of tools, though, and a brief search in the barn uncovered a similar implement.

As Hettie and Nora held the half conscious man's shoulders, Paulie did his bloody duty, his wiry hands and arms, strengthened by years of farm work, twisting the broken teeth from the front and side of Crispus' mouth.

Two teeth had been so badly cracked by Brown's blows that they broke as Paulie tried to twist them out. He had to probe for fragments, causing Crispus indescribable agony. While Paulie worked on the second tooth, Crispus gave a deep sob and passed out. This made the rest of the ministrations go easier, relieving the three of the tension they felt over his pain.

Crispus bled profusely, making it unnecessary to bleed him formally. The extractions would reduce fever, they believed, and the bleeding would cleanse the wounds.

Crispus slept.

Nora kept watch over him for five nights, sleeping upright in a hard chair and waking to any change in Crispus' breathing. Her vigil did not exempt her from the heavy duties Brown imposed upon her and all the other hands. Nora could rarely escape notice anywhere on the farm. A delicate beauty dressed her features. Her carriage, attained by nature and not by rote, caught every eye as she passed barn, house or hut. Her disposition was as gentle as her beauty was fair. Before the death of Mrs. Brown she had learned to read the scriptures and had become a devout Christian. Conversion marked her out for the mistress' special protection and this, plus the girl's natural restraint, kept her from the promiscuity associated with the other servant men and women. The men left her alone because they knew of Crispus' interest in her. Years before, the Rhinelanders had tried to force themselves on her while in their cups but had teen terribly beaten by Crispus in fair fights and had never crossed him after. They were long gone now, having served their terms and been replaced by a succession of four and seven year indentured men. Brown could have had convicts for a full fourteen years but though it might be more economical, a slit throat would not compensate for the extra advantage.

Tom Walter had paid little attention to Nora, his tastes running to a grosser strain of person.

The mating of black men and Indian women was characteristic of colonial America because of the simple facts that black women were a minority in the slave trade and Indian men were killed in wars.

xxxxxx

Weeks passed and Crispus mended. His spirit was greatly tried by Brown's cruelty but he also recalled the generosity of Mrs. Brown's children. And Nora's kindness drove his feelings for her even deeper into his consciousness. Yet, thought of Nora only gave Crispus anguish. He had not yet examined his face but knew he was hideously disfigured. A long ugly scar rode a crooked path from under his eye to the left side of his upper lip, pulling the lip upward in a permanent sneer which gave him a frighteningly sinister appearance. When he tried to smile, the gaps in his mouth, added to the crooked lip, were clearly repulsive.

Crispus had not prepared himself for this. Like most men, he had taken his normal looks for granted, being neither especially proud nor humbled by them. His face was his, he kept it washed and shaved and thought no more of it. Now his looks were a great barrier between himself and the beautiful creature he loved. How could she have him, he thought, when he was so disgusting? When he had awakened occasionally during her long vigil by his bedside he would steal a glance at her, dozing or reading his copy of the Scriptures. His love, nourished by this attention, overflowed. Yet her beauty was as great a wall as his disfigured face. There was no hope, he thought.

Crispus' vitality repaired his torn body, while his deep faith restored his mental balance. He returned to his bench almost greedily, taking great pains to produce work few cordwainers could master. The cowhide boots he made for Paulie made his younger friend the object of envy among all the youth of the region. And the slippers he fashioned for Hettie made Crispus' name and fame a topic of household conversation among all her female friends.

Brown grudgingly gave better terms to his slave, knowing how valuable he was to the economy of the farm. Crispus was a productive and versatile worker able to fashion everything from buckle to dressed fashionable footgear for formal wear to heavy clogs for use in the ever present mud of the farm.

Crispus made no fancy shoes for Nora, who went barefoot most of the time and gently refused his offers of deerskin slippers as too rich for her station. A maid of all work, she busied herself around the farm at a thousand duties, including the painstaking candle-making, soap production, and preparation of flax. No hands could be idle on Brown's or anyone else's farm. Goods of any kind brought from Boston or overseas were prohibitively expensive; thus the farm lived on itself excepting only the most necessary items. Nothing was wasted. Not for Brown the crackling delicious odors of beef fat dripping into the fire when a rare roast was being prepared. All fat must be collected, stored, and used for candles or soap.

Crispus tried to be present at candle-making time when Nora and Hettie applied themselves to this autumn activity. He loved to watch Nora's delicate fingers manipulating the sticks to which the wicks were attached, dipping a set, holding them momentarily in the huge tallow-filled kettle then lifting them deftly and swiftly and putting them in a rack to dry. Layer by layer, more tallow adhered to the wicks until a full candle was made and stored away for use. The candles so made were poor, smelly, sputtering things which shed only the weakest light. But compared with the store-sold whale-oil candles, they were a bargain.

It was on a candle-dipping occasion that Crispus first spoke his love for Nora. He had filled the heavy kettle and started the fire, working close to her all the time and feeling almost overpowered by the cleanness and freshness of her. Nora kept herself clean in clothes and body. Unlike most New England white women, she did not shun a complete immersion bath, although a deep-seated modesty prevented her engaging in it frequently or for too long. She brushed her lustrous black hair often, keeping her scalp free from scabies and other unhygienic ailments. Her teeth she kept clean with cold water, rinsing them often and so delaying the condition most New Englanders faced of tooth decay and toothlessness by the time they reached adult life.

As Crispus bent near Nora, he had to speak. "Nora," he said, in one of the few times he had used her name.

She became instantly alert, never having heard that tone in his voice before.

"Nora, will you, would you...?" he stammered shyly, trying not to think of his disfigurement.

"Yes, Crispus?" she asked quietly.

"Uh," he paused , " I...

At that moment Hettie entered, holding several balls of wick twine in her apron. She sensed the awkwardness and tension and prepared to withdraw.

"Oh," said Nora, "you brought the wicks. Now we can start."

Crispus withdrew in embarrassment.

Darkness came early in autumnal New England and as Crispus prepared to retire that night, he heard steps upon the gravel outside his door. Paulie and Hettie entered, bearing a small tallow candle.

"Crispus," Hettie said, "we wish to speak to you."

"Yes, mistress," Crispus said instinctively.

"Today at the candle-dipping, I interrupted you as you spoke to Nora, didn't I?"

Crispus reacted shyly, narrowing his eyes and looking a little embarrassed.

"Yes, mistress," he admitted.

"We, Paulie and I, think you were going to ask Nora for her hand. Are we correct?"

Crispus shuffled awkwardly: "Mistress, she wouldn't have me... yes, I want, I did, but she wouldn't have me."

Hettie and Paulie grinned widely. Paulie said, "She'll have you, Crispus, she'll have you. She told Hettie."

Crispus could not credit his ears. His heart beat as if to burst its cage.

"She told you?" he asked Hettie.

"This very day," Hettie said. "Oh, Crispus, we are so happy. You have suffered so much."

Tears filled Crispus' eyes but could not come, held back by his inborn reserve and by a life of self-discipline.

"I'll speak with her," he said, leaving the two in his hut and hurrying to the servants' quarters. By the time he had covered the brief distance he was unsure that he had heard Hettie correctly and almost drew back.

But Hettie had spoken the truth. Nora was waiting for him, her deep brown eyes seeing past the ugly scars to the soul of the man. They walked for hours that night under the rich yellow moon of harvest, heedless of the chill, or curfew or of time itself.

The joy felt by Crispus and Nora was diluted by the realization that they were both in perpetual bondage. They could not escape this great burden yet vowed to live their life around it, marrying the next fall. They would have no child while either was in slavery and neither would leave slavery without the other.

Late the following winter, Brown gave Crispus a new assignment. He was to take a dozen of the best cattle from the farm's herd and bring them to the cattle fair at Bristol.

"Take Paulie," Brown said, "I can't spare the blacks or the other servants. The stone walls have been so damaged by ice they must be built up again."

Paulie and Crispus set out one frosty morning, driving the cattle down the narrow road to Bristol. Ice still gripped the countryside but a few signs of the thaw were evident. Ponds and streams seemed solidly locked in ice but here and there a crack had appeared. Squirrels, much of their stored winter fat now dissipated, sprang hungrily from branch to branch seeking bits of food to see them through until spring time. Crows fought raucously on the upper limbs of tall maples. Some dug diligently for grubs in the pulpy stumps of winter broken branches.

The morning wind brought the temperature well below freezing.

Paulie and Crispus were well-used to such discomforts and were prepared against it. Both men dressed alike in deerskin trousers, coarse kersey stockings, and heavy coats of broadcloth over which they wore loose-fitting frocks. Their best articles of dress were their shoes, made with great care by Crispus himself. In his pack, Crispus had several pair he intended to sell in town. His "freedom" money, stolen by half-brother Tom, had to be replenished whether Brown changed his mind or not about his freedom.

Paulie walked carelessly along, swinging his food pack and occasionally darting after a steer which strayed off the road. They stopped for lunch as the sun reached its zenith above them. The johnnycake disappeared quickly as did a few pieces of beef, washed down with stream water. The cattle rooted indifferently nearby, pawing through the snow for a chance blade of grass.

Paulie stretched out on a large dry rock, while Crispus sat nearby, eyes narrowed, detained in thought.

"Why does my father want to sell the cows now? It's winter and there's been no fodder to fatten them up. Won't they bring a poor price?"

Crispus thought, then answered. "He sells for hides, not for tallow or meat. The hide is good for sale any time of year and he needs the money, since the farm pays poorly."

A fearful bellow brought them to their feet. Being higher, Paulie was first to see the cause of the animal's distress. A steer had strayed onto the icy skin of a stream nearby and fallen through. Struggling to stay afloat, it thrashed about in panic, slipping away from the black opening it had made by falling in.

"I'll get him!" Paulie called, racing toward the stream.

"Wait," Crispus warned. "Stay off the ice. I have a rope." He rummaged quickly through his pack and brought out a length of sturdy rope.

"Paulie!" he called. "Don't go!"

Paulie ran swiftly to the bank of the stream, tested the ice with the pressure of one foot, then skimmed lightly toward the floundering beast. It shook all the more as he approached, eyes bulging and terror stricken. Paulie removed his broad belt, intending to hook it around the horns to pull the beast to safety. He leaned too far, the ice gave way under him and he was swept into the water.

He slid quickly past the steer, clutching frantically at its slippery horns without success. The current took him underneath the ice and he disappeared.

Crispus watched with horror from the shore. He had no time to lose. Spying a stretch of ice downstream of a somewhat different color from the rest of the covering, he raced heedlessly along the solidly packed shore. He bounded into the center of the stream, leaped high and brought his feet crashing into the melting spot, plunging to the bottom for a moment. The desperately cold water engulfed him, squeezing inexorably through his heavy clothing and within seconds assaulting his skin with icy blows. Breath driven from him by the shock, Crispus flexed his legs against the stream bottom and shot himself to the top. As he rose, a heavy object collided with his body. Whether steer or man, Crispus could not know. His hands lunged for any hold he could get. By good luck his first grasp was of Paulie's arm, strangely flaccid.

Crispus' propulsion from the water's bed kept him rising to the surface, even with the added drag of Paulie's limp form. He broke through the pulpy weakened ice, lungs nearly bursting with the need for air. As he breathed deeply he pulled Paulie above the surface, treading water and surveying his plight.

The stream's current pulled strongly at him but Crispus managed to get an elbow onto firm ice. Holding Paulie firmly, he took out his powerful knife and began to chop his way to the shore. Legs numb, Paulie limp, the shore far away Crispus realized this was a futile tactic. Something else would have to be tried. Strong though he was, his strength was ebbing fast, drained from him by the frigid water and the physical struggle.

With his knife he cut enough ice away to allow him to float Paulie's body horizontally. Balancing his friend gingerly, he ducked under the water, then came strongly to the top and half-lifted, half-pushed Paulie's body onto the ice. The limp form was held firmly and did not break through. Crispus pushed the body as far away as possible. Again he went under and this time he came out high above the ice, diving onto it and spreading his body to get as much of himself on as possible.

The ice broke, plunging Crispus back beneath the water and sliding Paulie's body into the stream again. Crispus barely had time to right himself and catch hold of his friend. The one good result of this accident was Paulie's revival, the water shocking him back to sensibility.

"Crispus," he groaned, "I can't stand this cold. I'm sinking."

"Hold on," Crispus urged and explained his plan. This time it worked and both men found themselves on solid ice.

A roaring fire and vigorous rubbing of their bodies soon returned them to near normal. With no spare clothing, they were required to don the sodden garb they had. The remaining cattle were rounded up and brought to Bristol before the sun had set. That night, sleeping in a friendly farmer's barn, the warmth of the hay and the animals never seemed more welcome to the two men.

Paulie lost no time in telling the story of his rescue on returning to the Brown farm. Old Brown sat impassively in his corner of the kitchen as Paulie described the heroism of his friend to Hettie, bustling through the dinner chores.

"He is our greatest friend," Hettie said, tossing her head firmly. "And we repay his friendship with ingratitude."

Brown had no reply to offer, busying himself with the dinner she set before him. When supper was ended Brown broke his silence with a laconic promise.

"I'll see Crispus tomorrow."

The following morning Crispus sat awkwardly on a rude bench in Brown's cubbyhole accounts room. Brown sniffed loudly, cleared his throat, paused and spoke.

"Crispus, you saved my son." The tone carried a greater measure of bluff accusation than it did of admiration.

Crispus said nothing, his big frame unmoving, his disfigured face impassive.

Brown looked away, at the bleak New England scene he had challenged every day for bread all his years. How could he continue without Crispus? he wondered. Life was hard, he bitterly mused, with no woman and no profit in farming. He never mentioned the lost steer. The price Crispus bargained for the rest he could never have gotten himself.

"I'll free you," he blurted out suddenly, in a tone at once pleading and final. Crispus found no joy in the moment. He had been morally free, he knew, from the day of Mrs. Brown's death.

Brown's greed had frustrated his early dream. A plan, however, had been formed in his mind for some time.

"I'll stay and work for you," he said. "For wages... ," he paused, moving uncomfortably, "...and for Nora."

"You want the Indian wench?" Brown said in surprise. "Ah!" he lapsed into silence, his mind racing with this thought to many possibilities.

"Five years you'll work for her on the same terms you have now," Brown said, fairly shouting his position.

"Three," Crispus said quietly and flatly, "and for higher wages."

Brown sucked in air. "She's my best wench," he argued. "Three years, yes, but on the same terms as now."

Crispus nodded. "I need a paper," he said.

Brown glanced hard at him, saw the metal in Crispus' eyes and thought better of any remark he might make. He grudgingly reached for a sheet of paper from the dwindling supply he had long ago acquired at great expense from Richard Fry, the Boston stationer, late of London. Taking pen he wrote:

Three years from this day, March 26,1750 will free
my bondsman Crispus Attucks. He has also agreed to
work three years from this date to earn the price of
Nora, my female servant.

Within himself, Brown gloated over his good fortune. The clouded - nearly invisible - title he had to Crispus was now affirmed, for three years at least. If Crispus left before the date of freedom he would officially be a runaway.

Brown flinched as he signed his full name, Praisegod Barebones Brown, blotted the sheet and passed it to Crispus.

That night, the cider ran freely in the servants' quarters as Crispus and Nora's good fortune was toasted. And in the Brown house, similar festivities were going on, since Hettie and Richard Pyle, a neighboring farmer, had also plighted their troth.

The next few weeks were taken up with wedding plans for both couples, since Nora and Crispus had decided to wed close by in time to Hettie and Richard.

Crispus worked mightily to prepare boots and shoes for sale and as gifts. Nora and Hettie span and sewed ceaselessly as did the other women. The farm pulsed with life as spring flowers pushed their way past the gray brown wreckage of winter. Summer sped by into harvest time and soon the weddings were upon them.

New England marriage was a combination of merriment and solemnity. From the early morning musket blast which signaled the wedding day's arrival to the last quaff of rum, the Lord was invited to watch his children give themselves to each other.

The wedding of Hettie and her Richard was a tightly structured happening, beginning with the very declaration of love for each other. Hettie had no problem with her father since she was no longer young. At her time in life, she was nearly a thornback, a thirty year old with no prospects. In her case, all the amenities were observed and Brown gave her no trouble with the dowry since she paid it herself from the treasures left her by her mother.

Crispus and Nora, out of their love for Hettie, decided to celebrate their union on the same day. Slave marriage, of course, was not on the same plane with the marriage of free-born white English persons, although it was solemnized legally and spiritually in the Puritan Bay Colony.

Crispus and Nora, being only servants for three years, had hope of a life in freedom together. Still they knew the weakness of their position and were all too familiar with the tale of Nero and Dido, two slaves owned by the Rev. John Swift right there in Framingham. When the Reverend died a few years back, Nero was sent off to Sudbury to Swift's daughter and son-in-law, Ebenezer Robie. And Dido and her little girl remained with the widow Swift. This after twelve years of marriage. The servants still gossiped over it and held it up as an example of the fragility of their state.

And the couple had been owned by the same master; imagine the case where two servants owned by different persons fell in love, they observed.

The great day came and at dawn horse drawn carts and ox drawn wagons began to leave Natick and Sudbury, both North and South, with loads of guests for Framingham. Some, closer by, came by horseback, the farmer in the saddle and his wife riding pillion behind him. The guests tried to travel in groups, since law and order in the Bay Colony, while strong and clear, was remote.

The day dawned much like a good marriage, sunny with occasional showers. But it was September rain and spirits rose, even as it pelted down. It was a blessed day for relaxation and conviviality.

In token of her age and the condition of her Richard, a widower with two children, there were few highjinks on Hettie's nuptial day. A crowd of older folk with younger children toasted the couple and enjoyed the feast Brown grudgingly allowed.

The celebration at both ceremonies was primarily gustatory. Fermented drinks of diverse kinds, including rum punch, brandy; Malaga wine and hard cider were available. And an overly laden table provided guests with a bewildering variety of food. Salmon, venison, and nut-stuffed turkey supplemented pigeon, beef, and pork as entrees and such late vegetables as beets and cucumbers garnished the meal. Puddings were enriched and sweetened with the maple syrup which had been running for the past month. Cakes stuffed with nuts and fruits abounded, making the day a delight for the young especially. Here, as on few days of the year, one could eat one's fill without fear of doing without the next day.

All classes mingled on this occasion, slave and free making merry from the same bowl. The infrequent sun showers only added to the gaiety, sending groups running pell-mell for shelter. The rain abating, the revelers returned to their cups or plates or games.

The children at the wedding were predictably boisterous and engaged in their games with great enthusiasm. The adults helped, settling disputes or just watching and applauding. A small pig was let loose, followed by a dozen boys whose shouts almost drowned out the squeals. Racing under carts and behind trees, through thornbush and field, the little porker tried to escape its pursuers. Some got a hand on it, but this did not count, only the boy who had a firm grip on its tail was pronounced the winner of the pig run.

Being good Puritan citizens, the wedding guests did not break Massachusetts law by dancing or engaging in other wicked practices. They did do some target shooting though, threw quoits and bowled avidly.

As the day drew on, the gathering grew more raucous. Two indentured servants newly arrived from Bristol were especially rowdy. These young men had recently been acquired by Brown to replace several servants whose terms had expired. Unseasoned, they were still good workers and gave every sign of being good farmers, too, once broken to the ways of New England and P. B. Brown. But they still carried with them the godless ways of old England, drinking overmuch, roistering and making free with the servant women. Crispus had already warned them off Nora but this was a festive day, they were filled with good rum punch, and they began exchanging stories of the old country.

"D'ye think they hold here for bride capture, Edgar?" the taller of the two, whose name was Adam, asked.

Edgar brought his cup down from his greedy lips and wiped his mouth with his sleeve. A sly smile played on his beard-stubbled face. "I hold for more than capture," he answered. "I'd like to board her for a prize."

Both men sought out Nora with their eyes, resplendent in her bride's gown. The beads and ribbons tried without success to disguise the lithe contours of her body but failed badly, only heightening her beauty and desirability.

"What about the black?" Edgar asked, watching Crispus as he chatted with Paulie at the table.

"He's a big 'un, but we be two," Adam answered. "Let's lay onto our task."

The weather had added just the right note to the festivities. Each time the skies opened, the laughing crowd fled, each person for her or himself. Standing under the eaves or in the doorway of a building, the laughter continued.

As the clouds began to threaten again, Edgar and Adam maneuvered themselves to a spot near Nora. The rain began and the party erupted. Nora, lifting her skirts decorously, ran lightly to a large outbuilding used to house firewood, lumber, and spare parts for farm machines. The two men followed, waving off several children who were going their way. Crispus and Paulie ran heedlessly to the barn directly across from the storage building.

When Nora reached cover, she smiled at the two men who stood beside her.

"Why Edgar and Adam," she began pleasantly but breathlessly, "I have not seen you all this day."

"No, mistress," Adam said, "but you'll remember us from now on."

Nora's eyes widened in terror as the two men moved toward her, forcing her back into the gloom. Adam lit a tallow candle, and placed it in a holder next to a post. Its sputtering light illuminated Nora's beautiful olive face. She cried out a shrill instinctive scream. "Crispus!" Thunder muted the call with its great drums. Adam stripped off his light coat as Edgar closed and barred the door.

Across the yard, the revelers waited for the last drops of rain to fall, greedily eyeing the sagging table with its load of richness well-protected by a canvas-topped covering.

"Where's Nora?" Crispus asked, looking about. Guests began to leave the house, barn and other buildings.

"Nora!" Crispus called as several guests joined him. Soon a chorus of lighthearted "Nora's" was raised and cries of: "She left you already, Crispus" or "Run off with the Parson" began to float good-naturedly about.

One of the children came to Crispus and pulled at his sleeve. "She's in the woodshed," he said solemnly, "with the 'dentured men."

Crispus' eyes flashed to the shed. The sun was out, drying the yard already, only a few drops still dribbled off the rooves. Yet the shed's door was closed tightly and finally.

The blood rushed to Crispus' brain and with a deep shout he sped to the building.

"Nora! Nora!" he called.

A shrill scream of pain cut through the air, stopping laughter and jollity instantly.

Crispus hurled his body against the shed door. The sturdy wood gave but little as he smashed and kicked in a frenzy. Soon, others joined him.

By now the whole party was awake to the situation, save for a few who dozed or lolled in careless stupors at the table. One of these was Brown, who had started the revelry early in the day before the guests came and was now practically torpid.

The bar across the door came out of its rest and Crispus entered. Unaccustomed to the darkness, he blinked, started forward and a heavy board struck him to his knees.

Adam, holding Nora down, called to Edgar.

"Quick, fasten the bar back before the others can come in." Edgar slammed the door shut, catching those outside by surprise and slid the sturdy bar back.

Crispus shook his head to clear it, his rage restored with each passing second. Adam shoved Nora, arms trussed behind her, clothes disheveled, to the side. Her head struck a beam and she fell into a pile of twigs and refuse wood used for kindling. The candle sputtered above her unconscious form, trying to cast a stronger light on the scene.

As Crispus rose, Edgar swung a board again, catching the black man's right shoulder and twisting him painfully around. Adam came at him and drove his heavy boot into Crispus' side. Crispus fell again to

44 • Arthur J. Hughes

his knees and the heavy board smashed against his back once more, driving him to the floor.

Outside, the clamor mounted. Voices were raised, giving contradictory orders. One, that of Paulie, called out above the rest. "Get axes from the barn! Hurry!"

That voice brought Crispus back to reality as he lay face down on the packed earth floor. He saw the form of his wife, huddled against a post, her body outlined dimly by the candle directly above her. The young servants paused to catch their breath, their fear of Crispus abating.

"He's not at all a tough one," Adam remarked. "These blacks is weak men else why be they slaves?"

Edgar agreed. "And he's a Bible nigger too. Turns the other che..."

UFF! Edgar's foot slid out from under him, caught in the steel grasp of Crispus' hand. The surprised man, slighter than Crispus by three or four stone, froze as Crispus seized his other foot and swung him heavily into Adam, off balancing the second man. Adam crashed heavily into the shed's side.

Crispus pulled Edgar roughly to his feet and drove his fist into the man's stomach. Mad with rage, he did not notice Adam behind him. The bigger white man threw his arms around Crispus, pinning him. Crispus struggled against the grip but could not break it. Edgar began to punch him with sharp, painful blows.

With a great effort, Crispus raised his leg, kicking at Edgar, who staggered back, stepped on Nora's leg and jarred the post heavily. The candle dropped unnoticed on the floor, rolling onto the hem of Nora's gown.

Chapter 3

The sound of axes came dully through the sturdy door. Shouts and threats sounded in the dark shed as the battle continued.

Crispus succeeded in wrenching himself free from Adam's grasp and the two men struck powerful blows against each other with their big fists. Edgar came to Adam's side and the fight began to turn against Crispus.

A flame leaped above the dirt by Nora's body, its golden finger brightening the dark interior of the shed. It caught Crispus' eye, distracting him momentarily. Adam moved in and dealt a dreadful blow to Crispus' jaw, knocking him unconscious.

"What should we do?" Edgar called in panic.

"Put out the fire!" Adam shouted. "We can always say we was funnin', jes' playin' bride capture."

"What about her?" Edgar asked. "She'll talk."

"No, she won't." Adam answered, rolling Nora's inert body closer to the fire.

The two men began to halfheartedly beat out the flames but reckoned without the speed it took dry wood to ignite. Smoke disoriented them and prevented them from even opening the door to the rescuers.

By the time the axes had done their work, only Adam showed sign of life. Edgar, lungs choked with smoke, was on his knees, retching.

Crispus was dragged to the yard and sponged off with water.

"Crispus! Crispus! Speak to me!" Hettie called, cradling his bloody smoke-covered head in her arms, heedless of her wedding raiment. Tears streaming down her cheeks, Hettie sobbed over the unmoving frame of her friend.

Paulie and some of the other men trussed up Edgar and Adam, making sure the bonds were tightly bound to insure maximum pain.

The inert body of Nora was carried over to the house and brought indoors, put on Hettie's bed at her instruction. All turned away sadly as it passed, the slender body seeming almost puny now, its blackened face so awful in contrast to the beauty that once radiated from it.

Slowly, almost imperceptibly, Crispus' chest began to move. He coughed, coughed again, then rasped violently in a paroxysm, his stomach emptying again and again as if to rid itself of all memory of the wedding feast. It took long moments for his head to clear but as soon as it did, he spoke the one word:

"Nora!"

Hettie and all those around looked at him, their faces filled with pain and pity.

An animal cry escaped Crispus. "Nora!" he roared, raising himself shakily to his feet.

"Where?" he asked fiercely, turning to Hettie. She pointed to the house and he staggered toward it, his will forcing strength into his legs.

Presently Hettie joined him, Crispus sitting on her bed, holding the still form of Nora.

"I'm sorry," she said, "I'm so sorry."

Crispus, too numb and angered to speak, clutched Nora's body more tightly to his own.

A short time later, he left the room, his stride filled with resolution. "Goodbye Hettie, I be leaving now."

Hettie knew his intention. "Goodbye Crispus. God go with you."
She pressed a folded paper in his hand.

Crispus emerged into the midst of the sad wreckage of the wedding
party. Twilight had nearly arrived, only enough light remaining to
make out figures. He walked to the group that held Adam and Edgar.

"Release them," he ordered.

Brown, by this time sobered by the tragedy, including the loss of a
valuable outbuilding, quickly intervened.

"What are you going to do?" he demanded.

Crispus looked at him, his eyes burning with rage. "Get out my
way," he said deliberately. Brown moved away.

Released, the two men now drew back in fright from Crispus. They
tried to resist his blows but they were no match for him. Soon both lay
in bloody heaps on the ground, bodies broken.

Brown had stood watching impatiently while his servants were
beaten into bloody pulps. The other guests had encouraged Crispus,
urging him to complete the job and save the township the expense of a
trial. Crispus ignored them all and crossed to Paulie, whose sadness
knew no bounds.

Grasping his hand, Crispus said softly, "Goodbye, my friend."
Paulie's eyes filled. He could say nothing.

Crispus went to his hut and gathered up his few belongings,
including a small food supply, a few tools, his freedom money, and his
Bible. As he left, he was confronted by Brown, a rifle held
menacingly.

"Get out of my way," Crispus ordered.

"No," Brown said, "I'll lose two servants to the hangman. Nora's dead. My woodshed burned. I won't lose you, too. You'll stay or be a runaway."

"Get out of my way, Master," Crispus said. "I don't want to hurt you."

Brown stood firm, rifle pointed at Crispus' heart. Crispus moved toward the old man.

"Boom," a flash of gunpowder and a ball spat from the weapon.

The shot went wild, though, as Paulie pushed his father's arm away.

"Go, Crispus! Go quickly." he urged.

Crispus vanished into the night.

Crispus' first few days took him deeper into western Massachusetts, where farms and towns were fewer. He drifted southward toward the wild Connecticut border and continued westward.

Some forests he passed were so thick and tall as to impose perpetual night upon the mossy forest floor. At other times he passed through areas where man had been or would soon be. These he tried to give a wide circuit to.

Brown had in fact wasted no time in placing a runaway advertisement. The Boston *Gazette* had carried one three days after he left, on October 2, 1750. A complete description of Crispus, including the clothes he wore, was given, along with a promise of a ten pound (old tender) reward for anyone recovering him.

Crispus had wide experience of the woods, having been raised on the half-wild frontier of the Bay Colony. He had spent many boyhood summer nights under the velvet New England sky. He could navigate by the stars without too much difficulty, although early and fearful encounters with wild dogs, wolves, and snakes made him loath to venture on once the sun had set. Besides, a black man gliding through little used terrain in darkness raised too many suspicions.

As he sped across the rolling countryside, Crispus watched the natural world carefully for any favors it might bestow with little effort. Berries and wild fruit he picked and consumed without thinking, along with dandelions and milkweeds. Occasionally, his keen glance spied a rich prize, as when he discovered a crippled wild goose partly hidden in the foliage along his trail. He wrung the bird's neck, then plucked and dressed it with his razor-like trimming knife. That evening he stopped early to begin his modest fire. The goose, half raw and gamey, was a feast to the big man, augmenting the depleted supply of johnnycake, dried fish, salt pork and vegetables he had brought with him.

Not all Crispus' days were as fruitful as the one on which he caught the goose. Some dinners were limited to a few small fish caught in the streams he crossed.

At night, he bedded down on pine needles, covering himself with leafy boughs to retain his body heat and partially screen himself from detection. His kit bag he laid next to his body for warmth and his deadly stone-honed trimming knife he kept grasped in his hand for protection. A light sleeper, he awakened without starting at any strange sound.

As he slept one night, he felt an object nudge his leg. He lay still, not knowing how much danger he was in. Presently, the thing slithered up onto his leg until he felt the loathsome body of a large snake, first on his calf, then his thigh and trunk. He was in no position to move or wield the deadly knife he held against his moist palm. The snake paused, then continued its explorations of its warm host. It found an opening in Crispus' shirt and poked its head in, feeling his body and hair with its ever-moving tongue. Crispus tensed to think of the dry flaky scales against his skin and a short rattle burst from the snake. Hearing the rattle, Crispus lay more still than ever, knowing that any movement on his part could trigger fangs delivering a full dose of venom into his chest.

Involuntarily, his skin prickled into goose flesh. His back hair stood on end, the urgency in his bladder almost overpowered him. As the beast continued its tour across his flesh, Crispus' heart beat so fast he wondered it didn't disturb it. Yet despite the fear and horror of his position, Crispus was more angry at the animal than anything else, coldly yearning for swift revenge.

After an eternity, he felt the last of the snake's suppleness slide off him. Without aiming, he struck with feeling at the intruder. The trimming knife drove straight through the rattler's body, slicing it in two. The head reared up to deliver a reflex sting but Crispus' knife was too fast for it, slicing it off the truncated body, the mouth still gaping for attack as it flew into the woods.

He watched with horrified fascination as the remaining segments of the body writhed a twisting dance of death before him, slowly losing motion like a freshly caught fish upon a hook.

For breakfast, Crispus dined on the white, savory flesh of his antagonist, cooked in thin strips on a flat piece of bark over a low fire.

Aside from this horror, Crispus liked his new life well enough. The smell of his smoky clothes; the sometimes quiet, sometimes noisy, music of birds; the bitter, long-lasting taste of hard-shelled nuts plucked from the trees; the spongy softness of the ripe, mossy earth beneath his feet; the crack of the forest as the deer started across his path, these were some of the soon familiar joys of his forest life.

But Crispus was a Christian man, much in need of his fellows. A civilized man, his place was with the civilized. Some evenings, as he watched the demons in his small fire leap and dance and crackle among the wood chips, he yearned for the comfort of another voice. Then he opened his well-worn Mrs. Brown's Bible. He could never bring himself to call it anything else but Mrs. Brown's book. "Justice and peace shall kiss," he read, as he randomly leafed through the Psalms. The promise of that line gave him the strength to think of the farm, the memory of Nora, and to have hope.

On his way, he occasionally passed rude frontier farms, skirting them with just enough distance to keep the dogs silent. He sometimes came upon a grove of girdled trees: silent, rotting, upright corpses, sacrificed to the blade of an ax that the soil beneath them might give sustenance to pasture grass or table crops. Dead branches, fallen from the lifeless torsos, lay strewn about and cracked irritably at him as he padded on them. Crispus paused not to marvel at the assault on nature. He accepted forest killing as a way of life, like cattle slaughter or hog butchering. His main concern was his open and exposed position as he trod through a dead stand of timber. He preferred shelter in the tall piney woods, where green boughs shielded him from potential captors.

Crispus feared not only the authorities and his owner but any straight laced "Goodman" who might demand to know where he was traveling to, particularly if it were on the Sabbath. Another source of trepidation came from fear of renegade whites and Indians who regularly roamed the backwoods of western and central Massachusetts. One of the books Mrs. Brown had impressed Crispus most with in her reading to the household during his childhood years was Mary Rowlandson's *Narrative*, an account of a woman's enslavement by Indians.

The book described the trials of a Massachusetts lady kidnapped and held captive by Indians for almost three months during King William's War in the previous century. P. B. Brown had bought his wife a copy of the book while on a trip to Boston. As a boy, Crispus had thrilled to the description of the surprise attack on Mary Rowlandson's farm and family and had huddled in terror in the corner of his imagination as one by one the Rowlandson children were "knocked on the head" by the savage "company of Hellhounds."

Grown now, Crispus still carried the impression of ruthless stealth with him. He had few dealings with truly "uncivilized" Indians in his life. The farm Indians and town types he had met were the product of intricate interbreeding and were as different from the genuine article as water from a waterfall.

Making his way through the countryside, he watched for signs of other travelers, sometimes hiding in the bushes to let others pass by unnoticed. But Crispus was no match in stealth for the practiced natives of the forest and his trip was not many days old when he was surprised one night at his small fire by two buckskin clad braves. Without warning, a rough blade was scrapped lightly across his neck. He knew that he had only to move and the edge would bite through his skin, severing the tubes which carried life to his brain and body. His skin prickled but he stayed quite still, mastering himself as he had when the snake crawled across him.

His senses were heightened as they had rarely been before. The damp foliage seemed frozen, no bird made song, nor did the forest crack beneath any weight as if in expectation of a deadly encounter between Crispus and the two visitors.

The braves worked quickly, binding Crispus' arms behind him and passing through the bend of them a stout stick. The deer skin thongs were pulled tightly around his wrists, through the crooks of his arms and tied securely to the rod. He was then pushed roughly against a tree as the pair squatted on their haunches to observe him closely. One fingered Crispus' prized trimming knife, grinning with satisfaction at the irony of slitting a victim's throat with his own well-tempered blade.

"Black man, why you here?" one of the Indians asked in a quiet voice. Crispus was startled by the man's easy conversance with the language. He studied his captors carefully before answering. If they were not fugitives themselves, they could claim the reward which Brown must have put up for his return. If they were fugitives, they would never chance turning him in but would rather kill him and take his few possessions.

He decided on his answer. "I am a free Negro cordwainer, a journeyman on my way to the northeast to open a shop for shoes."

One of the Indians spat, then held up his hand. "You are no free Negro. The signs of the collar are clear. The fur does not grow smooth overnight." He paused and fixed Crispus' eyes with his own. "You runaway."

Crispus locked his teeth and glared at his captors. They shrugged at his silence, then fell upon the scraps and crumbs in his kit bag, devouring his remaining food supply in minutes. Frequently, they stopped chewing to identify a noise somewhere in the forest. Now it would be a falling bough, again a small animal or even a deer. Once they remained still for minutes trying to resolve the meaning of a cracked branch.

Their stomachs satisfied, Crispus' captors dozed off, waking dog-like and alert at intervals when something disturbed them. Crispus watched his small fire burn low, then smolder out. He reviewed his position carefully, considering every possibility. Crowding out his other thoughts, though, was one which had no place in his immediate situation - he was still free from bondage. Hunted by Brown, captured by Indians, he still preferred this tenuous freedom to the secure misery of chattel bondage.

Also interfering with his orderly thoughts were his painful bonds. The deer-hide thongs tightened as the evening grew damper, numbing circulation in his arms and hands.

A loud snap woke the Indians and shook Crispus out of his painful musings. Clear-eyed, their hands on their weapons, the braves drew into the bushes to listen further. A bird call sounded, triggering great relief on their faces. One returned the call and then both stood at ease, awaiting the arrival of friends.

Crispus strained to hear the approaching footsteps but could not. His first indication of the new arrivals was the almost magical appearance of a dozen figures gliding from cover. Largely covered with fringed buckskin, only their open blouses and faces revealed the copper tint of their skin. Hard, dark eyes stared at him, measuring a man several inches their height and many pounds their weight. When Crispus' knife was thrust at them by its proud new owner, they made no effort to conceal their eager envy.

Rapid chatter between the new arrivals and Crispus' two captors led to a quick decision to break camp and push on. Crispus was the subject of some discussion, he knew, and was much relieved that, instead of being killed, he was to be brought along with them. He was roughly lifted to his feet, then led off by the two braves, who evidently wished to retain their exclusive claim to him.

Then he realized! Slavery! He was to be sold into slavery. He stiffened and stopped dead on the road, the Indians following him bumping into him and roughly pushing him forward. Crispus struggled to master his rising rage. Never, never again would he be enslaved. Death would be a friendlier host than bondage.

For the next hour, Crispus fell often, his rage blinding him to the perils of the unfamiliar path. He was beaten severely each time by the prodding sticks carried by his captors. Finally, he became aware of his aching and bleeding body. This was no way to win his freedom, he realized, and attended better to walking.

From early morn to sunset they traveled west, stopping not at all. From time to time, single individuals were ordered up pine trees by one brave, most likely a chief of some sort, to espy the countryside. The haste they were making convinced Crispus they were in flight but where from or to he could not guess. It really mattered little anyway, for if the whole lot were captured, Crispus would most likely be returned to Brown. If the band was not captured, then Crispus' lot was the same - to be sold into slavery.

Toward evening, they came upon the broad Nesquonset River, swollen by recent rains and swift in its course. They traveled some miles upriver, wading in the shallows to blind any pursuers. Crispus watched the leader carefully and guessed that it was his intention to cross the party before nightfall. Several fleet braves were sent upriver with crude coils of rope around their shoulders, while the rest waited in the shadowy cover of the overhanging trees.

Soon they spied one of the Indians, swimming powerfully toward the far shore against the choppy current, paying out the rope as he went. After a struggle which took him nearly a half mile downstream from his point of entry on the near side, he reached the opposite shore. The braves with Crispus brought him along the river to join the smaller party upstream. By the time they arrived the rope was securely fastened between two stout trees.

After three Indians had gone across, Crispus was untied and he was pushed forward. Knowing exactly what he was going to do, Crispus stood near the rope, rubbing circulation back into his hands, cramped arms and shoulders. He watched intently upstream, waiting for his chance. Finally, catching sight of an uprooted tree covered with large branches far away and centered in midstream, he plunged into the water, pulling himself hand over hand along the rope.

After a few yards, his tired, tortured arms began to give way on him, forcing him to rest. This was almost as taxing as going on, since the water pulled ceaselessly at his wet clothing. He struggled on, always watching the fast approaching tree. His timing was barely right, he reached a branch just as it snagged upon the rope.

The sun was dipping into the trees, its life slowly ebbing into the gold-green leaves. Occasional flashes of brilliance made their way to the river, capping its blueness with liquid gold, promises of tomorrow.

It was the best time for escape. Crispus let go of the rope, clutching fast to the branch, his weight freeing it as it swept away. The first brave to notice the action was perhaps twenty feet behind him on the life line.   Heedless of his own safety, the Indian struck out after Crispus, swimming furiously after the tree.

Crispus looked back to watch his pursuer gaining on him. Aided by the current and his own efforts, the Indian was fast approaching. There was nothing to do but fight. Crispus reluctantly tore a limb off the trunk of his tree raft, worked his way around so that he was facing his pursuer and mounted the tree, straddling it with his legs.

As the brave came near, he unsheathed his knife and slashed at Crispus. With a movement so swift it nearly escaped the eyes of his attacker, Crispus fastened one hand on the Indian's wrist and with the other drove the jagged branch into his eyes. A cry of agony escaped the injured man as blood spurted into the river, reddening the water around. Still clinging to his wrist., Crispus snatched the knife from the Indian's hand. He could have slashed the attacker to death. Instead, Crispus released him. Losing blood, blinded, and nearly overcome with shock and fatigue, the Indian dog-paddled, floated, and swam, half-drowned, to the shore.

Crispus had already been swept several miles from the Indian party. He faced forward on his makeshift raft, still straddling the main trunk. There were no signs of further pursuit. Nothing disturbed the tranquil scene along the shore.

The black man took stock of himself in the fading twilight. His first thoughts were to get ashore, since it seemed to him that the current was picking up speed. This could only mean rapids ahead. He lay belly down on the bough, reaching through the leafy branches to paddle and steer with his arms. He tested his skill, dragging a leg and an arm on one side to change the course of his makeshift vessel. Some minutes of maneuvering put him along the shore in water shallow enough to stand in. It was none too soon. The water was beginning to churn and bubble with white foam as it hit submerged rocks, then rocketed down in a series of small cataracts to other rough spots.

Crispus dragged himself onto the bank of the river and fell upon a mossy patch underneath a tree. Dripping wet and overcome by fatigue, he turned over and fell asleep. He woke when the sun was powerful enough to bore through the foliage next day. Then, stiff and hungry, he washed himself in the icy flood which sang past his open bed and set forth on his travels again. His kit bag, food, shoemaking tools, and fine trimming knife were all gone. He had only the poor blade he had snatched from the attacking Indian the night before. But he had his freedom again. And he still had his Bible, soaked but safe.

After a few miles of traveling, he came upon a dilapidated farm, fences down, doors hanging off their hinges, and weeds growing everywhere. He settled himself by a wild corner of the cleared area where the weeds reached high enough to conceal him. For several hours, Crispus patiently watched and rested until he was convinced that no one was nearby. Then he walked quickly to the house.

It was deserted, but like most places of human habitation, yielded up a few primitive treasures. The root cellar housed the wreckage of a bounty of a once well-fed family. Crispus found several roots which he cut up with his knife and chewed. Outside in the yard was a small orchard with a number of gnarled apples strewn about. Crispus consumed these ravenously. The roots and apples gave him back some of his strength and spurred him on to new searches. Not far from the orchard, he found a grave site. The graves, three for adults and two for children, were still mounded, a sign that they were less than a year old. A wooden marker, meant for all, had already fallen. When Crispus righted it, he read: "Wilkens family kilt by Indians" scrawled on the rough board.

Crispus sat wearily down, back against a tree amid the rank overgrowth of what had been a good family farm. He murmured a short prayer for the family, then took stock of himself. A literate, skilled man, he knew the Colonies needed him, as much as he needed them. The labor hungry settlements of North America used up human energy as greedily as modern times devour fossil power. But, as a slave and a black he was an object of fear and suspicion. How could he join civilized society without risking capture and return to Brown?

Musing in this way, Crispus fingered his treasured Bible, thumbing its worn pages. A paper fell out, surprising him. He could not recall - yes, he could - it was the one Hettie had given him the night . . . the night. He could not bring himself to think the words.

Unfolding the paper, he read its well-formed letters by the flickering glow of his small camp fire. A second time he read it until its import reached him fully.

Crispus Attucks, once a bondsman, now released from all such obligations. He goes free on this day, September 21, 1750.

Signed
H. Brown
Framingham

The paper had no legal standing, he knew, since he was Brown's property, not Hettie's. But Hettie had sufficiently clouded the issue as to give him an identity which would pass all but the most careful scrutiny.

At that moment, Crispus made his decision. He would go to Boston and seek his fortune there. It would not be easy, he knew, since there were so many hazards. No ferryman, for example, would take him across water without proof that he was a freeman. Any constable, selectman, or indeed any "Goodman" could question or even arrest him on suspicion of being a runaway. As for working, he would need a license to engage in his trade as shoemaker. And since it might give him away, Crispus decided not to follow it for the present.

He was then on the eastern side of the Connecticut River only a few days - perhaps a week- from Boston. He would go in easy stages, skirting populous centers and working his way up to Boston from the south.

He tested his identity several times by begging bread in return for work at isolated farm houses. Careful to keep his retreat open, he would show Hettie's paper legitimizing his existence, then offer himself for any Christian work. Wary though they were, New England farmers were also keenly conscious of his powerful physique, the broad massive shoulders which marked him as capable of manual labor. Repelled by his face at first glance, the observer would be equally attracted by the dignity and inner peace which also characterized him. Some of those whom he worked for were eager to retain him, offering him good, comfortable lodging and a small wage for his services. Crispus would not be persuaded. Instead he would ask questions about Boston, its customs and rules, its opportunities for advancement.

As he reached within a day of Boston, Crispus became increasingly nervous over the prospect of entering the Bay Colony's major city.

Stopping at a well-kept farmhouse in Braintree just east of the Blue Hills, he saw a farmer and his son zealously cutting marsh grass, the swamp water soaking their trousers to the calf. The boy worked stolidly, without looking up, his wiry arm wielding the sickle with practiced stroke. Crispus struck at a swarm of mosquitoes, attracting the attention of the older man

"Good day, master," Crispus said, without obsequiousness, doffing his cap.

"Good day to you, Goodman," the farmer replied, wiping his streaming forehead with a red kerchief of extra size. "How may I serve you?"

"My name be Crispus Attucks. I am a freeman. A former slave to a farmer over to the West. Here is my paper."

The farmer scrutinized the paper, nodding. "I did not believe you would come out of the woods as you did to announce yourself a runaway." He wiped his hand along his trouser leg and extended it to Crispus.

"I am John Adams." Inclining his head toward the teenager, he added, "and this is my son, John." Adams cast his eye toward the sun, now nearly overhead. "Will you stop to sup with us? We would welcome the company and any news you might bring from the west."

"I mean to work," Crispus said proudly, holding back.

The farmer looked at his tall frame, grinned warmly and said, "And so you shall." Crispus smiled back; farmers in Braintree differed little from the Framingham kind.

At the table the Adams' ate plentifully but plainly, in style befitting Puritan yeoman farmers.

Pork and bread and cheese, pies and milk disappeared magically around the table as the three boys, John, Peter Boylston, and little Elihu compensated for their long forenoon's work, urged on by their mother, Susanna.

"Well, Mr. Attucks," John Adams said. "You seem a man of some education. Have you a trade?"

Crispus decided to reveal this part of his secret. "I'm a cordwainer," he said.

Adams' eyes lit up as did those of the rest of the family. He smiled broadly. "That is my craft, too."

Susanna Adams added proudly, "along with many others."

The dinner hour passed quickly and was even extended somewhat over the customary time, to the delight of the children, who took their bat and went outside the house to play a rousing game of ball.

Crispus spent the afternoon in the cool shade of Adams' well-stocked barn tending to leather work which had long been neglected. For several days he stayed at the work bench, completing half-finished work long deferred. Occasionally, he would venture out and offer his help to undertake a task he knew to be beyond the strength of fourteen years old John or his younger brothers.

Spying the younger John Adams ditching one morning, Crispus offered his help.

"My father says I'm to do it," John said, in a thin but commanding voice. "I don't know if he wishes me to share the task." The New England conscience had John Adams in its grip. He wielded the iron-edged wooden shovel handily, and grubbed out roots and heavy rocks with a clumsy looking grub ax.

"Why does your father wish you to work on this ditch?" Crispus asked, squatting on his haunches Indian fashion, a weed dangling from his mouth.

"I think he wants me to know the life of a farmer that I may decide between it and becoming a minister like my Uncle Joseph." Adams spat a stream of brown tobacco juice against the rough of the ditch.

Crispus nodded. "Are you called?" he asked.

The shovel bit deeply, striking a heavy stone. "To be a Christian, but not a divine."

"And to be a student?" Crispus asked. He jumped lightly into the hole to help John wrestle the huge stone over the side.

John sat heavily on the ditch's edge, wiping his face with a red bandana. He refreshed his tobacco from a supply carried in an upper shirt pocket, biting a deep piece of the plug. "Some subjects I love and some teachers. For the rest, I have no heart."

"I had only one teacher in my life," Crispus said, looking away as the image of Mrs. Brown rose in his imagination and Nora...Nora.

"Did he teach you school subjects?" John Adams asked, interested in this mysterious black man who inspired such feelings of security in spite of his horrid appearance.

"She. 'Twas was my Mistress taught me," Crispus said. "Yes, I learned some school subjects - sums and spelling - but 'twas the Bible she taught best because she said learning could take us anywhere but the best place to go was Heaven."

Crispus took out Mrs. Brown's Bible and held it fondly. John Adams asked, "what passages do you favor?"

Crispus grinned, almost impishly. "The selling of Joseph."

John coughed and clapped his hands at the answer. They talked for some time, trading their knowledge and enjoying the warmth of the sun as it rose toward midday.

"Should I go back to school?" John asked Crispus, as matter-of-factly as if they had known each other all their lives.

Crispus studied the boy. Lean and tense, he lacked the black man's height by eight inches and his weight by many stone. That would not keep him from succeeding as a farmer, of course. The elder Adams was of modest proportions, too, but heavier.

But in John Adams, Crispus saw a restless light few men possessed. It was a burning to do something. "If not to serve the Lord, then what?"

"I can not say," Crispus replied slowly. "Whatever you do you will do well, that I believe. Can't you serve God and man?"

John Adams smiled broadly. "Thank you, Crispus. I will speak to my father."

Chapter 4

Crispus reached the south shore of the Neponset River at about noon time on a crisp November morning in the year 1750. The point from which he stood, on a high bluff overlooking the river, gave him a sparkling view of the approach to Dorchester Bay which washed up into Boston Harbor. His identity paper passed muster with the venerable Neponset ferryman and Crispus enjoyed a brief river trip watching the old fellow polling his flat scow across. No physical obstacle now lay between him and Boston, toward which he had been striving for so many years.

Before traveling the half dozen or so miles which lay before him, he turned off the narrow path he had taken and found a leafy glade. Resting on the mossy floor, his back against a century old oak, Crispus ate a simple lunch of the food the Adams' had pressed on him when he left. He tried to recall everything the elder Adam had told him about Boston.

"It's a city of widows," he had said, "nearly one in seven wears mourning, and much of it newly woven. That's natural enough in a seafaring town but it's especially so now after Louisburg."

"I had not heard of that," Crispus said.

"I fancy not, where you were. Five years ago the King called upon us to rid the fishing grounds of the French once and for all. Our boys went and gave all they had, capturing Fort Louisburg, that stinger on the tip of Cape Breton. We left near one thousand on that cursed island from wounds and distempers back in '45. And what value was there in it? Three years later they gave it back to the Frogs."

Crispus mused under his tree, remembering the fire which the elder Adams showed as he related the tale of Britain's crass betrayal of the sacrifices made by the four thousand colonists, most of them from Massachusetts, who captured Ft. Louisburg and thereby destroyed a powerful French foothold in the New World, some said the most powerful. It was pleasant to recall Adams' very tone, his precision of speech and his wide command of vocabulary. The talk had been more than just general information, though. Adams had tried to warn Crispus about the perils of being black in Boston.

"You need not be told," Adams had said, "that submission is the only way for you to survive in Boston. Women, little children, anyone has command over you because of your color. And as quickly as possible you must learn what you cannot do in Boston. Stay away from spirits and crowds of your own people and above all stay away from fire. The people of Boston fear nothing more than fire and any fire of doubtful birth is blamed on the Negro, slave or free. Carry no stick or cane. When I was in Boston last a black man was fined twenty shillings for carrying a stick with a nail in it. And remain off the Common, especially after sunset or in the company of other blacks."

Crispus had never known how involved urban life could be or how regulated the people of Boston were. Brown's farm was a haven of openness compared to the coming environment. He decided he could delay no longer, gathered his possessions together and made his way to Boston town.

His arrival in the late afternoon at Boston Neck was uneventful except that he had not been prepared for the vastness of his new home.

Stretching before him were nearly two thousand buildings, more than he had ever seen before in his entire life. The port bustled with life. Dozens of ships tied up at the Long Wharf were in various stages of loading, unloading or repair, their masts and riggings like myriad spider-like entanglements. From every corner, small boats made their way toward the center of the city, carrying provisions, people, and above all firewood. It being early November, the more prudent Bostonians had begun laying in plentiful stocks of firewood against a winter expected to be severe. The town's voracious appetite for fuel for heating and cooking had driven woodsmen farther and farther afield seeking fresh supplies. Some hoped-for relief might come if coal could be introduced, but this source of energy was still a long way in the future. Massachusetts had thought that Cape Breton coal might be used but the return of Louisburg snagged that hope.

Through the streets Crispus walked, keeping close to the side of the road as carts, horsemen, hackney coaches, and foot passengers hurried by. The posts lining the sidewalks, linked by heavy chains, were a reminder of the dangers of the streets. Few days went by without reports in *Courant* or *Gazette* of the death or maiming of some luckless tyke who strayed into the heedless traffic. Heavy fines for galloping or other reckless offenses did little to deter the thoughtless.

Tremont Street stretched before him as he neared the town center. As he reached Boylston Street, wondering what connection John Adams' middle son had to this byway, a chill swept his body, deep into the bone, stopping him short. He shook himself and walked on, even slower this time.

Surprisingly, he did not feel out of place, only awed by the vastness of it all. Everything took on larger proportions, as though through a magnifying glass, in Boston. Crispus had thought the poor conditions of his clothing, permeated with dark forest stains, would make him stand out like a leper to nose and eye. Instead, he blended in well with the town's general squalor. The streets abounded in filth of every description, hogs rooted and dogs snarled everywhere.

Crispus continued along Tremont Street, on the fringes of the Common, enjoying the wide spaces of the open area, livestock grazing, idlers lolling about, and children playing. He crossed School Street and stopped to note the construction going on outside a simple wooden church. Granite walls were being thrown up around the old wooden building as if to dress it in a cloak of stone.

A poorly dressed black passerby took note of Crispus' interest in the church and sidled up to him.

"She's a nice 'un, ain't she?" he asked.

Crispus nodded, aware that this was his first contact with a native of the town he had chosen to adopt.

"Why do they enclose the wooden building?" he asked, pointing to the workmen busying themselves on a scaffolding.

"The inside church be King's Chapel of wood and the outside skin be King's Chapel of granite. The worshippers and elders didn't want to tear down the old church while the new was abuilding so they keep the old one 'till the new one be complete."

Crispus smiled at the ingenious idea.

"Ye don't be Church of England, do ye?" the black man asked, glancing sideways at Crispus.

To Crispus that was a new term. No one had ever told him "what he was" except Mrs. Brown. He could not imagine being anything but a Christian or a nonbeliever.

"I am a Christian," he answered proudly.

"Well," the older black answered, "there's some of those among the King's church people, too, most likely, but I don't think we'll go far down this road."

He changed the subject. "My name be Abel Hayrood, what be yours?"

Crispus told him, waiting for the glint of recognition which might come if Brown had advertised his name widely. Hayrood showed no special interest in the name. They exchanged some more of their lives, Hayrood describing his own background as a slave in Barbados until good fortune put him aboard a vessel bound for New Bedford where he became the personal slave of a whaling master. Freed by the master on humanitarian grounds, he made his way to Boston, seeking employment.

"Are there places here for men like us?" Crispus asked.

Hayrood asked "Have you a trade?"

Crispus hesitated; he had better not, he thought. "No, but I'm strong and can learn."

Hayrood said: "There'll not be much to learn. See this?" He pointed to the outline of a pine tree with a number on it pinned to Hayrood's cap.

Crispus had wondered about the symbol but had decided not to ask.

"That be my license from the town as official porter," Hayrood said proudly. "None that hasn't this sign had better cry for porter work or he'll be hauled before the magistrate forthwith."

Crispus was impressed. "How can a stranger get work?"

"There's work at Boston, no doubt about that. Them's what are in the Alms House be there lacking limbs or some such. But a strapping man such as you can always be used. Only thing," Hayrood added, "there be two hundred Irish new arrived September last and these be mighty tough birds to digest."

Hayrood gripped Crispus' arm and drew him aside. "There be two now," he said, nodding toward two ragged figures ambling down School Street toward them. Bearded and dirty, their thin leather wallets stained and begrimed by thousands of miles traveled, the newcomers still had a cocky air about them.

"They be papists," said Hayrood, "and had best stay indoors tomorrow lest they lose some hide."

Crispus looked bewildered. "I don't know what you mean."

"Oh, you mean you don't ken papists? Why them be the devil's disciples, prayin' all the time to idols. They use magic and mumbo jumbo and their priests forbid them take a breath without their leave."

"But tomorrow," Crispus asked, "why tomorrow?"

"Why, that's Pope Day, man. You mean you lived in Massachusetts your life long and don't know Pope Day?"

Crispus smiled, somewhat abashed by his ignorance. In his memory were dim recollections of such celebrations but his tutor, Mrs. Brown, had been too kind a woman to preach bigotry or to allow it to be celebrated with much enthusiasm. He had learned what the Godly stood for at her knee, not what they disvalued. Her Christianity was the product of her own conscience not any contentiousness. But to the Englishmen of the 1750's, Pope Day or Guy Fawkes Day, celebrated on November 5th, was a major feast day. Established in recognition of the abortive Gunpowder plot planned by Guy Fawkes and other fanatical Roman Catholics in 1605 to blow up Parliament and assassinate newly crowned King James I, the holiday had been transferred across the sea by succeeding generations of colonists. It was the American link with the old ways of Merrie England, a country in reality as remote from them as France or Turkey but one to which they were tied by every bond conceivable.

"On Pope Day," Hayrood continued, "we dress up and parade and feast and clamor to our heart's content. 'Course you and me be part of the nigger parade and not the white one but we have ourselves more fun, anyhow."

Crispus was much more concerned with shelter for the night and the possibilities of employment than he was with any imminent celebration. He spoke of his problems to Abel Hayrood.

"Why, you needn't fret on that score, young fellow. You're to come home with me. Martha and the children will welcome you. As for work, you can help me out with my burdens, if you will. I'm allowed helpers and first thing day after tomorrow we'll introduce you to the magistrate and get you started."

Crispus accompanied his new friend to the Negro Quarter, a section of South Boston made up of crazy, dilapidated structures ranging from venerable one family houses converted into dwellings for a dozen families to ramshackle sheds, stables, and outbuildings into which people were stuffed by force of circumstances and the color of their skin.

Abel's home was a fairly spacious two room building, the rear wall of which was made from the converted barn against which it leaned. Probably a tool or wood shed of some sort in earlier days, it now served to house his wife and three children. Crispus' hut on the Brown farm was in area larger than the entire Hayrood house.

"Martha," Abel called, lifting the metal latch on the heavy door. "I have a surprise fer you."

A little ferret-like woman, thin and anxious, Martha put aside a wooden spoon she had been using to stir a black cauldron filled with savory smelling soup. Her hands went automatically to her apron as she saw Crispus, instinctively drying them although they were perfectly dry.

"Here's Crispus. He comes from Framingham Way," Abel said proudly.

"Pleased to know you, Crispus," Martha said pleasantly, "ye be staying to supper?"

"'Course he'll stay," Abel boomed. "Ain't that why I brang him home? And he'll bed here tonight, too."

Martha, apparently accustomed to her husband's impulsive generosity, offered no objection. Crispus enjoyed his first meal in Boston immensely, laughing and teasing with the children and with Martha and Abel.

"Have you no woman, Crispus?" Martha asked at one point. "A stout fellow like yourself must be sought after."

Crispus was much discomforted by the question and could not bring himself to answer.

"Hush, woman," Abel interjected, sensitive to the big man's embarrassment. "Can't you see he's had no chance to socialize, bein' a farmer and so young and all."

They were patent lies, but kind at least.

"I just thought him and cousin Phillis..." Martha's voice trailed off.

"She's a slave!" Abel roared. "Crispus here's a free man, He don't need no nigger slave woman as a noose 'round his neck. 'Specially that one."

Turning toward Crispus, Abel said: "Crispus, there's no sense stayin' here to hear this nonsense. We got 'bout an hour to curfew. I want for you to meet my friends."

Crispus and Abel left Martha and walked the short distance to the local grogshop. It was not a pretentious place. A hole-in-the-wall room in a larger building, it consisted of a few rough tables and benches of split logs, a large plank bar and a number of stools. A sooty fireplace dominated one wall and a few greasy prints decorated another. A dozen black men, in appearance and dress little different from Crispus and Abel, lounged and talked in low voices. Several greeted Abel as he entered. It took getting used to the light thrown by three smoky tallow candles. Abel introduced Crispus guardedly, volunteering little information.

There were only one or two slaves in the tavern, permitted by indulgent masters to stay out until 9 P.M. this special eve of Pope's Day. Two women, recent widows of seafaring men, conversed quietly over their rum on a wall bench.

The door opened and all eyes turned to see the new arrivals, a tall, handsome dusky woman and a light-skinned man. They both looked quickly about, spied Abel and came over, "Evenin', cousin Abel," the woman said, ignoring him to scrutinize Crispus closely. Abel was plainly uncomfortable and nodded peremptorily.

"Who's your new friend, Abel?" the woman continued. "He looks so big and strong he could be a runaway from the circus came by here not long ago." Crispus felt a sharp stab within him. Turning to the man with her, she added, "Remember that strong man who heisted the heifer no one else could lift? Looks jus' like him." Her male companion said nothing.

"This here's my wife's cousin Phillis," Abel said. "And that be Mark. They be owned by a man name of Codman over School Street way. A rich man, too."

Mark snorted and broke his silence. "Rich and stingy. Works us all the time at no pay and poor vittles."

"He's a mean and cruel master," Phillis added. "Not a spot on my hide that hasn't felt his cane. He hits me 'cause he knows Mark won't let him do no other things to me."

Phillis said this as she slid over toward Crispus on the rough bench. She grew coy, drinking from his mug and leaning provocatively against him. Mark observed this with growing chagrin. Crispus did not reciprocate Phillis' attentions, but could do nothing to discourage them.

Bending close to him, Phillis whispered: "You had a handsome face once. Who robbed you of it? Mind, you still handsome in every other way - in lots 'a ways, I bet. Tell me, who took away your good looks?"

Crispus was clearly embarrassed and despite her lowered voice, Phillis' words were heard by all. In fact, her tone called attention to them.

"Now, Phillis," Abel said, "don't you bother Crispus. He just come a long way an' he's tired."

"Oh," Phillis said," an' where is it you come from, big man? You a slave or free man? Where you born?"

Crispus rose, seeking Abel's eyes. "Time I was goin'," he said quietly. "Must get up early tomorrow."

"Right." Abel boomed, getting to his feet. "We got to go right now. Watchman bound to be by soon, anyhow."

The early November night was clear and star-filled, a moon of pale yellow illuminating the puddle-pocked paths. Few lights continued to burn within the houses they passed, although some civic-minded citizens had begun to put whale oil lamps on posts outside their homes to guide neighbors and ward off thieves and caution roisterers. Street lighting at public expense was not far away, having been introduced in Philadelphia the previous winter, thereby making it mandatory that Boston would soon follow to maintain its position as chief rival of its Quaker competitor.

The slight wind sweeping in from Boston Bay brought with it chilly vapors that portended the approach of winter. And the breeze was of little use to carry away the city's many unsavory odors. The city smells, earlier masked somewhat by the pleasant scent of cook-fires, became more ugly and stark as the fires were let die, by order of the town authorities as a precaution against fire. Bostonians never felt secure in their homes against fire even though stringent rules required builders to avoid wood as a building material. Fires in the '40's had caused great damage, especially the one three years earlier when the famed State House was reduced to ashes with the loss of priceless records and documents.

Out of the darkness appeared burly men with clubs, one carrying a lantern. Crispus did not need to be told they were the watch. Since curfew was still a few minutes away, they contented themselves with eyeing the two men suspiciously. Crispus and Abel cast their eyes submissively downward in the time-honored dumb-show of humility.

Abel sniffed when they passed out of earshot. "Curs," he muttered in a low tone. "They like to poke fun at us every chance they get. An' they're no help when you need 'em. Why, couple seasons back some gay boys stole the door right off the watch house when they was sleepin'. An' no sooner did they put a new one up then it was stole again."

Crispus smiled at Abel's anecdote.

Martha greeted them, her thin hands entwined nervously.

"Children all bedded down," she said, "and asleep already. Can't wait 'till Pope Day tomorrow. Gonna eat themselves sick I just know it."

"We seen Phillis," Abel said, half accusingly.

Martha brightened and asked Crispus, "You like my cousin? She a handsome woman or not?"

Crispus' cheeks burned. He grinned and nodded.

"Woman, leave it alone, I say," Abel demanded impatiently. "She no good, she a slave. Crispus' too good for her. And there's Mark."

Martha sniffed. "Mark's a no 'count."

"He's a mean one," Abel said. "Somethin' 'bout him that's no good. He's got a streak a' mischief in him wide as King Street. Now let's forget all this nonsense and get some sleep. Up early tomorrow an' Pope Day," he added exultantly.

"You as excited as the children, "Martha said, smilingly.

Before he dozed off on the straw mattress provided for him in one corner of the Hayrood's house, Crispus reflected contentedly on his first day in Boston. It had been a busy, happy one for him. He had made a friend and he would have a job. The morrow and its festivities he was indifferent to. He would go along but stay in the background. Crispus looked about the darkened room, barely making out the shapes of the rude tables and chairs which made up the only furniture. He lay back sleepily and rested fully for the first time since the wedding which took his Nora from him.

xxxxxx

Bonfires crackled on the open fields and rifle shots ripped the late afternoon air. Gay crowds surged over the Commons and up and down streets groups roistered, grog mugs and cider jugs in hand. Children ran, skipped, and jumped from one delight to another. Here and there a young blade pressed his maid against a house wall, took a kiss or subtle pinch where he could, always wary of the authorities, who looked upon this day with reluctant indulgence.

The general public was wary, too, of Pope Day, since only five years earlier, in '45, many deaths and injuries had resulted from Pope Day rioting. Sentiment had even been voiced in favor of abolishing the holiday, since so many acts of violence occurred on this day. Popular pressures restrained the bluenoses, though, and it still brought out the worst in the least. Sailors and apprentices, idlers and miscreants, used the day as an excuse to drink and be boisterous.

Crispus stayed close to Abel and his family, sharing in the laughter but never really enjoying it. His heart was too heavy with thoughts of Nora. And, he was surprised to note, he missed his old place, friends, Hettie and Paulie, work bench and all.

"Boston's a busy place," he called to Abel as they relaxed upon the grass, their backs against a tall pine tree. Abel pulled at his pipe, sending white puffs aloft. "Aye, there be many would knock you down and walk over you 'fore they'd trouble to go 'round. I don't like Boston but it be where I be so I don't question."

Crispus thought Abel was about to share some of his life with him but Abel stopped speaking to gaze at some young sailors passing by. Apparently he was not yet ready to confide in his new friend. Crispus was curious but cautious, he knew a confidence from Abel would have to be matched by one from him and he was still too reticent for that.

"See the tars yonder?" Abel said, pointing to four young skylarks racing about the Common. "Those boys be off a King's ship. See the scrubbed trousers and striped bright jerseys they sport? Them's the new uniforms Commodore Anson's made up for them. Never had 'em in my day."

Seeing the quizzical look on Crispus' face, Abel explained. "Anson's the Navy man who took the Spanish treasure years ago. Now he's takin' his own Navy in tow. There's many don't like the fancy duds. Costs too much, they say."

Leaving the crowd behind, Crispus and Abel strolled to the Long Wharf past crowds of festive celebrators. Young boys seemed to be everywhere, racing after each other, dodging horse and cart traffic and bumping into anything in sight. Their heavy clothes were out of place this day because of its crisp clemency but they could lay aside few garments since winter clothing had already been given them by their parents. Most were already sewn into their heavy woolen underclothing, not to be released until spring. The result was an assault upon the sense of smell as each youth streaked by.

Boston was a wharf with a city attached. The great two thousand foot Long Wharf and its lesser companions were roots drinking nourishment from the sea and transmitting it to the homes and businesses of the mainland. Along the Wharf were warehouses and mercantile establishments rising to three stories in height, covered and dressed with the precision of a line of marines in Anson's new Navy.

All manner of boats plied their trades in Boston Bay. Sloops and schooners, shallops and slavers. Even a few whalers put in, although New Bedford was the coming place for that enterprise, now that sperm whale were chased more than right whales. Some formidable merchant vessels were in port on Pope Day 1750, including the *Rachel*, a vast three master armed with twenty-four guns to ward off buccaneers, French or Spanish raiders, or any other peril.

Crispus and Abel eased themselves onto a heavy timber edging the pier, unmindful of the layers of tar and debris. Their legs dangling over the undulating water, they took in the scene with every sense. Gulls circled in the air, watching their opportunities to strike at uncautious fish swimming too close to the water's surface. An unusually high and strong tide washed at the hundreds of mooring ropes which linked Boston's treasured fleet to anchors, moorings and piers. For every hull in harbor, one, two, three masts pointed skyward, some short and stubby, others tall and commanding. From the cross trees joined to the masts hung shrouds and halyards in profuse confusion. Furled sails, the engines of sailing fleets, awaited calmly the hands of swarms of seamen to put them in action. The ships at their moorings seemed like listless skeletons to Crispus, those under sail in the harbor like graceful birds in flight.

In all the Colonies no place made such ships as Boston. Its shipbuilding yards, rope walks, sailmakers, and chandleries were legendary. Only in New England could the King find the mast trees he needed to keep his warships at their highest levels of performance.

Special royal agents marked such trees to warn off any who might seek their timber and heavy fines punished transgressors.

Bostonians loved the sea. To them, the feel of the halyard was far more preferable to that of the reins of a plow horse. There were no lands they had not touched, including Oregon, the South Seas, China, the Mediterranean, and Africa both east and west. Voyages of ten or twelve thousand miles, through perils undreamed of, including the fearsome Cape Horn passage, were common to Bostonians, some of whom captained their own ships at nineteen or twenty years of age.

Abel lit his pipe and looked about him with contentment The sun was low against the sky, no clouds obscured its majestic passage into the Atlantic waters.

"I guess I be a sailor at heart," Abel said, wistfully. "I still feel the roll of the waves as I walk the cobbles here."

Crispus asked if he had sailed to many places.

"Enough," Abel said. "I shipped aboard a whaler in '39 as a lad and spent two years in the South Sea, huntin' sperm whale. The work was hard but I ne'er complained. Fer complaints they had a cure, right across your back."

He went on, "And 1 served on a King's ship, too, the *Centurion* it was, in '44. Spent four years aboard her and got this."

Abel pulled up his trouser leg and showed Crispus an ugly jagged scar on the inside of his right calf.

"A splinter they called it. More like a dagger to me. The surgeon said it was fourteen inches long. Near ripped the inside a my leg right off. Screamed, I did, aplenty, you can be sure o' that."

Abel's jaw set as the memory stirred him. "But I kept my leg. Surgeon he was fetchin' to saw it off 'til I told him leave off."

Seabirds across the bay called to each other shrilly, perhaps announcing troves of shell fish or other edibles. The sun was a half disk now on the horizon. As if determined to be remembered, it glinted powerfully off the upper windows of the city, momentarily dressing their drabness in a coat of gold.

"I never was to sea," Crispus said quietly, looking at the scene around him. "But I'd like to, I think."

"Maybe you can," Abel said. "I know many a captain would give a lot to have you in his crew, you bein' so steady lookin'." He grinned and added: "So watch out for the press gang, big man. You be just what they want."

"'Course," he said, "the King's ships is much more careful now than a few years ago. Why, they used to break the doors down and steal our men from their beds or come aboard our firewood boats and steal their crews. Even took men with exemptions. My half-brother was took in '47. Started a riot. I was in the crowd that broke the State House windows that night. I didn't much like the crowd, but we made ol' Gubnor Shirley hightail it to Castle William."

Night had fallen and torch lights blazed everywhere. Worthy citizens hurried to their homes and barred their doors against the evening's rambunctiousness.

Crispus and Abel returned to Abel's street to eat a feast which was the high point of the day. Half a dozen families had pooled their food and cooking talents to prepare a memorable meal, each contributing a specialty. To those who shared in it, its greatest feature was its abundance, since on so many nights they went to bed only partly full.

The following morning, Crispus and Abel went to the Long Wharf, where Crispus was registered to work by a magistrate, his paper from

Hettie passing scrutiny. His day was long and arduous but no more taxing than on the farm. All morning he loaded and unloaded ships. Occasionally, he and a gang of men would be assigned to a large vessel, of eighty or more tons, but much of his work consisted of emptying or loading the little ketches and pinnaces that plied the harbor. He unloaded barrels of food, firewood, crates of dried cod, and a hundred other items waiting to be fed into Boston's hungry body.

As he ran up and down the gangways, or balanced on a gunwale ready to step ashore with a heavy load upon his back, Crispus tried to take in the bustle around him. Blacks and small boys, sailors and Indians, gentlemen in frock coats, pinch-faced clerks at dockside desks, all busied themselves with one thing alone - the pursuit of profit.

Lunch was a hastily eaten affair of johnnycake and beer. On the dock few workers felt the need to stop for a formal lunch. Every cargo of food unloaded yielded a small percentage for the dock workers, porters, even passersby. Strange fruits from the South, apples ripened in Vermont, and occasional cured tobacco leaves were part of the wharfside spoils. The afternoon's labor tended to slacken as tired bodies slowed down from the forenoon's efforts.

Crispus kept his pace, his powerful muscles gleaming in the afternoon sun. His natural energy provided the motivation but the thought of earning a few shillings to pay his own way and repay Abel and Martha for their kindness was uppermost in his mind.

Paid off by Abel at day's end, Crispus stopped at the local shops near Hayrood's to make a few purchases. Several lengths of cured leather, a bottle of spirits for the table, and a portion of ham were about all he could afford, but they raised the Hayrood's morale and the quality of their table measurably. That evening, Crispus turned his leather working skill to good effect. He made a fine wallet for Martha and belts for the children. The scenes of domesticity touched Crispus deeply, the more so when he realized how near he had been to realizing them for himself and Nora. Still, the sight of the little Hayrood children spooning down the last of their milk and pumpkin gladdened him for them and for his new friends.

After supper, Abel and Crispus visited the grog shop once more. A few rounds of rum and a pipeful of tobacco spread contentment all about.

"How do you find work here, Master Crispus?" the proprietor asked cordially.

"Fine, Mr. Barnley," Crispus said, "it suits me fine."

"Abel pays you handsomely, then, I suppose?" one of Abel's close friends asked, smilingly.

"More than I am worth," Crispus answered, sensing the mild jesting at Abel.

"He must be gettin' old," another said. "Most of his journeymen get 'prentice pay and 'prentices must squint hard to see what he has thrown to them."

Abel took the joshing goodnaturedly and the evening flew on in genial camaraderie.

A few minutes before curfew, the shop's doors swung open, Phillis and Mark entering quickly, followed by several burly white men, one of them an extremely well-dressed well-fed burgher, obviously a man of substance. The shop's patrons froze. Few persons of quality came near their street let alone entered one of their shops.

All knew him, except Crispus. Hats doffed, the men sat submissively while the two armed watchmen took up positions flanking the magistrate.

"Good evening, Mr. Warren," the proprietor said.

"Only a good evening, Barnley, for those who live within the laws of God and his servants. Is that not so?"

"Yes, Mr. Warren," Barnley answered quietly, "as all here do."

Warren's face reddened. Barnley was politely telling him there was no trouble in his establishment and that he was not needed. An air of tension sped through the room. No one fidgeted or drank or even breathed heavily. The familiar smells of tobacco, beer, rum, and stale human odor, usually so welcome and comforting, grew oppressive.

Warren stared Barnley down. "All Godly men here, you say?" As he spoke, he removed an old copy of the *Gazette* from his pocket.

"No fugitives, runaways, law-breakers, or miscreants of any sort, I suppose?" he asked sarcastically.

Crispus' stomach turned over; blood rushed to his face. His heart beat wildly against his ribs. Quickly he sized up the situation. It was unlikely that anyone else was the target of this visitation. Could he run, could he overpower those two sturdy fellows at Warren's elbows? Even if he were able to overwhelm them, would not all the shop's patrons be required as law-abiding citizens and under penalty of fine to apprehend him? For a moment, he looked at the lone window with its heavy wooden sashes. Could he crash through that, he asked himself?

No, it might not even be him they were seeking. Thinking this, he saw Mark standing by the door, smiling sardonically at him. Then he knew. Brown must have advertised his escape offering a reward.

"Crispus Attucks," the burgher called, "by virtue of my power as warrant server, I charge you to accompany me to Boston prison there to be detained until such time as you are reclaimed by your master, Praisegod Barebones Brown of Framingham." At this, the guards moved forward to flank Crispus, who was now standing.

"Shall we bind him?" one of them asked.

"As you please," Warren answered, whisking a scented handkerchief under his nose.

As one guard went to fetch a canvas bag placed by the door, the other stepped behind Crispus, grasped his wrists and roughly pulled his arms behind his back. A feeling of entrapment gripped Crispus and triggered an almost insane desire to escape. Instead of pulling against his captor's grip, however, he slammed his heel hard down on the guard's toes and threw himself backward, knocking the man off balance. Crispus fell on top of him, knocking the breath out of him. Spinning quickly and springing catlike to a crouch, Crispus drove his big fists twice into the man's stomach and face, smashing him into insensibility.

A crash behind him forced Crispus to turn, awaiting attack from the second guard. It never came. He lay stretched out on the packed dirt floor, rum and blood streaming down his face, thick pieces of heavy glass forming a halo around his head. An oak club lay on the floor, inches from the unconscious man's fingers. Abel stood, nearby, the neck of a bottle in his hand. The door stood open and Warren the warrant server was gone

"There's no time to waste, Crispus," Abel called. "We must be away." The other patrons called good wishes and two or three pressed coins into Abel's hand. Abel murmured his gratitude and the two men sped swiftly into the night. Passing along the dark alleys and byways of Boston's labyrinthine black quarter, they kept to the shadows, avoiding the moonlit portions of the roads where possible.

It was no use, a hue and cry was abroad and all Boston's eight watchmen, together with as many worthy fellows as Warren could immediately muster, began to scour the area. As Crispus and Abel turned a corner, they fell right into the hands of four watchmen armed with muskets and swords.

"Surrender or you die," one threatened, pointing his heavy piece directly at Abel's chest.

It was all over. Arms behind their backs, they were securely bound at wrists and upper arms. Removed to Boston's stone prison, they were cast into a dark cell, its stones slimy with moisture. The cell was bare and light entered only through a small barred window far above the floor. The chilly night air soon penetrated their clothing and set them to trembling. Their bonds cut the blood from their arms and set their fingers tingling with numbness.

"Why did you do that? What will happen to you?" Crispus asked.

"I will be flogged and fined," Abel said matter-of-factly. With a trace more concern, he added, "and I'll lose my badge," referring to his license as a porter.

"I'm sorry," Crispus said. "I should never have put you in this danger."

"You be my friend, Crispus." Abel said warmly. "And that Mark he be marked by me for a visit someday." He gritted his teeth as he said it.

As faint pink rays began to play upon the upper walls, the heavy iron bound oak door was opened. Several men came in, one holding a horn lantern. Crispus blinked, trying to make out the faces. One of them was Warren's.

"Is that the one?" Warren said, pointing to Crispus and addressing himself to a man behind him.

As the figure moved into the faint light, Crispus almost started. It was Paulie. He showed no recognition at the sight of his younger friend, only glaring in front of him, his sadly scarred face quite in keeping with the hideous surroundings.

"He's the one," Paulie said. Pointing to Abel, he added, "And I'll take that one, too."

"It will cost you fifty shillings more for me and twenty each for the guards they struck," Warren said.

Crispus watched as Paulie counted out the price in good Spanish money. The warrant server's eyes gleamed greedily over the heavy pile. He quickly stuffed the loot away in the big wallet he wore at his side and ordered the prisoners released.

Crispus and Abel barely had time to thank Paulie as they were hustled out into the deserted street.

"Quickly," Paulie urged, "to the dock side. There's a ship waiting."

Chapter 5

Crispus clung to the rail of the ship with both hands, using all his strength. But as the vessel rolled and pitched in the rough seas, his hands would be ripped away from the slippery rail. Dizzy with seasickness, he had not yet vomited but Abel and Paulie on either side of him were retching in misery, their color ghastly and their bodies limp against the gunwale as if to invite the sea to wash over them.

Unaccustomed to the sea, Crispus was adjusting to it in the hardest possible way. His eyes and mind described the beauty of his surroundings to him, the majestic splendor of sky and the crude strength of wave. But his stomach sharply vetoed any appreciation, rolling within him as if he were a ship and it the sea.

The *Whippet* was not overly large, 105 tons burthen. It had a crew of eighteen, the three seasick defectives being the newest arrivals. Eli Dunstan, captain and sole owner of the *Whippet*, did not interfere with them, knowing how intensely they suffered. Pushing seamen was not his style of leadership, although he could do so when necessary. He had enough hands to man the sails for now, even though the wind and sea did not combine well for the speediest run.

It was dawn of the second day out of Boston and Dunstan stood on his small quarterdeck, marveling at the good fortune which brought three such sturdy bodies his way. Prepared to up anchor from his berth along the Long Wharf the previous day, he had been surprised to see the three figures speeding along the dock. They had looked the harbor over and seen that his vessel was the readiest to sail, came aboard and offered themselves as able seamen. Only one, the black called Abel, had any experience aboard ship but the other two would learn fast or suffer sharp reminders from the Bosun's rope, Dunstan thought.

Dunstan realized the risk he took if the new crew members were fugitives, that is, if they were fugitives who had been seen coming aboard the *Whippet*. But life on the sea was chancy at best and much could happen in the months before the trip homeward. Both blacks would bring in a good price in Barbados if it came to that, he knew, and it little mattered what happened to the white man among them.

The following day, all three began to gain their sea legs and for the first time in several days took some ship's biscuit.

On the deck that night, Crispus and Paulie spoke for the first time since the lightning release from jail.

"How did you know where I was?" Crispus asked.

Paulie said: "'Twas by chance. I overheard Warren, the warrant server, talking about your capture in the tavern where I was staying."

He corrected himself, adding, "I should not say I found you by accident. After all, I have been seeking you since September."

"Why have you been seeking me?" Crispus asked, his curiosity roused.

"To tell you my news, Crispus," Paulie said, smiling broadly, if a little mysteriously.

Crispus searched his friend's face for clues. The moon over the water coated everything - ship, sails, and rigging - with an emerald cloak. The wind in the rigging sang a light song which kept tune with the sound of the waves rushing past the sleek hull of the fleet schooner. A strange peace prevailed.

"Nora lives," Paulie said.

"Nora lives!" Crispus fairly shouted the words, displaying more emotion than he had shown in all his adult life. Tears flowed down cheeks which had not felt their weight since childhood. "But how... how?" he asked, gripping his friend's arm. "I held her, she seemed...I held her for hours."

"Hettie stayed with her all night and into the next day. She would not let them take her, even though she was sure she was surely...uh...gone," Paulie explained. "She bathed her with cold water constantly, especially the places where the blood beats close to the surface. She passed camphor 'neath her nose, too. One minute Nora was still as stone, the next her eyes were wide open and she was asking for you."

Crispus heard the words but his heart so filled his mind he could not sort them out. They came into a different place in his mind. He would store them and recall them later to savor their meaning for now and in the future.

"Crispus," Paulie said, seriously. "Nora was badly burned. You must remember that. She is not the Nora we knew before the fire."

"That does not matter to me," Crispus said, adding, "it did not matter to her with me."

Paulie relaxed, he had done what Hettie and Nora had urged him to do. Particularly the last part, which Nora had insisted he tell Crispus. Paulie bade his friend goodnight and went forward to the fo'c'sle to leave him alone with his joy.

The ship rushed on, its sails straining, the stern breeze carrying it southward, ever southward, Crispus thought, and farther away from Nora.

xxxxxx

Life aboard the *Whippet* soon fell into a taxing and inflexible routine, four hour watches followed by four hours off duty and return to duty for the next tour. Since they were new men, Paulie and Crispus had the added burden of learning everything new. Nautical terms, knots, sail changing and a hundred other details immersed them.

Endless hours spent on bilge pumps left them lying in their hammocks soaked with perspiration and aching with fatigue. The seasickness passed while they were on deck, but a sailor's true value - like that of a sea bird - was best measured while he was aloft. High above the deck, standing precariously on the shrouds preparatory to taking in or letting out sail was the best place to learn seamanship.

Crispus at first could not bring himself to look down at the deck. Even less did he wish to look down and see the deck swing away as the vessel heeled over, leaving him hovering over the open sea. The swaying aloft left him sick and spent for hours afterward.

The crew was small but varied. A few New England Yankees, several twelve year old boys, two free blacks, an Irish fisherman newly arrived at Boston, and assorted nationals or colonists from here and there made it up. New England used thousands of men, young and old, to sail her ships.

Crispus, being ignorant of geography except for the few names such as Barbados and Jamaica that he had heard all his life, was at first unconcerned about his destination. He assumed he was on a typical merchant ship, perhaps a coasting vessel or at most on a voyage to the Caribbean or to old England. The ship was so stuffed with goods, it could have been bound for any destination. One of his duties was that of assisting Taylor, the ship's pursar, in inventorying the cargo. Barrels of pickled beef, crates of candles and huge quantities of corn, dried fish, hay, and peas filled the hold. Lumber, including well dried barrel staves, without which no community could exist for long, took up the bulk of the space but more refined goods, such as pewter products and clothing would bring a better return. Crispus took a professional interest in the supplies of leather goods, especially shoes, in the cargo.

The cargo hold had to be checked regularly to make sure that all lines and guy ropes were secure. A loose rope could mean disaster for all aboard, since a crate or hogshead, once freed of its restraints, would smash relentlessly at hull or bulkheads until the ship's life was in danger. And no force on the ship, least of all the men charged with the duty, could recapture a shifting cargo without paying a price in crushed hands and shattered legs. The *Whippet* was especially vulnerable since it had departed late in the autumn and could expect considerable buffeting from the inevitable Atlantic storms.

He crawled into one tight compartment, a candle well guarded in a wrought iron lantern being the only light to pierce the gloomy air. Taylor came after him and Crispus went through a now familiar routine, counting containers, reading shipping labels, and testing restraining ropes. They were in the most remote compartment in the ship and all about them was the sound and feel of water. The bow of the ship cut through a heavy sea which slapped back at it, sending spray against the hull. The bilge gurgled with water taken on during the night, and the ocean kept the vessel rising and falling to the beat that it set.

Crispus balanced himself, holding the lantern close to the sides of the supplies.

It was a huge quantity of hard corn and dried fish they tallied, corn of the coarsest variety and fish he knew to be nearly indigestible.

"Where is this bound, Mr. Taylor?" he asked.

"That's slave food," the officer answered nonchalantly.

Crispus looked at the stores and wondered aloud how there could be so much of it. "It must be for one of the slave colonies," he said.

"Colonies nothing," the officer snorted. "Those are for our slaves."

Crispus recoiled. "This, this ship is a slaver?"

"'Course, didn't you know that?" the officer replied.

Crispus was silent, only shaking his head in disbelief. The seasickness he had felt until recently could not compare with the revulsion now gripping him. He sat down heavily on a wooden chest.

"No," he said, "not a slaver."

"What did you think, black man," the officer said impatiently, "that you were on a pleasure ship? Get you up and about and be about your business."

Using his pen as a goad, Taylor poked Crispus' bare shoulder.

In an instant he was slammed into a bulkhead, Crispus' hands at his throat, their faces only inches apart.

"My business?" Crispus answered. "Slavery is not my business." The officer gagged, his face contorted.

"Please," he rasped. "Let go, please." His face reddened, slowly ripening to a near purple. The sight of his pain caused Crispus to relent and he slackened his grip. Taylor fell. Weakly, he muttered almost inaudibly: "I could have you flogged for this." One look from Crispus silenced him and left him trying to regain his breath and his composure. Reflecting on it, Taylor decided it might be more prudent for him to forget the incident for now. After all, the big black did have two friends.

In the fo'c'sle that evening, Crispus told Abel and Paulie what he had heard and his resolve to do nothing to help in the search for slaves.

"By God, Crispus," Abel said feelingly, "I had no idea she was a slaver when we came aboard her. I thought she was a coaster, aiming for New Bedford or the Great South Bay at the most. My family," he said sadly, "when will I see my family again?"

The others fell silent at Abel's words, but the tiny space allotted for the crew continued to speak in a hundred voices. The rush of water past the hull, creaking of hammock bolts, clanking of the pumps below them mingled with the snores and groans of the human sleepers who shared their watch and their off-duty time.

Good Massachusetts men as they were, Crispus and Paulie were horrified at the prospect of sharing in the world's most depraved trade. Even old Brown, who readily held slaves, legally or not, was vigorous in condemnation of the trade in humans across the seas.

"But what can we do about it?" Paulie asked. "To refuse would be mutiny and we could hang."

"Better die than be drawn into so foul a business," Crispus said, his teeth clenched, eyes fixed on the rough beams only inches from his head. "I refuse...to do the work of the Devil."

Abel asked: "And of what value will you be dancing from the yards above the deck?"

"What should we do?" Paulie asked.

"Live." Abel whispered harshly. "Live and fight."

The three vowed to live and fight; to learn seamanship until they rivaled the captain in their knowledge.

Running southward down the coast of British America the next few weeks, they selected the oldest and wisest salts among the crew and sat with them, extracting what knowledge they could squeeze out of them. Among the drops of gold were gallons of myth and legend to be jettisoned. One shipmate, a grayish wizened ancient with six decades of wind and ocean on his face, was particularly valuable. A former top man himself, he had been lamed by a runaway hogshead of tobacco which ruined his knee and ended his climbing career. He cooked now, took the wheel often and proved an invaluable asset on board for all purposes. Aaron was his name. He freely shared lore with all, welcoming questions and spending hours naming the constellations and other celestial navigational aids, discussing tides and currents, and dispensing advice on weather and wind.

Life on shipboard was routine, but too fastpaced to be dull. Always requiring quick reactions to the sea and wind, each response was tailored to the exact needs of the minute. It was as if the *Whippet* and its crew were in a play, whose plot and setting changed constantly at the whim of an unseen director.

On one cold morning in early December Crispus and his watch were at mess. The food stores were still fairly edible and their friendship with Aaron had provided them with a bonus consisting of the full ration due a seaman and not what a stingy captain and a conniving cook allowed. This morning the men ate a rich and rare concoction called dunderfunk, made from crushed biscuits mixed with fat, water, and molasses, heavily salted and fried brown. Washed down by coffee, the meal was filling and tasteful. What gave the food its best zest was the salt air and the hard work preceding and following it. And eating ship's biscuit that had already been broken up had the great advantage of making it unnecessary to tap for weevils. Otherwise, a whole biscuit could be teeming with them and the only way to avoid swallowing them was by crumbling the biscuit into a hot liquid and letting them rise to the top to be picked out.

Dunderfunk was a rare meal and the crew relished it, knowing that it might be many days before they enjoyed another hot meal.

"All hands on deck!" came the cry, instantly cutting short all talking and eating and driving the men pell-mell up the ladder to their stations. Crispus' weary watch showed few signs of fatigue as they tumbled onto the deck. To Crispus the scene was amazing. A few minutes before, when he had gone below for breakfast, the faint rays of dawn had already splashed themselves across the modest mounds of the waves. The swells had not been large and no ominous clouds could be seen anywhere. Now, the whole picture was changed and black ragged storm clouds scudded over the masts of the schooner, postponing the promised daylight and prolonging the night. The sea began to heave at a heavy rhythmic pace, forcing the ship to roll and pitch. The wind began to blow at gale force but not consistently, erratically striking the sails from south and southwest, driving the vessel far off the coast.

Within minutes, the *Whippet* was gripped in a furious Atlantic gale. To take in the sails required every hand available. Crispus was fortunate in being spared the perilous climb up the rain-soaked rigging. As he reached for the rat lines to begin the dreaded climb aloft, a hand tapped him roughly. It was the Captain.

"Attucks," he said, his head just barely visible in his rain gear, " go aft and help Carr handle the wheel. You'll be more use there."

Gratefully, Crispus made his way sternward to the giant wheel that directed the ship's rudder. By the time he reached it, the storm was nearly ripping the helmsman's hands off its spoked handles.

Crispus gripped the handles with his massive hands, bringing a fleeting look of gratitude from William Carr, the Irish fisherman, an excellent helmsman of long experience.

"Never mind, black man," Carr shouted to him above the roar of rushing wind and water, "we'll pull through. She's a fine ship and the Cap'n's a first rate skipper."

Crispus could only grunt and nod, his full attention spent on keeping the bow into the waves to keep the ship from broaching. As the waves grew steeper, *Whippet* pitched into them more deeply, buffeted by the unending but fickle high winds.

Down, down, it glided into one trough after another, the bow barely breaking through each crest before it folded over them. At times, the waves were nearly mast high when the ship was in the lowest point of the trough.

Green, slimy water washed every part of the deck, found every crack and opening to spill below on cargo and crew alike.

The slick decks were death slides for anyone who ventured on them. Crispus and Carr, the captain and one or two crew men were the only ones on deck. Just enough sail was set to stabilize the ship, any more would have been torn to shreds by wind or might have caused it to heel over and never come back up.

Crispus could not understand how the ship could take so much punishment and survive. Carr seemed to understand his wonderment.

"The cargo!" he yelled.

"Eh?" Crispus asked.

"The cargo! It keeps us set well in the water. Without it, we'd be bobbin' like Halloween apples."

Crispus nodded, feeling through the soles of his feet the strength and sturdiness of the little vessel. In the hour or so he had been on the wheel, fighting desperately against the sea, he had gone through several changes of feeling. At first a hopeless fear had been on him and he had not given himself five minutes to live. This had altered to a feeling of confidence as the rudder met the challenges forced on it, regaining course after each wild wave swept the ship around. Then came an exhilaration, an almost wild urge to pit himself and this little vessel against all nature, no matter how savage and tempestuous.

This wild feeling gave place to a resigned calm which steadied him, but which was brought about by almost total exhaustion. The captain had been eyeing his helmsmen, his practiced gaze measuring what was left of their strength as if they were fluid in a bottle. He leaned close to a seaman and ordered him to call two replacements from below. The seaman went quickly, snatching at every handhold the ship afforded him.

Soon, Crispus and Carr were able to open their soaked and cramped hands, surrendering their grip on the wheel to fresher men.

"Follow me," Carr said over his shoulder as he led the way down the low poop. It was necessary to wait for just the right moment before embarking on the hazardous steps to the crew's quarters up forward in the fo'c'sle. The Irishman waited while the ship lumbered up from the depths of a trough. As it approached dead level, he let go his handhold and raced forward. Too late, the deck rose up to a thirty degree angle.

His shoes slipped against the sodden deck and he fell heavily, the wind knocked out of him. His body slid rapidly toward the rope rail, hands clutching at everything in sight to catch hold of something.

Crispus watched in horror as his shipmate reached the ship's side, clinging precariously to a cleat and a hanging line from a bit of broken rigging. Without thinking, he hurled himself up the deck as the ship plunged into the waves, green water and spray flooding toward him. Crispus caught both hands tightly around a two inch cable running along the deck and brought his legs crashing into Carr's body, scissoring him securely. Together, they crawled away from the side of the ship to safety.

Both men were soon below, wet clothes clinging to them, mugs of rum held between their near - frozen hands.

Carr adjusted the blanket cook had thrown over his shoulders and looked gratefully at Crispus.

"I'm your man, Attucks," he said with feeling. "Count on that for good."

xxxxxx

The life of a sailor appealed to Crispus and he and Paulie often spoke of making it their life. On star-filled nights, as the moon and sea painted everything an iridescent green, there seemed no better place to be than the deck of a ship. When the sun rose or set on placid seas under cloudless skies it was possible to forget the hurts of life in the midst of nature's spectacular scenes.

Adjustment to discipline was no problem since it differed little from life on shore for that matter. Captain Dunstan was not one to flog his

men as so many did in the boisterous slaving trade. They'd take
punishment enough, by God, he always said, before they turned a
copper from their slaver's earning.

As the *Whippet* beat south toward the West Indies on the first leg of
its African run, the sun remained longer in the skies, shone more
strongly on the glistening backs of the crew as they went about their
duties. They were reaching the tropical Caribbean, where the sun
shone directly overhead and huge seabirds wheeled in flight, searching
endlessly for food.

Aaron sat against the mast in the sunlight, resting from the rigors of
preparing lunch and keeping an eye on his twelve year old ship's boy,
his galley servant, as the youth scrubbed the pots and utensils clean
with sand.

"Harder, brighter," he urged, watching elbows flying as the heavy
iron vessels took their customary dark shine. "Crispus, sit ye down by
me," Aaron called.

Crispus was practicing his knots, his deft fingers racing over a
supple half inch line. He could do these blindfolded now and often did
at night while waiting for sleep to claim him. He squatted next to the
maimed cook and offered his tobacco to him. Both lit pipes and
settled back to watch the slow rolling swells and feel the gentle lift of
the ship as it yielded to them in its course southward.

William Carr came by and, off duty, settled himself comfortably on
the deck against a hatch, lit a pipe and watched the smoke drifting with
the light wind.

"We'll soon be in the King's own lake," Carr observed.

Aaron smiled as Crispus asked, "Where is that?"

"Why the Indies, of course, the Caribbean, where English ships and Englishmen rule the roost," Carr answered lightly.

"Come over here," he said, moving over to the sand tray the galley boy had just left. Carr smoothed the sand out, then proceeded to draw Crispus a map of the approaches to the Caribbean Sea.

"We be's here," he said, jabbing a finger into the sand to the right of a big cigar-shaped outline he had made. "And this," pointing to the long indentation, "be's Cuba." He punched his finger all along the northern waters off Cuba to the Bahama Islands, then drew a line through the passage to reach Jamaica directly south of Cuba. "This be's called Jamaica."

This island Crispus knew, since several times in his life he had met slaves from there.

The lesson continued and Crispus learned how Britain had acquired a handful of islands from the Spanish, and had even established a beachhead on the Mosquito coast of Central America and the Yucatan peninsula. The sailors could not know that within a dozen years, Britain's rule would extend over the greater part of the islands of the Lesser Antilles and would even dominate Florida for a generation.

The West Indies was a world in itself, its climate, current, history seemingly very remote from far New England. Yet the North American colonies and the Indies were twins in Britain's experiment in colonization. And were almost wholly dependent on each other through trade.

Through the windward passage the *Whippet* surged, her sails bellying full and her bow foaming through the blue crystal waters. On clear days the lookout spied out land and even from the deck the surf which washed the southern shores of Cuba could be seen. Within a few days they reached Kingston, a drowsy pearl in the King's urban crown, its streets filled with slaves, sailors, rum wagons, donkeys laden with trade goods and wily vendors selling every type of ware. At Kingston the triangular slave trade made one of its sharp points of contact, as Northern ships laden with trade goods made a major shift in cargo before heading across the South Atlantic to Africa.

At dockside the *Whippet* loomed over sheds and warehouses, its masts and yards part of the forest of rigging which festooned the port.

An army of slaves swarmed over the ship, helping the crew empty the hold of crates and hogsheads. Tackle screeched as bulging cargo nets were swayed gingerly out of the dark corners below. Tobacco, dried corn, molasses, rope, window frames, and dozens of other manmade goods came out of the hold in an endless stream.

Using this time and the favorable sunshine to good advantage, Capt. Dunstan turned some of the crew to replacing weak and frayed rigging. Crispus, Paulie, and Abel were among those chosen. High above the deck they worked, checking lines for signs of wear, enjoying the warmth and dryness after weeks of storm and sway.

"We have leave tonight, Crispus," Paulie said. "Let us see the port." Dunstan allowed a few crew members off the ship each night, the majority staying aboard to protect the cargo and act as fire guards. Tonight it was the turn of Crispus' watch.

"Good," Crispus agreed, deftly splicing a line.

"T'will be good to touch dry land again," Abel said from his perch. "And since I have been here before, I'll show ye the best tavern a sailorman could hope for in any port."

At sunset, Crispus' watch, of seven men, went ashore at Kingston port. Abel and Paulie, William Carr, and three other crew members were with him, but the three strangers took their own route, heading for the less innocent pleasures of the town. Lights now shone brightly in the windows of crowded houses and darkness descended from the green-topped mountains which ringed Kingston Bay like the ascending seats of a stadium. Citizens hurried to their homes, shuttering their windows against the fears of night. Black policemen, in groups of five and armed to the teeth, patrolled the streets in gorgeous white uniforms trimmed with blue and gold. They looked suspiciously at the sailors, taking in every aspect of their walk and clothing. Crispus and Abel were eyed more keenly than their white companions. Jamaica was a black colony with a thin layer of whites in control. Firearms and weapons of all kinds were rigorously controlled and punishments for infractions by blacks, whether native, free, slave, or visitor, were ferocious. A quick death was a blessing compared to the lesser punishments dispensed under British law.

"Here she be," Abel said cheerfully, leading the way into a smoky tavern filled with sailors and dock workers. Many were black but there were enough whites to prove that all races mixed amiably on Jamaica. Loud but well behaved, they looked the newcomers over lazily as they made their way to a back table.

Soon, hot cups of steaming rum and heaping plates of stew arrived from the kitchen brought on a tray carried by a black Jamaican girl, her dazzling smile and flashing eyes capturing those who admired her. The men fell to, loudly enjoying their first shore meal after weeks of plain ship's fare. The plates were soon empty and filled again and just as quickly emptied. Then, filled and refreshed, the friends settled back with their pipes and pulled at their rum mugs generously, savoring the friendship they felt for each other.

A face appeared above them through the smoke.

"William Carr," he said, an uneven grin split his face, revealing tobacco-brown teeth.

Carr's face lit up. "Jeremy," he cried, "Jeremy Adkins Otis! A great pleasure to see you. How be you here?"

"I'm off a slaver out of Guadeloupe, didn't you know? We was nearly took by the blacks last June and near done for."

"Tell us," Carr urged. "Tell us how it happened."

The newcomer settled himself comfortably on a rough bench next to Paulie, pulling his pipe out as Carr slid a pouch across to him. He sucked contently at the stem for a bit, then sipped the full mug he brought with him, enjoying the attention he had created.

"We was sixteen days out o' Bonny when it happened. The captain was a good man - not cruel like some o' them what starves the poor devils so they fight to eat each other's fleas and munch on rats and insects when they can. He give 'em bonnies and coarse corn and a pint o' water a day. Oh, and even a pipeful now and then."

"We had 300 aboard, mostly young bucks and every day in good weather we brang 'em up on deck in lots of fifty. Then some of us goes below and makes sure the holds and platforms are swabbed, bringin' some o' them along for to do the work. We checks the chains and locks and looks for hidden weapons."

"Believe me," Otis said firmly, "while them fifty devils is above deck, exercisin' and breathin' deep, we don't get much rest, there bein' only thirty-five of us and some men down with the flux all the time."

Paulie asked: "How do you keep 'em from takin' the ship over?"

"We nearly didn't!" Otis said, winking at the rest amid the general laughter.

"You mean how was we '*sposed* to keep 'em from takin' us, I calculate?" Otis said as Paulie nodded smilingly. "Well, whenever they was on deck, we had ten muskets trained on 'em from the quarterdeck. And next to each marksman was another loaded musket so they'd know each of us would get two of 'em."

"What happened, then?" Paulie asked.

Otis scratched his head. "Nobody knows. One minute they was lined up peaceful as you please under the wash pump, scrubbin' the grime off. Then, all of a sudden, one of 'em leaps on top of a hatch cover and yells to the others. From nowheres comes knives and metal staves. They jumped one of our poor boys servin' on the pump and near cut him in two. Stabbed him nineteen times they did. By that time, the marksmen had shot twelve of 'em but they didn't care. They kept killin' and stabbin' and throwin' our boys over the side. We came at 'em with cutlasses and pistols but they didn't stop 'till we'd wounded or killed every last one of them. We threw them over the sides, dead or wounded alike. All but the ringleader."

"What happened ta him?" William Carr asked.

"Captain tied him to the mast and killed him real slow-like; the hundred little cuts." Otis shivered as he said it. "Just bleedin' him to death little by little for days. I'll never forget the screams if I live to be a hundred."

All those present had heard of this. It was a horrible fate since the victim was always awake and acutely aware of the pain, not as in the case of a flogging or other traumatic punishment where there was no time to reflect and all the pain blended together. Usually madness came before death, which was a blessing.

"My slavin' days is ended soon's I get back ta Boston. All that blood shed by Christian men in a devil's cause. There's no use on 't."

The little group sat quietly for a while, pulling at their pipes.

"Well," Otis said, rising, "must go. Good luck with you, William Carr." Glancing around he added, "You too. Ye'll need it."

Crispus watched Otis as he slowly edged his way toward the door. The candles flickered as the door opened and closed. A cool evening breeze blew in across Kingston Bay, cleansing the harbor of the stench of man's day time activities. The voices rose and fell about them, raucous laughter greeting some particularly well-told tale.

Crispus brought his fist down with a crash on the heavy circular tablet, its thick timbers bouncing from the blow.

Several sailors nearby looked bleary-eyed at him.

"By God," Crispus said, "I'll not do it. I'll not go back aboard that ship to treat men like dogs and worse."

"What will you do, Crispus?" Paulie asked, "where can you go?"

"I don't care," his friend answered fiercely. "Any place would be better than a slave ship. And we bein' Christian men. No. I'll have none 'a that."

Abel interrupted. "You have no choice. You don't know these islands or their people. Once offend them and they'll make sure you don't do it again. Why, jumpin' ship will get you slavery for life. And on this island, boilin' indigo dye 'till you turn purple yourself or choppin' cane 'till you drop. And what of your Nora? What good will it do ye to be here while she pines to death up north."

William Carr added: "Dunstan won't mind. He'll list you as an escaped slave and sell the right to catch you to a bounty hunter. And he'll keep your seaman's pay for himself."

For long minutes they argued with the big man, in no way convincing him of the foolhardiness of his plan. Crispus remained firm until Paulie spoke.

"Crispus," he said, laying his hand on Crispus' arm, "let's sell our lives dearly, not throw them away. From what Otis told us, I have a plan. And I think it's the only way...and may be the safest as well."

For the next hour or so, they sat huddled around the table, refining and polishing the plan till each man knew exactly what part he would play in it.

Three days passed, during which the ship took on its major cargo, rum, for the African leg of the voyage. These casks, lashed securely below decks to cargo rings, would be the basic trade goods for the *Whippet's* human cargo. Iron bars, some tobacco, and several cases of muskets were also included to tempt the hungry traders of West Africa's delta area, the destination selected by Dunstan for his craft.

The next few days and nights were spent under devastating tropical heat which turned wood to stove tops and metal to fire. The tar between the deck planks grew soft as putty, and not a breeze stirred for long enough to ease the solar downpour. Sunsets were blood red, turning the bay into every shade, pinks and roses culminating in deep oranges under burgundy clouds. Then the darkness fell like a heavy shade over everything, followed just as quickly by spots of diamond as stars pierced the dark curtain of night. Nature in the West Indies was more alive, more fertile, more wakeful than in Crispus' New England.

The ship sailed early on a morning to catch a fresh breeze which had sprung up from the southwest. Back to sea went the *Whippet* with its new cargo and old crew, the new members now accustomed to sea ways.

Crispus had mastered the fear of falling which climbing to the high yards had first instilled in him. In fact, the fresh air and rolling seas were a relief from the heat of Kingston so that he even enjoyed competing against the wind to take in or let out sail. The sea birds were left behind and soon there was nothing but ship, sky, and ocean, as if these three alone existed and all the rest of the world had vanished.

Occasionally, a sail would be sighted by the lookout but little attention was paid to it since the world was in one of its few peaceful remissions. Only pirates were feared - those free enterprise beasts of prey who knew no nation and took no prisoners, except slaves. The nations of the world: Britain, France, Spain, and the Netherlands (and their colonies) had been so busy fighting among themselves as to neglect the savage forces of disorder which lived outside all law. But the days were fair and the wind blew strong and the *Whippet* sped toward its goal, heading toward its fate.

xxxxxx

Ros-Ibo and his brother Wallesa had a vital errand to perform. It was exactly one week before their sister's marriage and the bride price had to be paid for their father. The two teenage princes were proud they had been selected from their fourteen other brothers for the honor.

"It is nine leagues to Creektown," their father, King Ibomin cautioned, "take care no evil befalls you. I can give you no escort, as you know."

The manpower of Rivertown, a small kingdom on the lower Cross River, was stretched fearfully thin. The greater part of it was engaged in a great retaliatory raid upstream against its traditional enemy, the Kingdom of Bonomayu (or little inlet). Every available warrior was needed for home defense, including the king, who had remained home only because of the significance of his daughter's wedding to the future king of Creektown. It was a marriage of state which would link Creektown and Rivertown politically, perhaps eventually into an empire.

"We will take care, father," Wallesa promised. Older than his fourteen year old brother by two years, Wallesa exercised all the rights and privileges this gave him but also felt a deep affection for the younger man.

The rains had not yet begun when they started off with their sister's dowry of twelve cattle, although before many minutes passed they were drenched by the warm tropical downpour. Palm leaves and other vegetation slapped at their legs as they pushed their way along the narrow pathway to Creektown. But the two young men hadn't a care in the world, skylarking all the way, eating the fruit which tempted them from low hanging branches and chattering happily together.

An hour passed. The sun now shone brightly on the roof of the jungle's leafy canopy but little penetrated through to the matted floor below. Moisture from the evaporating water created a pleasant hot house effect. Bird and insect noises filled the jungle with reassuring natural music.

"How long before we are there?" Ros-Ibo asked, readjusting his heavy sack for greater comfort.

"Two more hours, I think," Wallesa replied. "We should be there by noontime."

"Will they have a feast for us?" Ros-Ibo asked, with a boyish grin.

Wallesa replied with mock gravity: "As befits two great warrior princes of Rivertown. After all, if our sister is to be princess and perhaps queen of Creektown some day, she will need strong allies."

The boys walked along, proud of their youth and strength and royal breeding.

The noises hushed. The jungle froze as even the rustling breeze seemed to die. Ros-Ibo and Wallesa stopped. Ahead of them was a small clearing. They tried to pierce the curtain of nature which shielded it from them. Slowly, Ros-Ibo, who was in the lead, stalked toward the clearing.

Twelve Mbytu warriors squatted around a slow fire over which a corn meal dinner simmered in a iron pot. Squatting, their sleek bodies balanced by a grip on their iron tipped spears, shafts resting on the ground. Along the wall of the clearing, six other Africans sat dejectedly, hands tied behind their backs and heavy loops of tie-tie bark about their necks, cords linking them together in a coffle.

"Slaver's!" Ros-Ibo whispered to his brother, fear showing in his eyes. They slowly backtracked, trying to avoid all contact with the still moist leaves and weeds. Their bare feet gingerly avoided twigs, seeking mossy spots to deaden the sound. The cattle would betray them, they feared.

But it was a runty brown jungle pig, its tusks gleaming, that burst from cover under Ros-Ibo's feet that brought them down. The boy leaped clear of the slashing curled ivory and the beast ran grunting toward the clearing. Stirred by the sound, the slave hunters dashed from the clearing to find many prizes instead of one. A deftly tossed spear pinned the pig to the mossy floor, its death nearly instant. But it would not do to kill such valuable game as the boys before them and their cattle. These had to be captured.

"Run, Ros-Ibo!" Wallesa screamed and dove into the jungle.

By prearranged practice, the brothers knew exactly what to do. Split up and race away in directly opposite directions, cutting their pursuers in half.

Ros-Ibo plunged into the thick jungle, heedless of the thorns and saw-bladed leaves which slashed against him. He had only the briefest instant to catch sight of his brother, hastily weaving his body in and out of trees. To Ros-Ibo, the race was maddeningly slow. He could hear the heavy panting of his pursuers as they closed the gap. Push himself though he did, he was unable to hold his own. The ground cover and vines snatched at his feet and lower legs as if they were human hands. Once or twice he tripped but quickly recovered before losing his balance. On, on, he ran, lungs bursting with pain, his brain not daring to consider giving up the race. He would win, he told himself, win this greatest contest of his life.

Eyes alert for any advantage, Ros-Ibo watched for openings in the undergrowth ahead of him. Directly in front he saw a massive tree, its gnarled roots grasping the forest floor like an old withered hand. Beneath the roots were spaces large enough for a tall man to hide. As he dodged around the huge roots, disappearing for a moment, he literally dove into a deep hollow, wedging himself in and freezing. Scarcely breathing, he heard the panting warriors crash by. Now, the waiting began. Minutes passed and Ros-Ibo's heart slowly returned to normal. He resolved to wait as long as he could before emerging. The jungle sounds returned, reassuring him of his safety. Slowly, he squirmed from the hiding place, orienting his sense of direction toward home. For the first time he thought of Wallesa, hoping he was safe, too.

"Do not move," a deep voice said menacingly. Ros-Ibo's blood ran cold. His skin felt the prick of a spear point and he knew it was all over.

Chapter 6

Eastward the *Whippet* sped, her great sails transforming her into a graceful, living thing, part bird, part sea creature. The long South Atlantic rollers held no terror for her, her sharp bow cleaving cleanly through them. *Whippet's* crew, now trained to be a well-oiled machine, worked good-humoredly at every task, even the hateful pumping to rid the bilge of sea water. Even the best caulked ship leaked and *Whippet* was no exception, although tighter than most.

Crispus' reliability had been as quickly discovered by Capt. Dunstan as his natural leadership ability had been by the crew. The pursar for whom Crispus had worked on the Jamaica leg of the voyage had drunk himself to death and his body, neatly sewn in canvas and weighted with a ballast stone, had been assigned to the ocean.

Having seen how quickly Crispus had grasped the details of the job, Dunstan made him acting pursar, offering him a few shillings more for his new duties. Crispus took the post to learn more about the ship's inventory and also to assure the crew their fair share of food and supplies, something which most of them had never known in all their lives as seamen. Pursars had the notorious habit of skimming part of every ration from the crew and doling out every item under their charge as if it were their own personal possession.

Dunstan was a lonely man, who had nothing to do with his officers socially. Educated in the scriptures, he had the habit of quoting them at odd times. Crispus and he often worked together, since the ship's stores and cargo had to be constantly watched, inspected, and tallied.

Crispus sat in Dunstan's tiny cabin one morning while the captain checked the accounts. Looking about the bare quarters, he spied a leather covered Bible on the shelf above the bunk. An almost physical pain came over him as he reflected on his own Mrs. Brown's Bible, lost when he fled Boston. Dunstan noticed his interest and asked gruffly:

"Do ye ken the Bible, lad?"

"I have read it," Crispus answered.

"And do ye live by the Word?" he asked, eyeing Crispus slyly.

"No," Crispus said, "I only try to."

Dunstan grinned and nodded to the Bible, "Take it down and handle it, seein' how you're so interested."

Crispus reached for the well-worn book and thumbed its pages, stopping here and there at favorite passages. He looked up, and the Captain was staring at him intently.

"Ye don't like slavin', I reckon?" he asked sharply.

Crispus looked him fully in the face: "Do you?"

Dunstan stirred and pointed to the book: "It's allowed in there, ain't it? The slave of Shem and Japheth, that was Noah's curse on Canaan. Besides, it's for the best that these savages come in contact with us. We civilize 'em, teach 'em the ways of God, show 'em how free men live."

Crispus shrugged and rose.

"You don't agree with me, Attucks, do ye?" the Captain asked.

"No," Crispus replied.

Eyes narrowed, Dunstan growled a warning. "See that your disagreement stops at thoughts and don't become words or deeds."

Three days later the coast of Africa was sighted, the lookout pointing to a thin dark line on the horizon. Within a few hours, clouds could be clearly seen over the land mass. The *Whippet*, which had been on an east-southeast tack for days, now changed course to head in a more southerly direction. This would take them along the coast where they could enjoy the favorable current until turning easterly again to reach their destination.

"Only a few more days now," Carr said from his hammock one evening, his fingers locked behind his neck.

Crispus swayed only inches away from Carr's head. The ship's motion kept all seamen in the crowded, dark fo'c'sle rolling incessantly. The closeness of the hold could nearly be felt. No air seemed to circulate despite the speed of the ship. The sense most taxed was hearing, ears being attacked on all fronts. Raucous sleeping noises split the atmosphere, creaking of timber and slop of bilges joined the chorus, and the rush and slap of water as the bow cut through the waves provided the main themes.

"We must not fail," Crispus whispered.

"We won't, my friend," Carr said.

"The Captain knows...I think," Crispus said.

"Little he can do," Carr sniffed.

"Is everything ready?" Crispus asked.

"Yes, Abel and Paulie have made copies of the keys. But you must pick the time. As pursar you are freer than we are and can roam the ship at will."

By the following morning, the ship reached the Gulf of Guinea, one of the world's richest sources of treasure. Here could be found every product sought by the white man from ivory to gold to a hundred other goods, including human slaves. Thousands made their living on this coast, most in the unsavory craft of selling, stealing, and buying fellow humans. Into the stormy waters of the Gulf flowed the rivers of

West Africa, the Niger, the Volta and the lesser ones: Crosa, Ogun, and Mono. These natural highways carried the produce cheaply and quickly to waterfront "factories" where "factors," those unholy middle men of trade, took over from there.

A full day's sail brought the ship into the Bight of Benin, on a direct eastward course to the Delta Coast, where the Niger River split into numberless branches to pierce the swamps and jungles in its run to the sea.

Already, Africa's unique atmosphere had taken command of the crew's senses. An unreal glow radiated from the mysterious coast, wrapping itself oppressively around them. The air they breathed seemed different, the colors of sky and sea and jungle were deeper, darker and more intriguing. Across the water strange sea birds wheeled, perhaps screeching their rage at the newcomers or demanding that the slop be dumped immediately. A white necklace of surf guarded the shore. Jealous of any sudden effort to penetrate it, the surf roared and swelled a challenge which made even the most courageous seamen draw back. Here and there the white water subsided, leaving somewhat calmer spots. Toward one of these channels Dunstan ordered the *Whippet* steered.

Although calmer than the breakers on either side because it was part of the Niger River estuary, the channel still ran fast, causing the ship to surf through crazily. One moment, the *Whippet* was rushing over the swells and the next it was bobbing gently within the estuary, its crew enjoying calm water for the first time since leaving Kingston. Sails filling with a mild wind, the ship tacked its way up the Mgotu branch of the Niger to its destination, the factory at Boorigha.

xxxxxx

His hands held fast behind his back with tie-tie bark, Ros-Ibo joined the slave coffle of his captors. Rough hands fixed a collar around his neck, ran a bark rope through it to the collar of his fellow captive. Then, prodded by spear shafts and musket butts, the coffle made its way to the coast.

A happy day had come to this, Ros-Ibo thought bitterly. If only Wallesa got away! He might reach Rivertown and father would start after him. No, all his brothers and the other soldiers were away, so there was no one to come for him. It was too late. Soon they would reach the coast and he would be delivered to the hideous pale people. Were the stories that they ate human flesh true, he wondered? But even if he was not eaten, he would be taken away forever in their giant canoes, past the raging white surf. He would never see his home or the ones he loved again.

Staggering blindly through the dense undergrowth, Ros-Ibo blinked the tears out of his eyes. Razor-sharp leaf blades slapped against his face and he could do nothing but hunch his shoulders to ward them off. Every step he took threw him off balance as the heavy cord holding the coffle together pulled roughly at his collar.

The joys of youth and nature were gone. What remained was an awful emptiness, a void that gave him intense pain. The horror of his plight was almost impossible to believe. It was as if this was happening to someone else far away. His ears and the back of his head burned, partly with fear and partly with shame at having been caught.

"Uff!" Ros-Ibo cried as a musket butt dug sharply into his back. He pitched forward clumsily, dragging the man in front of him down.

Soon, all the captives were down, writhing and twisting against each other in their effort to rise. Too late, the enraged captors began to beat them, thrashing arms and legs and buttocks with bamboo sticks which stung and cut.

Nursing their wounds, the captives set off again, carefully treading to avoid another fall, each blaming the one behind for causing the misery. At nightfall the parade stopped in a clearing where a small fire was lighted.

A half-cooked pig torn to pieces by hand satisfied the warriors, while a few pieces of dried yam were fed to Ros-Ibo and his fellow prisoners. It mattered little to him anyway, since the capture and beatings had taken away his hunger. The one thing he longed for was water and he waited anxiously for it. An hour had passed since they had eaten and no water came.

"Water," he called, "water."

His fellow captives laughed harshly at him and the guards took it as a great joke. Then Ros-Ibo took the time to notice the other prisoners. Lips cracked and bleeding, white foam around their mouths, they were drying out before his eyes, literally mummifying. Their dry skin showed few signs of sweat, only grayish powder mixed with the dirt of the jungle and its floor.

Two hours passed and the captives dozed fitfully against each other. A light noise stirred them awake and Ros-Ibo noticed how alert they became. Across the clearing, one of the guards took a gourd and waterskin from a tree branch and brought it over.

Ros-Ibo felt the desire for water surge within him, crowding out all human feeling. He hated the fellow prisoners who surged toward the water bearer, begging to be first. He could have killed anyone then and there for a gourd of the rankest swamp water. As the water was ladled out, the captives greedily eyed each drinker, begrudging every swallow taken. At last Ros-Ibo knew the meaning of relief, as the gourd's contents slid down his parched throat. Thereafter, life revolved around the water skin. Over several days, the thirst he felt became an obsession which cast out of his mind all thoughts of home or rescue or escape. The only relief came from the jungle showers which occasionally drenched them on their travels.

He was now a veteran of the coffle, longer in captivity than those poor dazed souls who had been added to it in the days following his own capture. Most of the newcomers were strong young men, caught as he had been by chance or taken prisoner after a skirmish with other slavers. The captives now numbered two dozen, worth a small fortune to their captors.

At midday on Ros-Ibo's fourth day in bondage, the coffle arrived at a clearing alongside the Mgotu River factory at Boorigha. The factory consisted of a dilapidated building, the center of which was a large circular barracoon made of upright logs held together by hempen cords. The captives were quickly herded into the barracoon. There was no shelter from the scorching sun in the stockade so the prisoners fought for the side of the walls where some shade was offered. At least they had been released from their human chain. Only the bindings on their wrists chafed them now and these would not be removed.

The Boorigha station was a small one, run by an elderly African factor who represented a group of towns from the Upper Niger. Between a factory run by natives and one under European control there was little difference, although the sight of a gray haired African struck far less terror in a captive's heart than a white man. Stories of white cannibalism and other atrocities were widely circulated among slaves, perhaps to maintain control through fear to make African bondage preferable to European. The end result was, of course, always the same: transportation overseas under the most barbaric conditions.

Studying the faces around him, Ros-Ibo saw the despair lining their features. A lifetime of fright came back to haunt him. Stories of just such captures as his, pure accidents that would never have happened had he been a quarter hour late or early on the trail or a quarter mile away from it. For years, his female relatives had promised him such a fate if he failed to obey and all his life the old tale teller of the tribe had described heroic chases and captures and escapes. His was not heroic, his was stupid. Had he not been impatient, had he waited just a few minutes longer in his hiding place, he would be a free man today instead of a wretched slave.

Soon, the mental misery he felt left him to be replaced by pangs of thirst and hunger. Night came and brought with it the gloom of despair and the depths of fear.

xxxxxx

"Drop Anchor," the mate ordered, as the *Whippet* stood off a few cable lengths from the broken down Boorigha pier. The ship, stripped of its sails for the first time in weeks, dipped slightly as the heavy chains rushed to find the sandy bottom of the Mgotu. Crew members, freed of their duties for a brief time, scrutinized the shore curiously. The ramshackle buildings and the barracoon stood out from the dense jungle surrounding them. Along a path of sandy beach, women labored, untangling and repairing fish nets, while a troop of naked children played nearby. A few canoes lay along the shore, but no one seemed eager to greet the *Whippet* after its six thousand mile voyage from the New World.

"Attucks! Carr!" the mate called out. "Report to the Captain!"

Crispus and his companion ran to the quarterdeck to stand before Dunstan.

"Go below and bring up a crate of trade goods, three muskets with ball and powder. And three iron bars. And four jugs of rum. We're going ashore to meet the Boorigha factor."

The ship's boat was hastily lowered and loaded with the goods. The crew pulled vigorously toward the shore, three oarsmen on either side. Crispus noted they were all heavily armed with pistol and cutlass, although he and Carr and the Captain were unarmed. Looking back at the ship he noticed the alertness of the crew, muskets on shoulders and the ship's guns in plain view although not run out and loaded. Nets were strung along the sides of the ship to make it difficult to board without causing considerable noise and commotion.

These preparations were clear signs of the vulnerability of Americans on this hostile shore.

"A bold front is needed," the Captain said, nodding to the bristling ship, "else we be taken advantage of."

Along the shore a crowd was collecting. A dozen or so tall warriors, bodies glistening in the sunlight, leaned easily on their spears. Bare breasted women in long skirts stood by, curiously eyeing the newcomers.

The boat scraped gently on the sandy shore and the oarsmen pulled their oars up smartly. Crispus and Carr leaped into the warm, knee-deep water and lifted the cargo out. The Captain splashed ashore with dignity and marched into the circle of blacks, then halted, waiting. Minutes passed: five, then ten. The sun baked down.

A door flew open and half a dozen richly dressed Africans appeared. Several slaves with palm fans joined the group, immediately beginning their work of circulating the fetid air above the head of the central figure.

He walked slowly toward the beach.

Dunstan spoke out of the corner of his mouth. "Damn! The factor's not here. Sent his interpreter instead. Means he's got good trading stock here so we won't get off cheap."

"How do you know he's not the factor?" Crispus whispered. "I thought this was your first time to this station."

"It is, but the Captain of the *Swallow* told me the factor here never goes about without a silver headed cane."

The interpreter came up, his eyes on the gifts laid out behind the Captain.

"You dash me plenty," he said pleasantly, "then you see FAC--TOR!'

The Captain ignored this and said: "Tell the factor I have trade goods and gifts for HIM... when I see him."

The interpreter looked hurt. "He no see. You come tomorrow. He maybe see you tomorrow."

The Captain wheeled on his heel and swept past Crispus and Carr. "Bring everything except one jug, one musket, and one bar," he whispered.

On the trip back to the ship the Captain was smiling.

"Very independent, these African snails," he said, "but that's all to the good. It means they've got good stock. When they see the goods I left 'em, they'll know that we have good stuff, too."

He swept his eye down the Mgotu, past his ship. "Now, if no other ship happens along, we'll have the trade all to ourselves." He clapped his knuckles into his palm. "And by God we'll get a good bargain!"

The next day the process was repeated but the factor came with the interpreter. Dressed in a combination European-African costume, he brought his wives, children, and other relatives with him. In appearance, this gray-headed patriarch seemed more a businessman or shopkeeper than a slaver. But beneath his calm features there lurked a cruel smile and what seemed to Crispus the most ruthless eyes he had ever seen.

The dickering over price continued for several days during which more coffles of slaves were brought in. Soon the baaracoon was overflowing with humanity, a fact which Dunstan noticed with satisfaction, since it meant that the factor would have to make concessions in order to make room for the newer arrivals and, indeed, for those yet to come.

A bargain was finally struck, based on the crudest laws of supply and demand. Two bars of iron for three slaves, one musket for two slaves, and one jug of rum for one slave. Lesser trade goods were lumped together for a set number of slaves.

While these arrangements were being made, the rest of the crew was on constant watch or engaged in reprovisioning the ship for the journey home. The water casks had to be scoured out and refilled and huge quantities of yams and other slave foods had to be taken aboard.

A shed was built on deck as a temporary holding pen for the slaves before docketing them below decks.

For Crispus, the worst day of all occurred when the Captain and mate selected the slaves being bought. A few at a time, slaves were brought to the beach for close inspection. Those chosen were quickly trussed up and loaded into canoes manned by native oarsmen.

Ros-Ibo watched as slave drivers removed groups of captives from the barracoon. He had seen the ship through the openings in the log fence and had also watched the bargaining deliberations. Now, peeking through, he saw the white captain and several other men, including an ugly black man, inspecting slaves.

The method was the same for each. Teeth were checked along with eyes and ears; the entire body was searched carefully for scars or malformations or any signs of disease. Close attention was paid to infections wherever bonds or shackles had rubbed the skin raw. Skin was carefully scrutinized to detect signs of doctoring to cover flaws. Standing on one foot or trotting back and forth along the beach gave some idea of the agility of a slave.

Ros-Ibo was pulled into the next group and left the barracoon gladly. Although fearful of the future, he saw no hope in continued imprisonment at the station. At least now he would have a better chance to escape...or die. And death seemed a good alternative to the life he had been living in the last two weeks.

Standing before Captain Dunstan, Ros-Ibo looked squarely at him, saying to himself: "Don't fear, he is just a man. You are a prince. You bow to no one."

"Uff!" he groaned.

He was not prepared for the roughness of the physical inspection. The ship's mate grasped his face in both hands and pried his jaws open as if he were a horse, poking around with a hairy finger for scars and lumps. No part of his body went untouched and the poking finger brought him close to tears several times.

"JUMP!" the big mate ordered, grabbing handfuls of skin under Ros-Ibo's arms. Without knowing the word, the young African leaped instinctively, to the laughter of all around him.

The mate turned him around, holding him by the shoulders. "He'll do," he told the Captain, who nodded.

With both hands, the mate shoved Ros-Ibo across the beach into the hands of two burly Africans.

Seizing him by the upper arms, they dragged him across the beach and up to a hill covered by dense underbrush and palm trees. Through the palm screen, a moan of agony escaped and Ros-Ibo tried to pull away in fear. The guards held him tighter, pulling him into a clearing where he was thrown on his back, arms and legs pinioned by his captors. As a filthy rag was forced into his mouth, Ros-Ibo saw the branding iron heating over a small charcoal fire. He squirmed to escape but his captors held him fast. Without delay, a third man grasped the wooden handle of the iron and deftly pressed it on Ros-Ibo's left breast. An acrid smell arose as his skin roasted under the scalding metal. Ros-Ibo moaned in pain. The branding had taken only a moment yet as he looked down he saw on the burned flesh a figure in the shape of two mountains. What Ros-Ibo saw was the initial "W" for *Whippet* upside down.

On board the *Whippet* that night, Crispus and his three friends made their final plans. Below deck, in a remote store room, Crispus had brought Paulie, Abel and William Carr for a council of war.

"Dunstan has purchased all he can carry," Crispus said.

"How many is that?" asked Paulie.

"Sixty-five...all men."

Carr said: "Good. That makes it easier."

"He won't be wantin' to wait here any longer than necessary," Abel said. "He's not the one to spend one penny extra feedin' them, now that they be his'n."

"He'll take them aboard tomorrow and settle them down," Carr said. "Then at nightfall, he'll sail."

"Did you learn the words, Paulie?" Crispus asked.

"Yes," Paulie said. "The natives taught me them."

"Teach us," Crispus asked.

At first light the crew was turned out. After a hasty breakfast of salt pork and ship's biscuit, they began checking the thousand items needed to prepare for a long sailing journey. By noon, the first canoes arrived, each carrying three or four natives. These were brought aboard and stripped of their few garments, by now mostly rags, inspected again for disease and sent below decks.

As a slave left the sunlight of the deck, he entered the hell of the Middle Passage, usually the worst part of his captivity. The capture and imprisonment he had suffered before would appear to be lenient when compared with the awful agonies he would encounter while aboard ship.

Ros-Ibo was one of the earliest to be brought aboard. Taken below, he was pushed to a flat wooden platform and shackled to another prisoner. All day long, slaves were tumbled onto the platform, crowding closer and closer together until each had only a bare eighteen inches to himself. The crowding of the barracoon was comfortable compared to this, Ros-Ibo thought. A constant moaning and clanking began as the hard wood platform punished flesh and bone for the offense of lying upon it. Soon there was no way to find relief from the numbing, bruising pains. Ros-Ibo did not know it but Captain Dunstan was a humane man as slavers went, allowing them many creature comforts other slavers never dreamed of giving.

Night settled over the ship. It made way slowly. Ros-Ibo felt the vessel moving but could not be sure since the ports were closed in the hold. It was a first night of terror for all the slaves. Taken from their homes and loved ones, they now suffered an almost equal loss. To be torn from their familiar surroundings and placed in the belly of this awful vessel meant that all hope was gone. Nightmare screams split the silence on occasion and broke in on the constant grunts and groaning. A movement on the ladder caught Ros-Ibo's ear. He saw four men quietly descending.

They divided into twos and came to each end of the platform.

"Be silent!" the big black man he had seen on the beach whispered in his own language. "We will free you."

Crispus climbed over the shackled slaves and pried the cover off the port opening. Ros-Ibo felt the coolness of the jungle evening creep into the stuffy hold.

Unshackling a dozen captives they helped them slide silently into the water. To those who shrank back in terror they repeated "land near," in their language. With barely a splash all sixty-five Africans dropped into the sluggish waters of the Mgotu. At this point, there was no more than two hundred feet to swim or float to.

Ros-Ibo reveled in the thought of having his freedom, even as he luxuriated in the swim to shore. But, his jungle instincts sharpened by capture, he was alert to anything that might take him back to captivity. Why was he freed, he wondered; why did those men take such a risk for people they did not know? Surely, Ros-Ibo thought, the punishment for their deed would be great. As he touched shore, his thoughts fled and he had to put every ounce of concentration into the work of escape. Before he did, though, he looked back at the ship. Looming over the jungle with only a few top sails set, it glided serenely down the river.

Crispus and the others carefully replaced the hatch covers and stole back toward the fo'c'sle. Filtering through the thin clouds, the moonlight etched myriad shadows on the deck. They reached the mainmast in safety and studied the best way to cover the few remaining steps to the fo'c'sle.

"One at a time," Crispus whispered. "Stay in the shadows. Paulie, you go first."

Paulie weaved around the tubs, hatches and coiled rope, then struck a misplaced block with his foot. The heavy wood clattered noisily across the deck. The group froze.

"'Vast," came a voice from the quarterdeck, "who goes there?" Feet pounded down the short ladder and soon the four were face to face with the mate and two other crew members.

"What're ye doin' above decks? 'Tis not your watch. Just what're ye up to? You, Attucks, speak up!" the mate demanded.

The four shuffled silently on the deck, each debating within himself what to do. There were only three opposing them, but the mate's pistols were stuffed into his broad belt and could be reached easily. It would not do to endanger the other three, each thought.

Besides, where could they go if they did escape? Only the dense jungle surrounded them an all sides.

"What's goin' on?" A gruff voice demanded. Swinging about, they stared at the angry Captain. Clad only in a nightshirt, the barefooted Dunstan made a comic appearance, except for the two menacing pistols he held.

"I said," he roared, "what're ye skulkin' about for? Speak! Speak up!"

The four stared at him in silence. It was too late for him to do much. The slaves were gone and within half an hour the ship would be at the mouth of the Mgotu.

"Tie 'em up," he ordered, "then search 'em. We'll find what they're about."

Soon the four were trussed up tightly and rough searching hands were seeking hints to their behavior. Items were tumbled out onto a hatch cover.

"Well," the Captain asked the mate impatiently, "what do you find? Speak up, quickly."

"Nothin' special, Captain. Not a thing except these keys off Attucks."

As pursar, Crispus would have access to many locked doors and chests. Just the same, Dunstan was suspicious.

"Hand 'em over," he demanded, "and hold these on 'em." Dunstan turned his pistols over to the mate and took the keys into an open patch of moonlight for a better look. The others watched eagerly as he turned them over and over, a quizzical look on his face.

He came back to the group and stared hard at all four, took the pistols without taking his eyes off them and in a low menacing voice told the mate: "Check the slaves below."

In a moment the mate was back, fury written on every part of his face. "They're gone, the slaves are all gone." His eyes opened wide as he realized the link. "Why, they must've...Why...the dirty blackguards!"

The speechless mate could only stare in rage at the four men sitting on the hatch cover before him. Both crew members looked at each other in dismay and rising anger. All these miles and dangers for nothing, was their thought.

Dunstan could contain his feelings no longer.

"You, Attucks, you're the ringleader," he said angrily, "you'll pay for this." Grasping a pistol by the barrel he struck Crispus across the face with the wooden butt. Crispus twisted his head quickly enough to avoid most of the blow's force but it still left a painful bruise on his cheek.

Dunstan raged up and down the deck in frustrated fury, almost incapable of containing himself. Suddenly stopping, he whirled and ordered: "Call all hands. We're goin' about."

Pipes whistled and racing feet sounded up the fo'c'sle ladder. Hands scrambled aloft to take in the few sails. The ship slowed to a crawl, only the river's tidal movement keeping it moving.

"Captain," the mate warned quietly, "goin' about in this narrow river could put us on the shoals."

"Damn you," the Captain cried, "shut your mouth! 'Twas on your watch it happened! I know the dangers."

Calculating the downstream flow and ordering the helmsman to keep the ship in the exact center of the river, Dunstan sent an anchor party forward. As the river widened at one point he gave the order.

"Drop anchor!"

The crew pulled back on the stops, releasing the cable and letting the heavy anchor plunge into the muddy brown water. The ship's forward motion stopped and the stern began to swing slowly to starboard as the current caught it and exerted its force. In moments the vessel had spun completely around, bow pointing up river.

"Up anchor! All hands aloft!" the Captain ordered and the crew scrambled to comply. Slowly the anchor cable rose, dripping with slimy green vegetation and shaking off its mud covering.

"Anchor's aweigh, Cap'n," a voice from the bow called. The ship began to move astern as the current caught it.

The sails flapped idly at first, then filled partially, fluttered, and finally caught the wind. The backward motion ceased and the ship began its laborious progress from dead stop to slow forward. Rosy dawn was beginning to light up the sky by this time and the dark jungle became clearer to the eye. The four culprits still sat on the hatch cover, bonds chaffing at their flesh, awaiting their fate.

"It was all my fault," Paulie moaned, "if I hadn't been so clumsy."

"Forget it," Crispus said, "it could have happened to any of us."

"We would have been accused anyway, I think," Carr said. "Who else would have done it? Ah, well," he added, "Dunstan will lose some good seamen over this."

The ship on its way back to Boorigha, the Captain could attend to the four responsible for his troubles. He strode toward midships, deep in thought.

"Stand up, you blackguards," he growled.

As the four struggled to their feet, Dunstan looked at them frowningly, a thunder cloud on his face.

"Flogging's too good for you," he said severely, "and keelhaulin' will kill you in these waters. I don't want to kill you for I'll need you presently, but by God you'll know from me what you did!"

He motioned to the mate: "throw four lines over the yards, two on either side of the mast. We'll see how these four beauties like swinging in the wind by their heels."

Heavy cords about their feet, Crispus and the others were dragged roughly across the deck and swung above, as crew members hauled the lines. Hands tied behind their backs, they could not fend off tackle and gear around them and were soon a mass of bruises and abrasions.

"You'll stay like that for a day or so, you blackguards, and then we may decide to hang you a different way," Dunstan called from the deck. Before he could continue, a lookout on the bow cried out:

"War party -- dead ahead!"

A seaman at work on the deck looked forward and gasped. "Oh my Gawd! It's the whole bloody country comin' after us."

Three cable lengths ahead were two huge war canoes, each holding over a hundred warriors. On their bows were two small cannons and before the shocked Americans could react, one of them sent a small shot screaming across the *Whippet's* deck. It splintered a cask and took a corner off the slave shed but otherwise did no damage. Still, the thought of two vessels attacking from either side was terrifying to the crew.

Orders to arm were given and the crew began firing without effect at the canoes. From the canoes, musket bursts returned the fire and several war hatchets sailed across the water, one of them digging itself into the mainmast.

The canoes, each almost the length of the *Whippet*, parted and expertly veered toward either side.

"Fire! Fire!" Dunstan called, using his pistols to shoot down into the packed canoes. Suddenly, remembering something from his younger days he called to several seamen:

"Bring over those cannon shot."

The men complied quickly and Dunstan ordered the heavy balls dropped into the canoes, now tying up at the ship's sides. Over went the heavy balls, plunging into the midst of the warriors crowded below.

Screams from those crushed and broken by the iron rounds filled the air but human obstacles still could not stop the heavy shot from crashing through the flimsy hulls.

Instead of saving the ship, the plan backfired, since the natives boarded the *Whippet* more rapidly to escape their sinking vessels. .

The crew fought well, retiring in decent order to the quarterdeck and firing their muskets and pistols in ragged volleys. The deadly bursts kept the attackers back, seeking safety behind every conceivable cover. Muskets and arrows took their toll on the crew, too, and soon the uneven sides began to tell.

The mate pitched over the quarterdeck rail, an arrow through his neck, his lifeless body glancing off a hatch and sliding gently onto the deck. A crew member sniped at the natives from his vantage point in the shrouds until a well-aimed lance tore him loose. He toppled from his perch and splashed noisily into the river, barely missing the ship in his fall. At these two victories the natives cheered and, under the leadership of their war chiefs, formed up to charge.

Dunstan ordered his men to hold their fire until they could make every shot count. As the ferocious natives reached within twenty feet of the quarterdeck, he gave the order. A dozen shots rang out and almost as many natives fell writhing and screaming. The rest retreated to the stern in haste except for those who made it up the ladders, only to be cut down by cutlasses.

Rather than risk another volley right away, the war chiefs fell back on another tactic. Concentrating their arrows on one or two of the crewmen they soon brought them down. This deadly attrition continued until Dunstan had only five able bodied men left and was looking longingly up at Crispus and his three companions swinging, so far safely, above the battle. With those four hands, Dunstan thought, he might have turned the tide. But now it was all over. The chiefs had been counting, too, and knew it was time.

With a bloodcurdling yell, the war party swept across the deck, several falling from the weak volley which greeted them. Two crew members died instantly, pierced by well-aimed spears. The captain, his second mate, and Aaron, the good natured cook, were the last to go. To them, surrender was out of the question. It would only be followed by a more agonizing death.

The decks glistened with the blood and gristle spread across them. Where men had slipped in the gore, toe marks scratched mad designs. Bodies lay sprawled at every angle the length and breadth of the ship.

As the fight subsided, Africans looked around slowly, fearful they should find some hurt hitherto unnoticed. Some appeared to breathe for the first time, expelling air cautiously. All knew they had been in the land of the dead for a while and none was quite sure of the permanence of his escape.

The crew lay dead or dying, Dunstan being the last to follow them, cut down by three natives. Maddened natives slipped among them, stripping them of any valuables and if one chanced to moan, quickly dispatching him with a short thrust of a bloody spear.

The victory celebration began after the blood-maddened soldiers discovered substantial quantities of rum in the ship's stores. While some were preparing to make a long day of it, a gray-haired patriarch, obviously the party's leader, was taking charge of details. He sent a young man over the side with a rope tied to his waist. The swimmer shot swiftly through the water, reached the shore, and dashed quickly up the low slope to tie the rope around the thick trunk of a tree. The ship swung stern around, threatening to pile up against the shore. Another swimmer carried a rope to the other shore, pinning the *Whippet* to the center of the river. The sails, still set, pulled against the ropes, the pressure almost snapping them. Aloft went a dozen acrobatic warriors, razor-sharp knives in their teeth. Beginning with the topmast sails, they cut and cut until rope and canvas lay crazily all over the ship.

Until this time, Crispus and the others had barely been noticed. Now they stood out clearly against the blue sky, swaying awkwardly and incongruously above the mad scene below. The gray-haired chief gave the order to cut them free and bring them down and soon Crispus and his comrades were on deck, trying to recover their balance and restore circulation to their bruised and swollen wrists and ankles.

As soon as he returned to the ship from his swim to attach a line on shore, Wallesa asked his father if he could look for Ros-Ibo below. The father readily assented but before Wallesa could go below, other tribesmen came on deck to announce there were no Africans aboard.

The natives conferred long and anxiously, puzzled by this turn of events.

At length, the chief turned to the four survivors, beckoning a native to his side. In his own tongue the chief spoke to the native, who translated into Spanish for him. The four looked at each other and shrugged, shaking their heads. The interpreter then tried Portuguese and finally French. Seeing they continued to stare dumbly at them, he repeated his question in the native language.

"Chief say, where are slaves?"

Paulie listened intently to the words to catch any hints of meaning. Cupping his hand around his ear, he motioned the interpreter to repeat the question.

"He's asking about the slaves," Paulie said. "Should we tell them what we did?"

The group exchanged glances, hesitant over what to do. If these were slave pirates, it might be certain death to admit to freeing the cargo. But there seemed to be no choice anyway, since they expected death regardless of their answer.

William Carr spoke first: "Tell him we freed the slaves. If we die, let it be for the right cause."

"Amen," said Crispus.

Turning to the interpreter, Paulie said simply "we free slaves."

The chief and the interpreter exchanged startled glances, as much surprised at the use of their language as by the answer given. On instructions from the chief, the interpreter bombarded Paulie with questions. He understood nothing so could only repeat the brief expressions he used. The natives became increasingly angered by the failure to communicate.

"Wait a moment," Carr said. "Let's show them."

A few feet from where they stood lay the body of Captain Dunstan, his jacket insignia announcing his rank to everyone. Carr walked over to the body and pointed vigorously to it, shaking his head over and over. He pointed to himself and his friends and upwards to the yards they had just been cut down from.

The chief nodded. He understood the message clearly. He spoke to the four directly, pointing at each one in turn and saying the same word four times:

"Free. Free. Free. Free."

The four well understood the meaning of that and broad grins split their faces. They shared in the rum and food brought up from below and lent a hand in ridding the ship of the corpses which had begun to bake in the risen tropical sun.

Crispus had not expected to see an hour more of this day - or any other, for that matter. Every breath he took, every glance at the jungle beauty surrounding the ship had a newness about it which only those reprieved from mortal danger could appreciate.

The celebration over, the chief ordered all the *Whippet's* boats lowered, the four remaining seamen showing them the way it was done. All the spoils of war were loaded into the boats - supplies, weapons, clothing, food, and any other goods which could be squeezed in. A generous quantity of gold and silver was found but the chief handed it over to Crispus and his friends as a gift. The chief then ordered the ship set on fire and cut adrift to float down the river to its mouth where the sea would take over and complete the task of destruction.

As this task was being completed, the chief muttered the word "slave" to himself many times, somewhat bitterly, Crispus thought, for a man who had just won a great sea battle over a well-armed foe. In fact the chief and his son Wallesa, for that was who the young man at his side was, were both extremely depressed and shared little of the joy shown by their fellow warriors.

The journey upstream took two days, during which Crispus came to respect the war party for its organization and discipline. Keeping a tight formation, they rowed the unfamiliar boats past hostile villages. But with the ship's pistols and muskets augmenting their own weapons, they were ready for any ambush. Too large a group to be attacked frontally, they were still vulnerable to cutting out when they sent water parties ashore. But because of their precautions, not a man was lost on the trip home.

As they approached the village of Rivertown, the chief nodded to a native who sounded a horn in a long, distinctive note. Moments later, the same note came echoing across the water. For the first time, the quiet discipline broke down and the men laughed and shouted happily.

Rounding a bend in the river, they came upon a narrow, crescent shaped beach bordering which was a town of substantial size. At the first sound of the horn, the people of the village rushed to the shore. Some still had their farm tools with them, others could be seen far off striding clumsily out of the fields. Many waved palm leaves in greeting. All strained to catch sight of relatives or friends; many would be disappointed, thanks to Captain Dunstan's fierce resistance.

Several youths plunged into the river, swimming strongly to the boats amid the applause and laughter of all.

As the boats scraped bottom a few feet from the shore, the villagers rushed their warriors and a melee of comradeship resulted. The Chief and Wallesa vaulted into the water and waded ashore, right into the arms of Ros-lbo. They stared in amazement before joining in a wild dance of joy.

The chief squatted on the beach, his two youngest sons beside him and the villagers crowding around.

"How did you escape the captors?" the chief asked Ros-Ibo, pointing at the "W" burned onto his breast .

"I did not. I was set free by some of the slavers," Ros-Ibo answered. "They freed us all and helped us escape."

The chief beckoned Crispus, Paulie and the others forward.

"Those are the men who freed us," Ros-Ibo cried, jumping to his feet. "Especially that one," he said, pointing to Crispus.

The villagers put aside all work for the day and devoted themselves to a three-fold task. Most spent the day in feasting in celebration of the victory and the party's safe return. Some went to their homes weeping and mourning, carrying the few possessions brought back from their slain kinsfolk. Another group treated the wounded.

Huge bonfires were lit and two slaughtered cattle placed on spits to provide meat for the feasting. Spitted chickens by the dozen were roasted slowly and huge kettles filled with rice and other savory foods simmered over other fires. Gourds of beer and wine made from grains and rice were passed around, as were mugs of rum from the ship's supplies.

"A far cry from the beef and biscuit we're accustomed to, eh lads?" Abel asked, raising a gourd overflowing with creamy African beer. The others grinned and returned the salute. For the first time in weeks they feasted on fresh food. Bashful serving women brought them platters of chicken and other fowl basted with strong spices. Vegetables and fruits were served in large wooden bowls and were consumed voraciously by the vitamin-starved seamen.

"Want to stay here, Crispus?" Abel asked jokingly. "You and I could be kings out here."

"At least, but what would we do with these two?" Crispus said, pointing to Carr and Paulie.

"We could make 'em honorary chiefs," Abel said.

"What are we going to do?" Paulie asked. "The chief's gratitude won't last forever. We should make a plan."

"'The last plan we made got us hanging by our feet from the yards," Carr answered. "What surprises do you have now?"

The town was miles from the coast through slave territory. During the days which followed the four learned more and more about their hosts. Their tribe was devoted to ivory hunting, collecting elephant's teeth, as it was called, and scorned their slave-trading neighbors. Still, as Ros-Ibo and many less fortunate than he knew, they could not relax a bit because of the slavers and their constant man-stealing.

Every few months, the tribe's traders, accompanied by a heavily armed escort, made the trek westward across the country to the port of Jebila on another branch of the Niger River. Jebila was an ivory port primarily, although precious metals, textiles and other goods were handled there also. The chief told the Americans that such a trip would be taken in a few weeks when the tribe had acquired enough ivory to make it worthwhile. At that time, they could go in safety with the traders and pick up a boat bound for the Americas.

In the meanwhile, he suggested they join the tribe in an elephant hunt and, if it was successful, they would share in its profits. The four eagerly agreed, since it promised excitement and a chance to earn a little wealth. The elephant hunt took them miles inland, past the heavily forested coastal region to the plains where vast herds of animals roamed.

To Crispus, the plains were a man's paradise. Every sort of game abounded, ready to be felled by musket, spear or bow and arrow with very little effort. The hides produced yielded many different leathers, some far stronger, others more delicate and supple than the deer and cowhide Crispus had worked with in New England. His professional interest awakened, Crispus used his free moments to fashion leather goods such as his hosts had never seen before. Soft boots and broad belts, knife sheaths, food wallets, and arrow quivers. All he gave as gifts to the chief and his kin, earning their gleeful gratitude.

At the end of a day's hunt, the tired warriors clustered around a huge fire, roasting the flesh of an impala or eland freshly killed and bled that day. In the early evening while the sun still sent a colorful glow over the sky, tribesmen feasted and sang, laughed and told stories. As darkness enclosed them, they drew closer to the fire, less confident and unafraid than during the daylight. Soon, each began to find it impossible to remain wide awake. Curling up under cloaks or sleeping cloths, they fell into deep restful sleep. Only a handful of guards remained alert, changing every few hours. These kept watch on the night, judging the distance between their camp and a nearby pride of lions by their distinctive cough. Hyenas circled the camp, keeping well out of range, their ugly eyes glowing yellow when caught by the firelight. Heavy crashing through the brush warned the guards to be alert to elephants. These usually, but not always, gave human camps a wide circuit. If, by chance they blundered into a camp, they often panicked and simply rushed right through, crushing unwary sleepers to death in their haste.

At the first streaks of dawn, the hunters stirred and with little ceremony and less breakfast set out to follow elephant spoor. At midmorning one day, they came upon a prize, a giant bull in a stand of mimosa trees on a hill a quarter mile away. The bull was alternately scratching its side against the bark of a fragile mimosa and feasting on the leaves of its upper branches. Its tusks were huge, so large they had begun to curl back toward the bull's head. The fact that a bull of that age and size was alone could mean only one thing: it was a rogue, displaced from the herd by a younger and stronger male. It would therefore be a beast of ferocious temper and great cunning, capable of outwitting even the best hunters.

At a signal from the chief, the tribesmen expertly fanned out, making a wide circuit around the beast. The purpose was to drive him toward the musketeers, of which there were six, including the chief, Ros-Ibo, Crispus and his three friends. They had been given this place of honor as a mark of respect by the chief. Standing with the sun at their backs would benefit the hunters but as they gazed on the elephant, its huge ears now wide with alarm, their muskets seemed to shrink in size against the target.

At a hornblow, the warriors began to beat spear against shield from every side except that where the marksmen stood. This left the elephant only one way out. Startled by the horn, the rogue took stock of the situation, then headed directly toward the musketeers.

It happened with incredible speed. One moment the beast seemed remote and far away, while the next it was charging down on them, looming high above and trumpeting in rage. At a range of less than twenty-five feet, all the hunters fired and six shots ripped into the elephant's massive head. It staggered off balance for a moment while the wounds began to flow with blood. None of the shots seemed to be at vital points so the beast, shaking its head and raising its tusks in anger, continued its charge.

"Run!" ordered the chief to the hunters, now holding empty firearms. Crispus and Carr raced away while Paulie and Abel, who had pistols in their belts, stood firm and used their small weapons. The balls whistled harmlessly past the elephant. Paulie dodged as the elephant's huge tusks swept toward his chest, escaping death by inches. Abel was not so fortunate. His foot became tangled in a vine and he pitched forward, directly in the elephant's way. It brought its foot down on Abel's back, crushing his spine and killing him instantly. Seizing his limp form in its trunk, the elephant lifted it high, then brought it down to earth again and again.

Taking advantage of the beast's preoccupation, the hunters quickly reloaded, and sent another volley crashing into the beast. This time several balls reached the animal's small brain. It dropped Abel's shattered body and turned its great bulk toward them, took a few steps in their direction, then pitched over on its side, completely lifeless.

The Africans rushed forward, leaping on its body and cheering, while Crispus, Carr and Paulie walked sadly toward Abel's body. They knelt by the battered form, now so small and shrunken.

The chief came over and laid his hand on Crispus' shoulder: "No shame to die from an elephant."

Crispus nodded. It was true. He met a man's death on a man's hunt.

They buried Abel where he lay, placing his body deep in the ground to discourage scavengers and piling stones on top of the site. Crispus recited the burial service by memory, while the tribesmen stood respectfully by.

Abel's death cast gloom over the three friends. They sat apart from the tribesmen, Crispus holding Abel's two meager possessions in his hands: the pine tree symbol he always kept pinned to his hat as a reminder of his position as a porter in Boston and a scrimshaw carving he had worn on a leather thong around his neck. These must go home to Martha Hayrood, Crispus promised himself.

The hunters worked feverishly, like ants on a sugar cube, some cutting out the massive tusks, others plunging their hunting knives deeply into the carcass to carve out choice organs and pieces of flesh. Some warriors lit a large fire while others stood guard against predators seeking to share the prize. Hyenas and wild dogs circled outside spear throw while hungry vultures watched the scene greedily from the upper branches of nearby trees.

The savory meat was soon crackling over the fire, its red juices splashing into the flames. The delicious aroma stirred appetites long neglected and despite their grief, the three friends found themselves looking forward to the meal. The chief brought choice pieces to them which they found remarkably tender and tasty once they overcame the aversion to the thought of eating elephant meat.

"Elephant!" Carr remarked smilingly, as he wiped off the juices running down his chin with the back of his hand. "Never thought I'd see the day."

"Not bad, though," Paulie observed.

"Bullock is far worse," Crispus said, tearing a piece with his teeth.

The chief joined them after the feast, bringing them a gourd filled with a sweet but potent liquor. As they settled down to drink and smoke, the chief tried to communicate to them in a language composed of his own tongue, hybrid European languages, and sign language.

"You stay," he indicated to all three, pointing to the ground. "Much hunting, many wives I give you."

The friends shook their heads but smiled their thanks.

"Be warriors," the chief continued, "maybe chief." He pointed especially to Crispus. "You chief."

Crispus answered him kindly: "Home...woman."

The chief understood, nodding sadly.

After a night's sound sleep, the hunters once again gorged themselves on the rogue's carcass, then left the remains to Africa's hungry beasts, still lurking at a safe distance from the camp.

During the next few days, they continued hunting but changed direction, heading back toward the town before departing for the Ivory Coast. Several more trophies were added to their tusk collection, but none so big as the rogue. The warriors, heavily laden with bundles of teeth, magical elephant tails, food stores and countless other by-products they could sell, were growing weary and peevish. The strain of absence from their homes and families was beginning to show.

All were glad when the Chief announced that they had reached the desired goal of ivory and sent runners ahead to inform the village of their return. In a few days the villagers were joyously greeting them and shortly after, Crispus, Carr, and Paulie were on their way to Jebila with the traders.

Before leaving, they had been presented with a fortune in gold and precious stones, in part for freeing Ros-Ibo but also for their share in the ivory hunt. The three pooled most of their wealth into one pouch, intending to give it to Martha, Abel's widow, upon their return home to Boston.

An uneventful journey through now familiar jungle terrain brought them to the Jebila ivory town. In plan it was much like the slave town but without the barracoon or the stench of human misery. Warehouses, trade buildings, native and European quarters made up Jebila. But, like all African port towns, its purpose was in its wharves and piers, which bustled with great activity. There were native and European boats tied up along the piers and in the river's center. All together, there seemed to be a greater spirit of trust in this town, compared to the suspicious tone which lay over the slave cities.

Arriving at Jebila, the three friends bade their African comrades goodbye and set about looking for a likely ship to take them home. The first evening found them aboard an ivory trader, the *Nellie*, out of Sag Harbor, Long Island. The *Nellie* was the fourth ship they had tried, the others being unsuitable for one reason or another. One of the rejected ships was, in fact, a slaver on its way upriver for a load of slaves after picking up ivory at Jebila.

The *Nellie's* captain was a rotund, red-faced Long Islander named Huntley who kept a pipe perpetually in the corner of his mouth. He had few back teeth, however, so the pipe kept sliding out of his mouth and dropping coals and ashes on the deck.

"So you want passage back to America?" Captain Huntley asked. "What became of your last ship? Did ye jump?"

Expecting to be quizzed about their former ship, the three had decided to relate part of the story, stressing the attack but omitting their role in freeing the slaves. The captain pulled at his pipe and took a sip from a metal tankard containing rum, listening to Paulie's account.

"There's been rumors along the coast about a ship lost. I didn't credit them but anything's possible in these waters. The *Whippet* she was, you say? Out of Boston? Didn't know her, but then I'm not in the dirty business that brought her here."

Huntley shook his head over the thought of slaving, losing his pipe for the third time and spreading red coals on the deck.

"I've a full crew," he said, "but you seem likely so I'll sign you on as supercargo at half wages and full rations, agreed?"

The friends could have easily afforded to pay for berths out of the wealth they had acquired in Africa but chose to work in order to have a bigger kitty for Martha Hayrood.

At dawn of a calm West African morning, the *Nellie* tacked slowly out of the Niger estuary, leaving the purple continent's sunrise behind. Reaching open water, the ship' s great sails caught the wind and began the race across the south Atlantic and north to New York.

The crew, including Crispus and his friends, took to their duties eagerly, happy to be away from Africa's oppressive atmosphere and glad to feel the swaying deck beneath their feet again.

Three uneventful days passed, the wind holding strong, enabling them to log 320 miles without taking in sail at night or even reefing sail more than a few times. Captain Huntley was not a man in a great hurry but neither was he a man to lose a good opportunity. He spared his crew but wrung from his ship everything that wood and canvas could give.

On the morning of the fourth day the lookout announced a sail. By late afternoon the hull was visible and it was obvious that it was following an identical course to the *Nellie's.*

Crispus was at the helm when Huntley decided to test the pursuer. "She may be trying to reach us for some innocent purpose," he remarked to no one in particular on the quarterdeck, "but then again she may be a buccaneer. There's plenty of 'em out here."

Watching the ship through his glasses, he ordered: "Helmsman, come up two points," thus taking the ship away from its previous course and in fact turning it southwest. Within minutes the ship following changed course to follow the *Nellie's* lead. Huntley ordered Crispus to repeat the maneuver twice more before he was satisfied.

"No flags flyin', no signals," Huntley said, sucking on his pipe. "And she's stickin' to us like barnacles to a hull. That means she's up to no good."

The Captain scanned the horizon, seeking a friendly sail or some other advantage. The only hope appeared to lie with the weather. Directly ahead of their southwesterly course was a black line, indicating an approaching squall.

"If we can reach that storm we may shake the blackguards yet," Huntley said. Then, turning to his first mate, he ordered: "lay on all sail. We'll outrun him to yonder squall."

"Captain," the mate said gravely, "that's a bad move. We may outrun him and get ourselves torn to pieces by that storm in the bargain. I suggest we heave to and give the pirates what they want."

"Damn your suggestions!" Huntley said. "Have you ever seen a ship that's been visited by one of those beauties yonder? I have, and there was not enough skin left on any crew member to tattoo the dot of an I. Even the ship's cat didn't escape; they cut his legs off and left him screamin' and bleedin' on the Captain's chest. Now lay on that sail, I say!"

The crew surged aloft, spurred by the mate's harsh commands. Laggards were inspired with sharp blows from the ropes held by petty officers for the purpose. But little encouragement was really needed after a bow shot screamed through the upper rigging, showing that the pursuer had closed the distance and could pound them into driftwood at whim.

Chapter 7

Alone on the vast expanse of ocean a small dory floated, its bow dipping gently into the low waves. The ten foot boat, badly holed high on the starboard bow, did not seem to be taking water at the moment. Neither was it the most seaworthy craft on the South Atlantic's waters. A benign sun smiled on the waves, making their oily surface shine brilliantly like multi-colored gems in a treasure box.

But beneath the splendor of scene an ominous strength lay waiting. The sea or the wind at any time could wipe out the life of the small boat and the three salt-caked figures sleeping on its rough wet planks could be snuffed out like candles.

For twelve hours they had been locked in a deep exhausted sleep, their bodies unable to shake off the struggle they had undergone during the previous day. Crispus stirred first, moving his arm from its numbed position under his head and lifting himself up to the rowing bench. Carefully, hoping not to disturb William Carr, he removed his foot from under Carr's leg. Carr turned over and fell once again into a deep sleep.

Crispus sank his face into his hands, resting his elbow on his knees and continued dozing. A large wave lapped through the starboard hole, drenching his dry right trouser leg and awakening him completely. He gazed first at the sleeping forms and then at the empty seas around him. So far from Nora, he thought. Would he ever see her again?

The jumbled events of the last day aboard the *Nellie* began slowly to sort themselves out. He remembered sighting the buccaneer and hearing the Captain's words because as helmsman he had to instantly respond to orders. And the mate...what had he advised? To heave to and take their medicine? He might have been right, Crispus thought. They are all dead as it is, he thought sadly. Huntley was a good man. Perhaps he had been right to try to run.

And the storm, no one could have judged the force of that wind. It whipped the canvas to ribbons in no time, nearly forcing the ship around in a 180 degree turn. Nothing they might have done could have helped. They were doomed from the start. The only consolation, and a small one at that, was in seeing the buccaneer, badly handled and apparently undermanned, go down before them.

Moments later it was their turn. Their ship was broached by the waves, and never came up again. Only a ship's boat, the very dory he was sitting in, escaped the sea's merciless pounding.

The third figure in the little craft stirred, opened his eyes and immediately closed them as the sun seared directly into them.

"Where, where are we?" Paulie asked. "What happened? I don't remember anything." He sat up and put his hand behind his throbbing head, feeling dried blood caked with salt.

"A spar hit your head, Paulie," Crispus said. "Just as we were crawling through a gun port. What were you doing down there, anyway?"

Paulie moved, winced, and rubbed his head. He thought for a minute, then grinned. "Remember that leather pouch you made for me?"

He pulled his jacket aside to reveal a leather container bursting with its contents. Tapping with his fist to make it clink, he grinned widely and said, "Abel's gold."

"You risked your life to get that?" Crispus asked, knowing they had hidden it below decks.

"He was our friend," Paulie remarked. Then, changing the subject to hide his embarrassment, he asked: "How is William?"

"No injuries that I can see," Crispus answered. "We were lucky we were on the starboard side when she broached. Otherwise, we would have joined the others."

"No other survivors?" Paulie asked.

"None," Crispus said.

Carr awoke soon afterwards and the three began taking stock of their situation. A few stores were found in the bottom of the boat, lashed to a bench, including a sealed cask of water-about two gallons-and a small package of ship's biscuit, crumbling and crawling with weevils. The best discovery was a broken oar and a few ship's tools.

"We can get back to Boston with these," Carr said cheerfully, holding up the hammer and nails.

"You're right," Crispus said, taking them from him and working his way to the stern. He checked the transom for rats and found none, then began building a seat for the oar to create a makeshift rudder. With this they could at least control the boat somewhat, keeping its bow pointed into the waves so it would not present its broadside to them and possibly be broached.

They each took swallows of water and tried the biscuit, then put their heads together to work out a direction, following their recollection of the sun's position on the last day of sailing before sighting the buccaneer's sail. Luckily, Carr and Crispus had spent many hours at the helm since Captain Huntley had early realized their steadiness. Remembering the course, they set off in high spirits, convinced that the Lord and their strength would get them through.

The year was 1751 A.D. and a time when peace prevailed throughout the world, even among the English and French, at least for a time. Commercial vessels plied the seas carrying cargoes back and forth across the Atlantic by thousands. All nationalities participated in the great economic game. But like all vulnerable creatures they tended to bunch together, keeping to well-used shipping lanes for their greater safety in numbers. Once they strayed from the well-charted path they were on their own. No naval patrol or passing merchant vessel was likely to pick them up. The three friends knew this, so hoped to bring their frail craft into a place where their chances of discovery were better.

Night was beautiful on the open sea but the cold enveloped them at sunset, forcing them to huddle together for warmth. The stars made it easier to keep on course, though, and all three were happy they had listened carefully to all the seamen on the *Whippet*. That ship had been a school for Crispus and Paulie and they had learned their celestial navigation lessons well. Carr needed no teaching, of course, since he had almost been born to the sea.

For nine days they drifted, blessed by the presence of good weather. A few short squalls had tested their skills but they had come through them well. A brief thunderstorm had burst over them as well, pouring life-giving water on them and washing off the days of salt that covered them like a second skin. They had removed their shirts and soaked them in the rain, cleansing them of salt. After a few rinsings the water ran clear and pure, and they were able to quench their thirst by ringing their shirts out. For the first time in nine days they finally had their fill of water. They even succeeded in replenishing their meager supply by ringing their shirts out over the water jug.

But in spite of these lucky breaks, the sea was taking its toll on their energy and strength. Each day the sun baked moisture out of them which they could not replace as rapidly as they lost. Food did not interest them greatly and this had its effect on weakening them. A string attached to a bent nail was hung over the side night and day but had produced no results so far. They began to lose touch with reality and even to dream fantastic dreams which left them wild-eyed and exhausted. Crispus dreamt often of Nora but always it was the same dream. Her bridal gown afire, she was beckoning him to her, inviting him to embrace her. He was forever striding toward her, never reaching her. It was a maddening time and had any of them been alone, he could not have lasted.

What kept them sane as much as any other factor was their organization. They divided the day into watches, using the sun and the stars as timekeepers. Each stood one watch of two hours around the clock, two hours on and four hours off. During their watches, each was helmsman and lookout at the same time. At first light each dawn they carried out a simple but vital religious ceremony. Then Crispus cut one more notch into the side of the boat as their record.

At sunset on the fourteenth day, Paulie was scanning the horizon during his watch. Suddenly he tensed, his hand gripping the rudder. "A sail," he cried. "Quick, a sail."

The others were awake instantly, straining their eyes to catch the direction of the ship before the light faded.

"He's bearing down on us," Carr said, "he'll be on us in a few hours. Probably pass us during the night."

Before dark they took turns standing in the boat, waving a light colored rag in hopes that they might be seen. The ship grew larger, its sails more visible every few minutes. Then...nothing. The darkness surrounded them and brought with it the worst despair they had experienced since the disaster. All through the night they kept their vigil, peering into the total darkness on all sides.

Toward morning a thick mist closed in upon them, cutting off vision for more than a few feet. The fog seemed to distort their senses, insulating them as if by a wall from their surroundings.

Suddenly, the bow of a ship loomed over them, white foam arching away as it sliced through the waves. Paulie put the oar-rudder over to keep the dory from being split in two. This action saved their lives, for the bow only hit them a glancing blow, nearly capsizing them but leaving them intact. All along the length of the ship they traveled, bounced away each time by the impact of striking its sides but drawn back by the rushing wake.

They waited their chance carefully, then spying a line dangling over the ship's side, grabbed for it. Crispus held it fast, feeling himself rise out of the dory. Carr seized Crispus, wrapping his own legs around the dory's rowing bench.

Now their direction was reversed and they were speeding parallel to the big ship, Crispus and Carr forming a human lifeline. Paulie shouted at the top of his lungs, beating the side of the ship with a wooden stick. The moments passed and Crispus' grip on the rope weakened. Water rushed into the frail craft, threatening to swamp it.

"I can't hold on much longer," Crispus cried. Paulie's eyes fell on a length of rope in the bottom of the dory.

"Hold on," he urged, "I'll do something." Slipping past Carr, he knotted the line through the dory's bow ring then searched for a likely place to catch onto the ship. Looking up, he saw a face peering down at them from a distance of a dozen feet.

"Well, I'll be!" the face said. "Look what the waves brought in." He disappeared for a moment, bringing other faces back with him.

"Wait and I'll drop ye a proper line, mates," he said, tossing a stout rope down to Paulie. Paulie quickly knotted the rope to the dory's bench, then helped Carr bring Crispus down.

Crispus let go his hold on the rope and eased his drenched and numbed body onto a rowing bench of the dory. They were now surfing along, a few feet from the big vessel's hull. Mist still enshrouded them so they could barely see twenty feet. But it was clearing and dim light was adding rosy tones to the fog.

A rope ladder went over the side and one by one they clambered up. Carr held the lower rope rungs for the other two, giving them a firmer hold.

When his turn came, he was whipped back and forth between dory and ship, banging into the latter's hull heavily. But, good seaman that he was, he made it over the gunwale.

As soon as he touched deck, he grinned to his comrades and said: "Blubber hunter, you can easy tell."

Crispus and Paulie looked about them, noting the long, sturdy whale boats, sharp prows fore and aft for better maneuverability. From their bows jutted ugly looking harpoons, taller than a man and attached to what looked like miles of rope. On deck directly forward were oven-like brick devices with huge kettles set in them.

"Them's the try-works," Carr said, "for renderin' the blubber."

The Captain was called and came hastily aft to greet them. He was a weather-beaten man with the strong features of one who has met many challenges and surrendered to very few.

"Welcome aboard!" he said gruffly. "What ship be you off?"

They told him and he said to the mate: "Make an entry in the log of all this." Turning back to them he asked, "and the buccaneer, could you describe it, in case it escaped the storm?"

On the Captain's orders Crispus and his friends were taken below and allowed to eat and drink their fill. The cook first gave them each a bowl of "longlick," a mixture of molasses, coffee, and tea, which they spooned down very slowly.

"Now get those clothes off and clean yourselves up," the cook bawled. "You'll find the wash pump on deck and I'll get the pursar to get you some new duds from the slop chest."

They were soon back in the galley, their skin free of the corrosive salt but cracking like old cowhide and dribbling blood in some places. The fresh clothes felt good and they were ready for some real food.

The cook gave them more longlick and added a bowl of scouse to the menu. They ate the portions greedily, savoring the combination of beef, hard bread and beans.

By the time they had accomplished all this, the morning was well along. Brought up on deck, they found themselves in the middle of a busy crew. Some were scrubbing the deck with sand, others were tending to the rigging, while a third group was hoisting the shipwreck's dory aboard the whaler. The carpenter stood by, professionally eyeing the dripping craft to see if it could be repaired.

"You're well taken care of, I see," the Captain said pleasantly, coming up behind them. "Then you'll rest today and do no work until tomorrow. Yonder little boat should pay for the food and slop advanced you. You'll be common hands like most of the rest and forced to turn to six days a week. The seventh is yours, saving a need for you."

He looked at the three men keenly, seeking any sign that they wanted to be treated as anything but crew members.

Paulie said: "Captain, we don't know which way you are heading but we can pay our way 'till you drop us off at a port."

"We're heading for the Pacific, my friends, and we won't sight land 'till we're 'round Cape Horn. That'll be Juan Fernandez and there's not much there to occupy us except its water supplies."

He looked again at them. "Save your money. I'll pay you decent wages for your labor. And you'll be home in no more than three years."

Three years, Crispus thought, and something inside him turned cold with despair.

xxxxx

Twenty-one year old George Washington huddled against Christopher Gist, trying to find some small warmth against the bitter January cold. It did no good, for Gist was colder than he, although Washington and not he had fallen off the raft earlier in the evening. Gist complained of his fingers and toes gradually losing feeling.

Stranded on a small island, they could almost see the ice slowly crusting over the Allegheny River, which they had been trying to cross for eighteen hours. Washington shifted his body slightly, his drenched buckskin trousers clinging fast to his six foot two inch frame. He had not slept in forty-eight hours and was almost at the point of giving up.

His mission a failure and facing slow death, he wondered why he had undertaken such a task at all, much less in midwinter. But, he recalled, when Governor Dinwiddie had summoned him to a meeting at Williamsburg the previous fall it was too great an honor to resist. He was exceedingly proud of being, at age twenty-one, a major, although commissioned by Virginia and not the English Crown. And he was further honored by the nature of the mission. He was to order the French at Le Boeuf to leave the Ohio Valley since they were encroaching upon the domains of His Most Gracious Majesty, George II. Lands, he thought, also belonging to King George's greatest province, his own beloved Virginia.

Gist shifted against him, moaning with the pain of the cold. Washington encouraged him, nodding to the lightening sky in the east.

"Hold on, Mr. Gist," Washington said, "it will soon be light and I can see from here that the river is almost frozen over again. We shall make it, after all."

That had been their undoing, Washington thought. The river. When they had left the main party with the horses and supplies, they expected to travel faster to get the news to Williamsburg. Plodding through the trackless terrain, Washington had been happy that Mr. Gist was such an expert guide. He might even now be wandering westward instead of on the proper course.

The hostile Indians had hurried them too, especially the braves they had encountered the day before yesterday. That was an interesting experience, Washington recalled. Not five yards away from him a brave had sent a ball singing right toward him. A clean miss. Strangely, he had felt no fear, only a kind of wild exhilaration. But that had hurried them on to the Allegheny River.

If only it had been entirely frozen over, he thought, they would not have had to spend an entire day hacking away at trees with their single hatchet to build the clumsy raft that had landed them on this forsaken island.

The night passed and the last day of the year 1753 dawned.

Hopefully, 1754 would be a better one than the last, Washington mused. At least it was gratifying to see the Allegheny River covered over with ice once again.

The two numbed figures proceeded gingerly to the eastern shore but had not gone very far when they met twenty Indians, war-painted and fully armed. Far from being hostile, they were fearful and excited.

Exchanging peace signs, Washington and Gist asked the Indians where they were bound.

"Home," the leader said, pointing northward. "We no go south. Death there. We no do."

"Where?" Washington inquired.

The Indians excitedly told of a grisly sight they had seen. Passing a farmhouse, they found the bodies of seven persons, all dead and scalped, their bodies half eaten by hogs. Only one young woman had remained alive. They feared they would be blamed for it.

"Who did it?" Washington asked.

"Indians. Ottawa tribe. That was their coup. We no do. No blame. We no do."

"We believe you." Washington said and bade them goodbye.

Pushing on, they left word at the closest town of the all too frequent tragedy.

By mid-January 1754, Washington and Gist had reached the town of Williamsburg, bustling capital of North America's largest colony. For over sixty years since it replaced dying Jamestown as Virginia's capital, the city had been in the making. It now consisted of several hundred private homes well laid out along spacious streets, as well as a substantial number of government, commercial, and manufacturing buildings. Central to the city were the Capitol, where the Virginia assembly met, and the Governor's house with its beautiful well-kept gardens.

Washington was ushered into Governor Robert Dinwiddie's palatial office, feeling out of place after months in the woods.

As Dinwiddie bent over to read the letter from Legardeur de St. Pierre, the French commander of Fort Le Boeuf, Washington studied the man. Fleshy and middle-aged, he was a thoughtful and decisive leader.

Looking up, Dinwiddie remarked. "Seems a polite enough fellow. Did he treat you well?"

"Yes, sir," Washington replied. "He was very cordial but firm in his refusal to leave the territory."

"So he says. Well, that leaves us no choice but to remove him." Rising, the Governor smiled and said to Washington, "You have acquitted yourself brilliantly in this affair, Major Washington, and the Journal you have submitted has earned an important place in our archives."

Washington left the office with mixed feelings. Glad that he had played a part in the event, he was also sorry that nothing had come of it. Was it worth all the suffering? Would any more be done?

Washington's fears that nothing more would come of what he started proved groundless when an expedition of forty men was sent from Virginia immediately after his return in January 1754. This contingent began the following month to build a fort at the point on the Ohio River where the Allegheny and Monongahela Rivers met.

For several weeks Washington basked in the fame he briefly enjoyed. He was delighted to see his report published and was gratified to receive 50 pounds from the Virginia Assembly. And when he was promoted to Lieutenant Colonel of the Virginia militia and named second in command of Col. Joshua Fry's regiment, Washington felt his star was soaring.

But honors usually do not come unless accompanied by duties which often exceed them in labor or danger involved. And Washington's case was no exception.

He had returned to Williamsburg in the dead of winter. On the second of April, while the soft breezes of Spring were just beginning to turn the frosty roads and paths to mud, he was departing for the Ohio Valley, this time with an advance party of a few hundred troops. Accompanying him were some cumbersome artillery and broken-down supply wagons which had to be brought through the pathways cleared by the troops as they proceeded. Most days they covered about a mile every four hours.

At this point, Virginia's militia forces in the Ohio valley were in three fragments: Washington's force, the main party under Colonel Fry, and those who had been sent in January to build a fort.

As Washington's small force reached a creek in Maryland they saw a group of armed men hurrying toward them.

"Hold your fire," Washington ordered, recognizing some of the stragglers. One of the men approached him, the others throwing down their arms and sinking exhausted to the ground.

"Mr. Ward, what brings you back here? Have you completed your assignment?" Washington asked. Mr. Ward was one of the officers of the original party sent out to build the fort.

The tired man, his face black with dirt and fatigue, took a mug offered him and drank, then replied, "Mr. Washington, the French chased us away. We built the fort and they came down the river by the hundreds and made us leave."

"How many were there?" Washington asked.

"A thousand, counting Indian. And they must have had twenty heavy guns if they had one."

Washington was overwhelmed by the information. His own small force was dwarfed by the French both in manpower and in guns. His convoy consisted of broken-down wagons and overage horses sold to the army by local farmers who got the highest prices for the worst goods. The only hope he had lay in fast action. Dashing off a quick letter to Governor Dinwiddie, he outlined his plan to push toward the French to scout and harass them.

By the end of May, he was deep in territory filled with hostile Indians and surrounded by French forts. His party found a suitable site for defense at a place called Great Meadows. Word came that a party of French and Indians was in the vicinity and scouts were spotted from time to time spying on them.

To Washington that could mean only that the French were planning an attack. He left the main portion of his force at Great Meadows and with forty men set out on a seven hour march to surprise the French.

Early on the morning of May 27, 1754, Washington and his Virginia troops, together with a few loyal Indians, came upon the French camp. The enemy scrambled for their rifles but were too surprised to react strongly. In a few minutes ten of them lay dead and twenty were captured. Washington's force lost one man.

Although he did not know it, Washington's action was the beginning of nine years of bitter war which would touch the lives of every person in the colonies.

Washington returned to Great Meadows realizing that his position was more perilous than before. At least one enemy soldier had escaped capture and would be racing to warn the French. They would not be long in coming.

"We must fortify this site to defend it against at least five hundred men," Washington told his officers and noncoms soon after their return from the skirmish. "Break your men into work parties. Set some to digging entrenchments, creating palisades of the dirt. Others should be set to work cutting and hauling timber for a fort."

Great Meadows was soon transformed into a fort, partly because its natural terrain made it easy to defend and partly because it was now strengthened by a circular wooden stockade with a log cabin inside it.

"Can we hold this fort against the French, Colonel?" Captain Robert Stobo asked, as he and Washington surveyed the works on a drizzly morning.

Washington looked at his handiwork, which had taken so much effort and which looked so meager. "I don't know, Captain. They outnumber us so greatly and have so much more fire power, that I fear we cannot do much more than detain them somewhat."

"Will the Governor help?" Stobo asked.

"He is doing all he can. I have requested reinforcements and more guns and ammunition. Let us hope all arrive in time."

"At least the Indians seem to be coming to us," Stobo remarked, watching a party of a dozen or so Indians approaching the fort.

Washington snorted: "The wives and children come and eat up our stores. We need lean braves but these prefer to fight for the French who pay them so well. We are running out of shirts and other clothing to give our own redskinned allies. And once we stop paying them, they will be on their way."

The little stream running north past the fort was swollen with June rain. Days of drizzle and hours of downpour filled the trenches with muddy water as well as casting a gloom over the fort's defenders. Isolated by miles of wilderness from the nearest settlements but ordered there because Virginia depended on them, the defenders gave the name Fort Necessity to their post.

The rain continued into July while scouts brought accounts of a powerful French and Indian force on its way. Fort Necessity's defenders prepared to meet the overwhelming numbers of the enemy.

On the morning of July 3, 1754, the French attacked. For hours, as the water continued to pour down from the heavens, the battle raged. With a hundred men ill, most of them unable to fight, Washington had only three hundred soldiers left to face a French force more than double that size.

The French fire was very effective and throughout the day nearly one hundred of Washington's men were killed or wounded.

The incessant rain had ruined most of the gunpowder in Washington's stores. Flintlocks would not fire, leaving the Americans defenseless except for the few bayonets they had. The situation seemed hopeless until a flag of truce appeared out of the woods from which the French were firing.

"Colonel," Captain Stobo asked, "should we let them inside the fort?"

"It could be an effort to gauge our strength," Washington observed. "Ask if they will parley halfway between the fort and their lines."

Stobo returned a few minutes later to report that the French were agreeable to this.

"Send Van Braam," Washington ordered. "He knows a little French. And tell Peyronie to accompany him."

The two officers cleaned themselves up as best they could, then sloshed through the mud to hear the French terms. Within a short time they were back with a rain-soaked copy of a document presented them by the attackers.

"Can you make it out for me?" Washington asked.

"Not all of it," Van Braam answered. "It's very difficult to read."

Night had fallen but the rain continued to beat down upon the fort's defenders. The officers huddled around Washington and Van Braam, holding candles which sputtered in the drenching flood. The ink ran and more blots appeared on the paper.

"Van Braam, what does it say? Get on with it," Washington demanded irascibly.

"We are allowed to withdraw with full military honors, as well as all our equipment and supplies except for the cannon," Van Braam said, squinting in the poor light.

"What else does it say?" Washington asked.

"They will take two officers as hostages to insure the return of those you took prisoner in May after the battle," Van Braam added.

The officer read on, his halting French stumbling here and there.

"I find nothing to complain of in that paper," Washington said, "although I would like a complete and accurate translation...no offense, Van Braam. But failing that, I'll sign it. The alternative," he added, looking around at the wounded and fevered men who carpeted the inside of the fort, mud-splattered and wretched, "is to lose the sick and wounded as well as all the living."

Washington signed and sent Van Braam and Stobo off as hostages. The following morning the little force began the rugged fifty mile trek to their own lines. It was the Fourth of July, 1754.

xxxxxx

Crispus stood on the deck of the whaler, his elbows resting on the railing. Peace had come at last to the ship, its rolling motion gone after months at sea. Thick mooring lines held it fast to the pier.

There was nothing to do now but wait, since they had docked precisely at sundown. Any later and they would have had to drop anchor in the bay and wait until sunrise to dock. Most of the crew had been permitted to go ashore, there being little fear that they would desert before receiving their lay or share of the oil they had worked so hard to acquire. Crispus elected to stay on board. There was nothing for him at the port of Dartmouth, later called New Bedford.

The summer moon bathed the houses of the town, glanced off the harbor and its forests of masts, and turned the world into a silver and blue scene of incredible beauty.

It had been a long time since he had seen this coast, Crispus mused. Not since the *Whippet* sailed nearly four years earlier. Those four long years had brought him to many climes and had shown him many faces. He had met the Japanese peoples of Cipangu and the Esquimos of the Aleutians. He had become an expert harpoonist, using his great strength to thrust deep into the whale's body.

Starting first as a common seaman, he had worked his way into the honored position by sheer ability.

It did not hurt that the first whale the ship took was sighted the day Crispus, Paulie and Carr had been rescued. After that, they had been regarded as lucky for the ship and that, added to their hard work and natural talents won them important places among the crew. All were to receive a lay (or share) of 1/60, meaning that the income from every sixtieth barrel of whale oil was theirs.

The stench of the try-works and the taste of whale brains would linger with him for as long as he lived, as would the dangers and exhilarating pleasures of the chase.

Crispus idly watched the town lights and listened to the snatches of sea songs coming from the waterfront taverns. The streets were full this night, since the day had brought in two whalers and several troop ships from Halifax, with their naval escorts. One of these fat-bellied transports was just across the pier from the whaler, their yards nearly touching. The troops, their scarlet coats easily visible under the ship's lights, were kept under close watch, only a few being allowed to disembark and these noncommissioned officers or officers of higher rank.

"Where from?" a voice asked from the dim pier. Crispus searched for it and found it in the form of a burly guard standing at the foot of the troop ship gangway only a few yards away.

"From the Horn," he answered. "And you?"

"Halifax," the soldier answered. "Bound for Alexandria. Put in here to escape a real blow off the Cape. Sank one of the escorts. Stripped its masts clean, then took them too, broached the ship and sent her down keel over stern."

"What will you do in Alexandria?" Crispus asked.

"I heard the French is actin' up out the Ohio way and we're 'sposed to teach 'em a lesson."

"Are you English?" Crispus asked.

"Some. Rest are everything, Irish, Scots, German, and Colonials. A fair amount of blacks, too."

The silver calm was shattered by sounds of fighting raging along Wicklow Street. Crispus leaned over to catch a glimpse.

"Sailor's brawl, most likely," the guard remarked. "Or a press gang. Heard the mate say t' other day how we could use more hands."

Crispus pulled on his pipe in silence, watching the press gang dragging five tormented souls along the cobbled streets. He could not make out all the faces but none of them looked familiar. Except... except for a tousled head bloodied and beaten which hung down limply, its body held up by two husky seamen.

"Paulie!" Crispus cried. "He's off this ship!" He dropped his pipe and bellowed angrily to the skeleton crew of the ship, grabbed a belaying pin and rushed down the whaler's gangway. A few crew members emerged from the fo'c'sle and joined him.

"You have no right!" Crispus said to the officer in charge of the press gang. "He's off this whaler and exempt from impressment."

Crispus took careful note of the strength of the press gang, some dozen armed men. He and only four crew members stood little chance against them. But noticing the arrival of a large party of sailors from his ship, he took heart. Carr was one of them and was soon at his side. The sides were now more than even.

"That man's off this whaler!" Crispus said. "Let him go. You can't hold him. He has the King's exemption."

The officer in charge, already far gone with rum, looked at him through watery bloodshot eyes. His leaderless gang shrank back defensively.

Other crew members took up the cry. "Let him go. Let Brown go. He's a seaman. Exempt from the press."

The noise attracted a good deal of attention.

Soldiers lined the railing of the troop transport by the dozens. And the officers of both ships began to grow interested. Dock hangers-on and idlers drifted around to swell the numbers to a near mob scene.

Some began to snarl curses at the dreaded press gang and one gray-beard, his leg off below the knee, leaned on his rough crutch and said: "Damn press gang got me this! Don't go, I say. Fight 'em, fight 'em, I say. If I did, I'd still be a whole man."

The cry went up. "Let them go! Let them all go!"

The bleary-eyed officer began to edge toward the troop ship's gangway. His men formed a tight circle around the prisoners. The ugly crowd closed in, a few shoving matches adding to the tension.

Crispus was worried about the outcome, since what had begun as a legitimate demand for an exempt captive was now becoming an illegal protest.

Brrum! the first sharp sounds of drumbeats split the air. On the troop ship's deck four black drummers began their frightening staccato tune. Ten, twenty, thirty musketeers appeared along the rail, their white cross-belts gleaming in the moonlight, muskets primed and aimed for the crowd.

An officer appeared among the musketeers. "In the King's name let those men go! You are interfering with the work of a King's ship. Back off or you'll be fired on!"

The crowd began to shout curses and some hurled debris at the troop ship, several pieces of rusty metal finding their mark.

The officer gave an order and a volley burst from a dozen guns. Bullets whistled over the crowd's head and struck the pier or the whaler's side. Like a live grenade the crowd burst into fragments, tumbling and scattering in every direction. Crispus and Carr were swept up by the exploding mob, keeping their footing only by flailing and pushing as fiercely as the rest.

Back aboard the whaler, they held a council of war. Crispus sat on the hatch cover, staring gloomily at the troop ship. Carr fingered a line, unconsciously knotting its ends.

"We could try to get aboard by stealth," Carr said, "and free him that way."

"No," Crispus said, "there are too many troops around and they'll be on guard. I say we go to the Captain and ask his help."

The following morning, Crispus, Carr and the whaler's captain stood on deck before the troop ship's commander, an officer named Captain Burket. The whaler captain had taken the precaution of bringing a selectman from the town as an official witness and spokesman.

"This was not a scheduled port of call for you, Captain Burket," the selectman chided, "why do you take advantage of our hospitality by seizing decent persons from our streets? We have given you water, provided you with cheap provisions and this is how you repay us?"

"This is a king's ship. It must be manned or it cannot properly do its duty. I have no choice," Burket said.

The whaler's Captain interrupted: "You have no right to seize my men, that we all know. I demand you release the seaman Paul Brown immediately as a whaling man and therefore exempt from your press."

"If you can prove that, I'll release him."

The Captain said to Carr: "Fetch the ship's muster roll and log. Tell the mate I need it."

While Carr was racing down the ship's gangway, Crispus looked about him at the ship. He had never been on a King's ship before and the difference was apparent in discipline and tidiness. The crew had no time to languish. While the meeting was being held they were holystoning the deck to a fine finish. Around the ship stood sharpshooters looking outward to watch for deserters. Orders were to shoot on sight without hailing.

Crispus' eyes ranged to the quarterdeck , then rested on a tall black soldier standing erect beside the starboard ladder. Memories flooded over him of a midnight fight, the theft of his freedom money, their mother and the Brown farm. Tom Walter, he thought, my brother Tom Walter. His emotions were mixed. Brotherly feelings mingled with remembered injustices. And curiosity. Had Tom been a soldier all these years since he had run away from Brown? But caution got the better of Crispus. His brother could not be trusted. He turned away -- too late. Tom Walter caught his eye, squinted, and then smiled that mischievous smile Crispus knew so well.

Carr came breathlessly back with the book and the Captain proceeded to show Burket the evidence.

Burket was unimpressed. "Brown is not a whaling man as you say here. He's a castaway, a shipwreck victim. The fact that he signed on for wages does not make him eligible for exemption. He is not a seaman by profession. Brown stays with me."

Burket looked closer at the book. "And his companions. Who were they? Attucks and Carr or something or other? Would you happen to know where they are now, Captain?"

Crispus and Carr froze, their hearts beating so loudly it made them feel their ribs would burst.

The Captain looked Burket straight in the eye. "Paid 'em off at Sag Harbor, Captain, long since gone."

"Humph! I'll have to be content with the one then."

Crispus moved but Carr quickly motioned him to restrain himself.

Out of the corner of his eye he saw red coats moving toward him. An officer came to Burket's elbow, waiting for recognition.

"What is it?" Burket demanded testily.

"Sir, One of the men knows these two -- and the prisoner." The officer nodded to Crispus and Carr.

"Oh?" the Captain said, a smile playing on his face. "Send him to me."

Tom Walter approached the captain obsequiously, saluting smartly and standing rigidly at attention.

"Well, tell me what you know," the captain demanded.

"Sir, that's Attucks -- he's a deserter from the Army. And that's his sidekick, I don't recollect his name." Walter did not look at either Crispus or Carr as he spoke.

"You, Tom Walter," Crispus shouted, "I'll pay you if it's the last thing I do." He lunged at the taller man, knocking him down. Before he could do any real damage a dozen hands held him fast.

Carr had been faster, leaping over the side of the ship onto a wagon load of provisions, he rolled off and landed on his feet. He broke into a dead run, bullets crackling around him and digging splinters out of the pier. In seconds he had disappeared.

Ignoring the struggle and the chase, Burket turned to the whaling captain. "Captain, it would seem your men know my men. Evidence enough, don't you agree? And even if you don't agree, good day to you."

As Burket walked away, he tossed an order to an adjutant. "See that Pvt. Walter receives a bounty. Fifty shillings should do nicely. Oh, and a double tot of rum."

Chapter 8

The rage inside Crispus was tempered by remorse that he had been the instrument which brought his friend to such a plight.

He shifted his numbed limbs, listening to the bilge slopping only a few inches below where he lay chained in the deepest and gloomiest part of the ship, its brig. Next to him lay Paulie, dozing fitfully and uncomfortably, his head lolling against the rough timbers of the bulkhead.

From the motion he could tell that the transport was under way, plowing through deep waves and plunging into troughs. The ship's roll meant that they had left the Cape's shelter and were in open water. They must be in a great hurry if they sail in seas like this, Crispus thought.

He sighed as he thought of his lost Nora. All these years and no word from him. Was she still alive? The darkness around him added to his gloom, sapping at his strength. But Crispus' nature could not pay heed to the lessons of despair for very long. Nothing will get me down, he thought, clenching his fists. I will face this and win, the way I did the whales and all else sent against me.

Looking up at the wet timbers overhead, he gritted his teeth and vowed: Lord, I will prevail. With thy strength. He thought of Mrs. Brown and the Bible she had given him, long lost now. But many passages stayed with him, giving him courage. He thought of St. Paul, and shipwreck, the Apostles and the storm, Jonah and his ocean perils. On the sea, Crispus thought, God tests a man's courage. Lord, test me. I will not fail.

No matter what lay in store for him, he would meet it and win, Crispus said to himself. It had to be that way. And he would return to Nora. Nora was alive, and they would live as man and wife one day, he knew.

A crack of light gleamed into the brig through the barred window of the heavy wooden door. Presently a key snapped back the lock and the door creaked open on its iron hinges. One marine held the light while three more crowded into the brig to rouse the prisoners and unchain their legs.

A few moments later, manacled only by their hands and arms, the two men stood before a grinning Captain Burket.

"Well, me hearties," he said mockingly, "'so it's the pressed man and his deserter friend. What shall we do with you? Will it be the army or the navy? Why don't we let you chose?

"First, though, I think our deserter should be given a taste of what deserters deserve. Where's Pvt. Walter? Let's ask his opinion."

Tom, off duty, was roused from his quarters and brought before the Captain, eyes looking fearfully about him to see what was in store for him. He stood erect and tall, the perfect image of a soldier. "Walter, you say you know this man," Burket asked, pointing to Crispus." How do you know him and where did he desert from?"

Never mentioning their kinship, Walter told a plausible story beginning with half-truths about their youth as orphans together and ending with a tale of desertion following a drunken brawl at a remote garrison town in Massachusetts. The Captain nodded, his clerk recording all the details.

Beckoning a soldier standing near him, Walter added: "Sir, Pvt. White here knows him, too. We all served together. Ask him, sir, ask him please."

Burket turned to White and asked: "Do you confirm Walter's story?"

"Every word, Cap'n, sir," the burly, blond-haired fellow said gruffly, "he's a deserter all right."

Turning back to Tom Walter, Burket asked: "Well, Pvt. Walter, and what do you suggest I do with Attucks? Being a drummer, you are accustomed to administering punishment. Suppose I select you and some of your mates to give him a thousand of your best? Would your acquaintance with him keep you from laying on full strength?"

Walter looked at Crispus. He saw the storm in his half-brother's eyes and replied: "Sir, it's amnesty time, ain't it, sir?" His voice was pleading, with a sincere ring to it. "Besides, we need every man we can get for the Indians and the Frenchies. They be good men, sir, and my friends, even if they do be deserters. Let 'em sign up and I know they'll be good soldiers."

Burket was genuinely surprised. "Walter, you are absolutely correct. It is indeed within the time of amnesty laid down by the Commanding General of all British forces in America. So few deserters have applied for the amnesty that I had quite forgotten about it."

Burket looked at Crispus and Paulie, nodded toward Walter and said: "You have heard the pleas of this generous man. Have you anything to say?"

Crispus and Paulie shook their heads.

"Very well, I am prepared to offer you two choices. You will be given one thousand or you will sign on as soldier volunteers governed by the Articles of War and subject to all rules and regulations of this organization. What is your decision?"

Crispus and Paulie looked at each other. A thousand lashes, they knew, was the equivalent of a death sentence. No one had ever survived it. Without speaking, they knew what they must do..

"We'll sign," Crispus said. Paulie nodded.

"Good, the army needs sturdy colonials. Oh, and clerk, remind me to write a commendation for Walter and to promote him to Corporal at the earliest opportunity."

xxxxxx

Fort Cumberland was a bustling town as Southern regions go. Not to be compared with Boston or New York, it still served a potentially large back country on the Potomac River. In the month of May 1755, it was a troop town, stuffed to overflowing with the baggage needed to capture the keystone of a continent.

Paulie and Crispus had little time to reflect on their new life as they were thrown into the hectic life of the British 44th Regiment. Drilling and muster were only part of a soldier's life in the Eighteenth century. Much time was spent in marching, bayonet drill, and marksmanship and it seemed that the most time was devoted to one's uniform. Cleaning the scarlet coat and keeping the white shoulder straps free of smudges and mud occupied most of their waking hours, they thought.

But army life had its satisfactions, too, as the friends found out. One of these was definitely not Corporal Tom Walter, whose merciless hazing taxed their patience to the limit. Tom's promotion had added to the new "volunteers'" woes, since they were put in his squad and constantly under his command.

Crispus and Paulie, being common soldiers, had little knowledge of the grand strategy of the British in America. This involved the struggle for the Ohio Valley and parts of the Great Lakes. The key to capturing these was Ft. Duquesne, located at the junction of the Allegheny and Monongahela Rivers.

This point marked the beginning of the Ohio River and was later called Pittsburgh. Young Washington had tried to take it the year before but his efforts had ended in honorable failure. This time, the British did not intend to leave the task to an inexperienced colonial officer. Instead, they were sending Major General Sir Edward Braddock, a courageous and battletrained commander, although ignorant of his enemy's war methods.

What Crispus and Paulie did know was that they were part of a huge military operation, involving two thousand troops, eight hundred horses, and 150 wagons. Mountains of salt pork, corn, bread, biscuit and dried vegetables competed with barrels of rum, wine, and whiskey for wagon space. Ammunition, explosives, swords, shovels, and hundreds of other necessary items completed the wagon inventory. After food, drink and military supplies, the most significant baggage was the artillery. This amounted to some thirty pieces of ordnance, including some powerful guns taken from a warship. These guns would, Braddock believed, pound Ft. Duquesne's star-shaped walls to rubble. But only if they could be dragged through the 110 miles of roadless terrain which included steep Appalachian Mountains.

On the morning of June 7, 1755, the 44th Regiment marched into the forest, following a party of road builders and followed by the other companies and regiments of Braddock's army. To Crispus, whose life had been spent among the forests and fields of North America, it was a welcome change from life on the sea. Memories came back as he marched along behind hundreds of other redcoats, avoiding roots and rocks and overhanging branches. He thought of the weeks spent in the woods after he left Brown's farm, of his Indian capture and escape. Then, he had been his own man, free to dress and travel and hunt as he pleased. Now, wearing the English red coat, he was a perfect target for Indian or French riflemen. And the line of march required of him and his fellow soldiers made them a perfect invitation for attack.

"It does not seem right, Paulie," Crispus said that night as they sat near the campfire, waiting for their rations to heat up.

"What's that?" Paulie asked.

"The way we march in the forest, the noise we make, the way we are telling the enemy how many we are and how soon we are coming," Crispus said.

"True, but it may be the general knows this and wants the enemy to know how strong we are. That way the French may not even want to seek battle."

Crispus stirred the fire and looked over it into the gloom of the forest. "Still, it doesn't seem right."

Strung out along a rough road, barely a path wide enough to drag cannon and narrow wagons through, Braddock's army camped where they halted for the night. Campfires glowed for more than three miles along the road and the clatter of dinner hour sounded throughout the forest. As darkness deepened, the fires were extinguished and except for guards and scout patrols the army turned in for the night.

At daybreak the march resumed, crawling along at the pace of two miles a day on good days. At the front of the straggling column were teams of road builders or rather, brush clearers. These hacked away at the thick and nearly impenetrable underbrush. The hundred axes listed among the King's supplies for this expedition would get plenty of use. Several hundred men, guarded by an equally large number of soldiers, labored all day, every day, at the task of clearing a path for the vast serpent of humans and supplies which crawled after them. Mosquitoes and flies, ticks and gnats feasted on the ax men's sweaty bodies. The eyes were special targets of the gnats, which flew right into the cornea and had to be blinked away. Hordes of these little beasts left a man's eye's bloodshot and his lids drooping and swollen within a few hours. At the same time, mosquitoes attacked every orifice, winging their way into ears with maddening insistence, penetrating under sleeves and up trouser legs. Accidents mounted, and the whole column suffered as its cutting edge grew duller.

Ten days passed and the army had dragged itself a mere two dozen miles. Stragglers who left the column often never returned, becoming victims of hostile Indians who watched every move. Fearful of attacking the great red coated army directly, the French allies satisfied themselves with hacking any stray members of it. The woods became an unconquerable enemy to the troops, their little path was their only safe haven. Any movement more than a few feet away from it struck terror in their hearts. Accustomed to steady marching and regular night bivouacking, they could not adjust to this limping along at a snail's pace. Walk and wait, walk and wait. And meanwhile the bugs made life unbearable.

Still, the troops had confidence in their leader, General Braddock. Sixty years old and looking every bit of it, he still had a reputation as a ladies' man, even on this expedition. He loved good food and dined sumptuously each night on well-cured ham, expensive cheese, pickled sturgeon, fresh vegetables and fruit. His meals were prepared for him by the large staff he kept solely to cater to his personal needs. These extras were accepted by the troops as part of the distinction between ranks and classes. They knew this was part of life and they did not hate so much as envy him his privileges.

This much they admitted -- he seemed to know what he was doing. After all, he had assembled and organized one of the biggest armed forces ever seen in North America. Even though it was also one of the slowest.

Crispus and Paulie sat by the side of the road, pulling on their pipes and watching the smoke rise in light blue clouds above their heads. Aside from the satisfaction the tobacco gave them the smoke had the welcome effect of keeping the bugs down.

"I never wanted to be in the army," Paulie remarked, shifting his weight against the tree they were both propped up against.

Crispus sucked at his pipe and nodded: "Nor me neither. My brother Tom always did, though, and now I know why. Look yonder."

In an open glade just off the road a small group had gathered. In its midst was a soldier and a sailor barely able to stand and stripped to the waist. Looming over them was Tom Walter, whip in hand and ready to begin punishment.

"What did those poor devils do?" Paulie asked.

"Same as the others," Crispus said, "drunk on duty."

"Every day this happens. There won't be a whole back left if this keeps up," Paulie said angrily.

"Not if my brother has anything to do with it. That's why he enlisted as a drummer, because they get to give the punishment out."

The sailor was taken first, dragged roughly to a slim pine tree and pushed against it. His arms, already tied together, were hoisted above his head and tied to a broken stub of a branch.

Tom Walter, sleeves rolled up, tested the whip several times by snapping it in the air, his long arm making a wide circuit over his head. With a clap that made nearby nesting birds flee in panic, he brought the whip against the sailor's flesh with excruciating force. The victim gasped and twisted, a small red welt rising from right shoulder to the left side of his lower back. "Clap!" the whip spoke again and a thin dribble of blood ran down the sailor's back onto his white duck trousers. Tom Walter worked himself into a sweaty mass, transformed by the pleasure he felt, from an expert executioner into an insane, sadistic butcher. Exhausted after 180 stripes, he had to rest before delivering the remaining twenty. The bloody victim kept lapsing into unconsciousness, only to be revived by water thrown in his face. Watching closely, the other prisoner trembled in terror at the prospect awaiting him.

The camp went about its business, little heeding the awful violence occurring only a few feet away.

"That sailor must be sorry he ever signed up to help wrestle the six pounders over these hills," Paulie remarked.

"He might have been pressed," Crispus observed.

The sailor was one of a party off the warship *Norwich*. He had been detailed to help transport, maintain and fire the big guns which Braddock was dragging with him to destroy Fort Duquesne. These were holding the column back, as were the heavily laden wagons. The horses purchased to pull all this freight proved unequal to the task. Weak, aging animals, they had been pawned off on the army as expendable. Why waste good livestock on generals, the farmer argued. The army did not appreciate either good men or good horseflesh. Give them the worst.

With such beasts of burden to begin with, it was no wonder little progress was made. The horses, weakened from pulling the heavy cannon, fell by the wayside and were replaced with other horses, or when needed by teams of soldiers. Wagons could not last in this terrain and axles cracked regularly, forcing the troops to load supplies into other, already overburdened wagons.

Stopped for midday rest one afternoon, Crispus and Paulie found themselves overshadowed by a grinning Tom Walter.

"Some a' the wagons needs pullin', an' I'm detailin' you two to help. Report to Ensign Disney over there."

Crispus and Paulie looked over where he pointed. A thin officer with brown wispy hair stood beside a horseless wagon. Several men were already standing in the traces, waiting to begin their task of replacing the horses. Crispus and Paulie reported as ordered.

"Put your weapons in the back of the wagon and be careful about it," Ensign Disney said, adding, "there's a sick officer back there."

Looking into the gloomy wagon, they saw a tall American, dressed in colonial garb. He was asleep but seemed to be fevered and in pain. Elsewhere in the wagon were boxes and luggage piled high.

As they took their positions, Paulie asked another soldier: "Who is the officer in the wagon?"

"Colonel Washington, Virginia militia," the soldier answered. "Some say he started all this fightin'. Been sick since we started...bloody flux."

The next few days were torment for Paulie and Crispus. Hauling the big wagon up the ever steep ascent was man-killing work. The woodsmen who cleared a path through the forest could not stop for roots or rocks. These had to be met by wagons and gun caissons. The only advantage the pulling, sweating mass of humans had was the dry weather they were blessed with in the summer of '55. This kept the pathway from becoming a muddy river and also made it possible to cross the many streams and rivers the army met without danger or great difficulty.

As Crispus and Paulie tugged the traces up a particularly steep hill, Ensign Dorsey appeared. "Four of you men fall to the rear of the wagon and push. The rest of you hold on as hard as you can.

Crispus, Paulie, and two others trotted to the wagon's rear and, using their combined shoulders, gave the needed momentum to reach the top. Then a new problem immediately arose. The heavy wagon began to lumber down the other side, clumsily threatening to run over those pulling it. Now the four men at the rear had to act as its brakes, holding the sides and rear tailgate to slow its progress.

The tailgate latch broke, bringing the gate smashing down with a loud noise and dumping some chests on the ground.

"Hold on!" Crispus cried, "stop the wagon."

Hands moved to check the wagon and brought it to a halt. Paulie put a large stone in front of the right front wheel while Crispus attempted to fix the latch.

"Where are we?" a weak voice asked from inside the wagon.

"On the road to Fort Duquesne, Colonel Washington," Crispus answered.

"I know that. I mean how far along are we? Will you find that out for me?"

Washington sat up with great difficulty, holding his temples with the palms of both hands. He groaned and lay back.

Crispus scrambled into the wagon. "Can I help you, sir? He found a water jug and poured a draught for the fevered Virginian. Washington sat up and drank deeply. The fact that the wagon had stopped seemed to help Washington, since the swaying motion was somewhat similar to the motion of a ship and often had the same effect on the stomach.

"Thank you. Now, will you go and find out where we are at this point? And bring back Ensign Disney."

Crispus found the officer and led him to Washington's wagon.

"Disney, I wish to see General Braddock. Can you find my horse and get someone to accompany me to him?"

"Certainly Colonel. I'll send an escort of your Virginia Colonials with you."

"And Disney, detail this man," Washington added, nodding to Crispus. "I think he may prove useful to me."

Crispus collected his gear and reported to the officer in charge of mounts. He was assigned a horse and joined Washington and his Virginia escort.

They rode several miles until they reached Braddock's party, camped at the site called Little Meadow.

Crispus and the others waited out of earshot while Washington, Braddock and his other officers parleyed.

"Who might you be, friend?" A tanned Virginia trooper asked Crispus. Crispus told him and the soldier gave Philip Drew as his name, 3rd Virginia Militia as his outfit.

"What are they planning?" Crispus asked.

"Don't know," Drew said, "but it could be a forced march. The only way we'll get to Fort Duquesne before we're all greybeards is by cuttin' loose from this miles-long parade and get to where the enemy's at."

He bit into a huge wad of tobacco and began to make great chewing noises as he spoke, brown drool mixed with saliva running out of the corners of his mouth.

It was a fine Spring day, green abounding. Bird songs matched in freshness and clarity the newness of the leaves. The rich smell of forest rankness caused by leaf and vegetative rot was a pleasant scent to the country people who made up the bulk of the army. Crispus and the Virginia escort stretched underneath the canopy of maples and pines which filled the woodlands to enjoy the brief rest.

"You from the Colonies or the Indies?" Drew asked Crispus.

"Massachusetts," Crispus answered, lighting his pipe and puffing lightly.

"Oh, you've no Indians there," Drew snorted, while the other Virginians looked on smilingly, knowing Drew was concocting another tale of Indian horrors to frighten Crispus as he had so many British soldiers on the line of march.

"Know what the Indians do to their captives?" Drew asked.

Crispus smiled sadly and looked Drew full in the face. "Yes, they captured me once," he answered quietly and, standing up, walked slowly over to another tree. He sat down, gathering his thoughts around him and thinking of what he would like the rest of his life to become. A few years with Nora, in Boston or Lynn. His own cordwainer's shop. A child, perhaps. Yes, a child most of all, after Nora, was his greatest desire. At his age though, thirty-five, he might not have many years to see a child grow to adulthood.

Drew sat down next to him. "Sorry, Attucks, we always like to make the strangers feel at home by tellin' 'em interesting stories. I should have known better with you. You act like you've been a few places."

Crispus accepted the hard brown hand and the two talked pleasantly through the late afternoon.

"Who is this Colonel Washington?" Crispus asked.

"He's a Virginia gentleman but a real man for all that. I was with him at Great Meadows a year or so ago when the French almost done for us. Lord, did it rain those days! But he got us out safe. Built a fort called 'Necessity,' 'bout as big as the necessary more like," Drew said, chuckling.

"A surveyor he is, by trade." Drew added, spitting a brown stream of tobacco juice on a column of ants struggling with their loads. "Owns five thousand acres of top tobacco land down Fairfax way." Drew eyed Crispus carefully and added, "and many, many slaves."

At that moment, the meeting at Braddock's headquarters broke up and officers began leaving to rejoin their units. Washington stayed behind and remained engaged in close and lively conversation with the General for some little while.

"This is suthin'else again," Drew said admiringly. "An English general listenin' to a Virginia officer."

"If he was here before," Crispus said, "then he should be the man to ask."

"I know that and you know that but the English don't ever seem to know that," Drew said matter-of-factly with a trace of bitterness.

It was the first time Crispus had heard the English spoken harshly of. Or that he had noticed it.

Washington saluted General Braddock smartly, then strode quickly over to the escort, which scrambled to its feet. Ordinarily a mild-mannered young man of twenty-four, Washington was not known for his temper, but his troops knew that he had a sharp one and was not afraid to unsheath it when occasion demanded.

As he drew closer, they could see the usually grave face pleasantly warmed by a satisfied grin. Washington said one word as he mounted, a little unsteadily, onto his horse: "Action."

Later, they learned what he meant by that word when half the night was spent in taking the great unwieldy military column with all its paraphernalia and splitting it into two parts. The confusion was a hellish experience more suitable for a nightmare than for a warm, peaceful June evening in the woods of colonial America.

By dawn on the eighth of June 1755, the faster of the two columns set off toward the Monongahela River junction with the Allegheny. By comparison with the former condition, this column was moving with great speed. With packhorses carrying the bulk of the supplies and few wagons to impede their progress, the column had only the artillery to struggle with. The rest of the army and its baggage was left under Colonel Thomas Dunbar's command at Little Meadow.

Crispus was still detailed to Washington's Virginians and was happy to be going along, feeling that he would at least know what was happening. Paulie's infantry unit was also picked for the advance force.

As they wended their way through the wooded countryside, the feeling of eyes upon them grew with each passing day. This suspicion was more than confirmed by signs left by the hostile Indians on trees they knew the column would pass. Unspeakable cruelties awaited them, they knew.

On a foggy dawn a few days after the forced march began, Crispus was sent into the woods with Philip Drew and six other soldiers to bring the horses in for the officers. As they reached the rope corral where the horses were kept for the night, they saw no signs of the pickets guarding them. Instead, the place was ominously quiet, although the horses were skittish.

Drew immediately took charge. "Hush!" he whispered harshly, crouching low. Flintlock ready, he edged slowly to the farther side of the picket line. As he reached it, he stood erect, shaking his head sadly and waving them over. As they drew near, they saw why he had shaken his head. Both guards lay dead, their throats neatly cut, bodies hideously contorted. Their rifles were gone and from the top of their heads blood and brain oozed slowly out. They had been scalped cleanly. Kneeling beside one corpse, Drew felt his skin.

"Still warm," he said, his eyes more alert than ever.

Before he could rise, a volley of shots rang out, dropping three troopers. Two died instantly, another twisted convulsively, then lay still. The others, resisting the temptation to fire blindly into the woods, waited crouching. Quiet prevailed except for the moans of a mortally wounded horse, its breath growing short, nostrils flaring.

Bayonets fixed, ears straining to hear every sound, Crispus, Drew, and the three remaining Virginians held their breath. The birds had fled and small animals hid.

The first sign Crispus had of danger came from his right side. A blur triggered all his senses and he wheeled around just in time to face a leaping, brown warrior, hatchet poised to strike. Too late to get off his knees, he dug the butt of his fourteen pound "Brown Bess" into the dirt in front of him, shoving its bayonet pointed muzzle diagonally forward. It caught the Indian in midleap, just under the sternum. His whole body collapsed over the rifle as the bayonet ripped its way through his vital organs and emerged covered with warm red blood. The one impression Crispus had of the split-second attack was that of the Indian's war-painted face. Hideous in the attack, it turned into a clown's mask in the surprise reaction to Crispus' tactic.

The warrior's body twisted sideways, enabling Crispus to slide his weapon out of the body. Out of the corner of his eye he could see other braves engaging the Americans. Philip Drew was struggling in hand to hand combat with a big warrior whose hunting knife was perilously close to the Virginian's throat. Crispus fired his Brown Bess and took the top of the Indian's head off. The shot also whistled past the other Indians, who broke away and disappeared into the woods. The action was over in less than two minutes. The body of rescuing troops was still thirty feet away when the threat had passed.

Crispus and Drew were unhurt and only one of the other three troopers was wounded. He had a bad gash on the arm but would recover.

Drew saluted the officer who led the rescue party and reported: "Sir, we lost three men dead from the surprise attack and one injured in the fight."

"And the Indians?" the officer asked.

"Attucks here killed two of 'em and we drove the rest off. Two of 'em looked to be in pretty bad shape."

The officer ordered a dozen Rangers to scour the woods for a few hundred yards in search of the wounded Indians. Blood stains could be traced quite easily in the dry terrain.

"Attucks," the officer said, "you're detailed to the Colonel's service, right?"

"Yes, sir."

"Good work. Be assured he will learn of this," the officer said confidently. Turning to Drew and nodding toward the Indians, he said: "Go ahead, Private. You've earned it."

Drew grinned and drew his razor sharp scalping blade from its leather scabbard. Leaning over the Indian whom Crispus had shot in the head, he looked up and smiled at Crispus. "Attucks, from the moment I saw you I knew you'd bring me some kind a luck. Looks like it was bad this time. You shot this devil's scalp off and that could cost you five pounds."

In response to Crispus' quizzical look, the officer explained: "General Braddock is paying us five English pounds for every scalp we bring in along the line of march."

Drew had gone back to work on the Indian's mutilated head. "I'll take the ears off this one with what remains o' the crown, but 'tis grisly work."

The first task completed, Drew strode over to the brave who had died on Crispus' bayonet.

"This one's a might easier," Drew said.

He cut an incision about one quarter inch in depth just above the brave's ears, slipping the point of his knife under the scalp to loosen it as far up as he could go. Wiping his knife on the Indian's leather trousers he put it away and prepared to remove the scalp. With both hands firmly holding the Indian's long hair, he gave an upward jerk and expertly pulled the scalp off. The watching soldiers cheered.

"Here, Attucks," Drew said, "you earned both of 'em, and saved my hide in the bargain, even though I probably would have downed that red devil you shot."

"We all share 'em," Crispus said, "two pounds apiece amongst the five of us left alive."

The. troops cheered Crispus, clapping him on the back. Brought back to camp as a minor hero, Crispus was struck by the irony of it all. He looked back at a burial detail digging shallow graves to keep the bears and other beasts from feeding on the corpses. Seven men died over that patch of ground, he thought, seven lives better spent in harmony and industry than in dreary conflict. Even in the midst of this little moment of glory, he longed for his cordwainer's bench and tools, for the smell of good leather and the other aromas of the Framingham farm.

His reverie amid the clamor was interrupted by the authoritative voice of Colonel Washington. "Private Attucks, you deserve great praise for your coolness under attack today. I shall dispatch a note to your Commanding officer commending you. You have raised the morale of this army greatly." His voice trailed off as he quietly added: "and Heaven knows we need that desperately. Have you any request to make as a reward for your conduct?"

Crispus thought a moment, then said: "I would like to become a part of your volunteers. And my friend would, too."

"Impossible," Washington said, "you wear the King's colors. You're a regular. I could not take you into the service of Virginia." The tall Virginian's mouth broke into a rueful smile as he added: "It is curious to me that you should want so much to get out of what I so want to get into."

Crispus briefly sketched his half-brother's betrayal and the innocent inclusion of his friends in the vengeful action.

Washington pierced Crispus with his deep, steady eyes and said: "I believe you. I shall write to General Braddock to that effect today."

By the end of the week, Crispus and Paulie were wearing the fringed buckskin of the Virginia Militia companies and had traded their huge muskets for the gleaming rifles of the American frontier.

"Attucks," Philip Drew said from his comfortable resting place on the moss-covered ground around a smooth sycamore, "ever since the Colonel brought you into the militia, things have been goin' right. We're makin' faster time, we're not losin' scouts or stragglers. I think you brought us good luck this time." He let a stream of tobacco juice strike a moth settling on a berry bush. It fell on its side, covered with brown spittle, its wings drenched and flapping wildly.

Crispus sipped his rum ration slowly out of his metal mug. "The leaders are good men. They know how to fight and how to prepare for it."

"But can they take a fort as strong as the one they say is at Duquesne?" Paulie asked.

"With the ship's cannon we have, there is no place in the world that can withstand us," Drew said. "We will be at the fort in two or three days. The real work is behind us. Now we crush the French, kiss their pretty girls, and bring home whatever we can carry. And...we teach the Indians a lesson they will never forget."

xxxxxx

The Allegheny and Monongahela Rivers flowed swiftly past a level triangle of land to become the mighty Ohio. At this smooth junction, the two lesser rivers met almost on purpose to create "La Belle Riviere," the beautiful river, as the French called it. The great Ohio then plunged powerfully into the West to water the richest soils in all the world. It had become an axiom that who controlled the forks of the Ohio controlled the Northwest...and who controlled the Northwest controlled the continent.

To protect their rights to the headwaters of the Ohio, the French now had a powerful new diamond shaped fort with massive walls covering an area of 150 square feet. It dwarfed any other French installation in the region and was appropriately named after the most important Frenchman in North America, the Marquis Duquesne, His Majesty's Governor-General in all New France.

All this grandeur would soon be ended, the French defenders of Ft. Duquesne knew, five minutes after the English guns were trained on their walls. Captain Claude Contrecoeur and his second in command Captain Daniel Beaujeu sat glumly in the former's headquarters contemplating their fate.

"In these past five days we have had only two English scalps," Contrecoeur said, "and it cost us four Indians to get those. A black madman in the English army killed two of our braves in the attack and two more died of wounds as they returned to our walls. I tell you these warriors will fade away at the first volley of the English."

"No, my Commandant," Beaujeu said gently, twisting his fine deerskin gloves in his hands, "they will fight...for me."

Contrecoeur, weary of war and eager to retire, knew his young handpicked successor was not boasting. Beaujeu had a way of dealing with the Indians. Never to lie, never to order what he himself would not dare to do; these were the rules of life of France's knight-errant whom the Indians called "father."

"A thousand braves outside our walls and only a few hundred French within," Contrecoeur said. "What can these do against so many English?"

"Let me meet the English before they arrive here," Beaujeu urged. "That way their artillery will be of little use and their huge numbers will not help them. Our Indians will not meet them if they come with their siege guns and continental-style attack formations. Now they are straggling along a line of march that is disorganized and indefensible. Let me lead the braves out to meet the English where we fight best."

Contrecoeur knitted his brows and looked out a small window high up on the wall of his headquarters office. The day was clear and cloudless. Such a dry day could only bring the English guns that much closer to the walls of the fort he was pledged to defend. Beaujeu could buy time. Perhaps in a day or so reinforcements from Canada might arrive. Surely, Governor-General Duquesne. might take a bit more interest in the fort that bore his name. And he, after all, knew as well as any Frenchman how vital "La Belle Riviere" was to the interests of France.

"I say go," Contrecouer said decisively, wishing he felt as confident as he sounded.

Beaujeu's face lit up with a smile of relief and satisfaction. He rose, saluted smartly and rushed to the compound to begin his task. The Indian allies, at first reluctant, were shamed into going when Beaujeu threatened to leave them, like squaws in front of a wigwam, while he and his French troops went out to do the work of men. Soon, the French and Indians were in place on high ground a few hundred yards from the Monongahela River where they knew Braddock must pass. On either side of the twelve foot path which passed for a road, the warriors grimly watched. Eight hundred fighting men, two-thirds of them Indians, with nothing heavier than muskets to fire, were going to challenge a great and well-equipped modern army.

xxxxxx

"We'll drink French wine in Duquesne tonight," Drew said cheerfully, as he swung along beside Crispus and Paulie. Drew's enthusiasm was felt by British troops all up and down the line.

"The worst part is over," Paulie agreed, "the part we did with our feet." Looking down he saw the once-bright boots he had been issued by the Quartermaster in New Bedford now scarred in a hundred places by brambles and mottled by stains from fording streams and rivers.

The vanguard of British troops was stepping along cheerfully on the early afternoon of July 9, 1755 when one of its road engineers ran back from his forward position.

"Indians! The enemy!" the advance troops roared, the cry being carried down the line from detachment to detachment. Riders were posted to the rear to carry the word to General Braddock. Weeks of inaction and uncertainty had made the British troops jumpy and anxious but the sound of gunfire ahead of them steadied them. The front rank troops dropped to one knee and fired off a solid volley. This caused great damage and, in fact, killed Captain Beaujeu instantly. But his second in command, Dumas, simply took up the leadership and proved as ingenious and resourceful as his commander had been.

Crispus and the rest of the American troops followed standard Indian-fighting tactics as soon as the firing started. They darted off to either side of the road and found trees, rocks, and hillocks to shelter behind, waiting for their targets.

"Look," Paulie cried, "the British are not seeking cover."

Crispus turned around, keeping his head low, to see the packed masses of redcoats kneeling or standing at their officers' commands and continuing to fire in volleys.

"They should find shelter," Crispus said, "or they will be picked off one by one."

The British troops stood firm for a time, firing at the unseen enemy. General Braddock rode pell-mell up at the head of his staff and the main body of the army, adding to the confusion. Now, close to a thousand British troops stood massed together under the withering fire.

Instead of facing fire from the front as they had at first, they began to experience it from all around them. Soldiers dropped by the score and those still standing began to fire at anything that moved.

Americans, spread out in cover, began to fall from British fire. Near Crispus, two comrades slumped over. An American officer stood up, waving his rifle and calling to the British to stop the firing. He fell, riddled with gunfire, his face an unrecognizable mass of blood.

"We have to stop them," Crispus said, pulling a large handkerchief from his pocket. He tied it to the end of his rifle, and raised it, waving it back and forth. The firing ceased and he scrambled up, raced toward the British units. As he approached the lines, he saw a black soldier take aim at him. Recognizing him, Crispus waved and called: "Tom, don't shoot!"

Walter's shot plowed into the butt of Crispus' rifle, glancing harmlessly into the earth. But worse was coming. Thinking Crispus was the buckskin clad leader of an attacking force, the British fired half a dozen more shots at him. Miraculously, none hit him, the nervousness of the soldiers probably accounting for their bad aim.

Recognized as a friend, Crispus made his way to the nearest British officer.

"Sir, your men are shooting us down like dogs over there." He pointed with his arm to the spot he had just left. The summer foliage made it impossible to distinguish anything very clearly.

"Soldier," the officer said with exasperation, "If you will tell me where the enemy is, I will gladly direct fire against them." As he spoke, a bullet hit him in the front of the neck and passed out the back. Blood spurted over Crispus as the officer soundlessly dropped to the forest floor.

Looking for another officer, he spied Braddock flaying about with the flat of his sword, driving men into formation. The horse the General was mounted on was hit by rifle fire, a stream of red flowing down the white flank. It collapsed in pain and Braddock barely escaped being crushed by deftly twisting off as the animal rolled over. Another mount was brought and Braddock was off to a different part of the line.

Crispus could find no other officers mounted on horseback. Most were either dead, wounded, or had dismounted to be less conspicuous. Only Washington, too far away to help, remained mounted. On that day he would lose two horses and would have four musket balls through his clothing. Braddock lost four horses...and his life.

The lines grew vague and haze and smoke blanketed the battlefield. Crispus lost touch with his Virginians. Blundering into a company of regulars, he saw the scarlet-coated form of Tom Walter loom before him. A great fury overwhelmed him, he dropped his rifle and dove at Walter. He began punching even before they had landed on the dirt. Again and again he drove his fist into Tom's face, heedless of the action swirling about him. His final blow snapped Walter's head heavily against the ground. Crispus stood up, watching the unconscious form of his brother. From behind, a terrific blow from a musket butt crashed against his back, driving him to his knees and across Walter's body. He twisted around and saw Pvt. Hugh White's form above him, bayonet poised to strike. Before Crispus could react, a long throwing knife flashed from nowhere and dug deeply into White's shoulder. He went down with a cry of pain.

In a moment, Paulie was standing over him, holding a bayonet-tipped musket against White's neck. "You blackguard," he rasped angrily, "make one move and I'll drive this through you...with pleasure."

White stared at him, holding his bleeding shoulder, hatred filling his eyes.

This scene was interrupted by the call for a general retreat.

"Fall back," officers ordered. "The General is dead, the Redskins are upon us."'

Abandoning the wounded, the British retreated in disorder, every man for himself. Paulie and Crispus left their bleeding enemies to seek their own units. A tall, bluecoated form rode by. Recognizing Washington, they ran after him and formed around him as he reined up, bullets whistling from every direction.

"Virginians," he called hoarsely, "rally to me!" Weary Colonial troops, sighting Washington, carefully left their cover to join him. Within a few minutes some three score men ringed the Colonel, their guns trained on the forest, their ears tuned to Washington's orders.

"We must cover the retreat and bring off our wounded at the same time. Officers and non-commissioned officers, split your force in two, half to aid the wounded, half to provide covering fire."

"But there are so many wounded, sir," a pale young Lieutenant protested, "we cannot carry all of them at once."

"Leap frog, then," Washington ordered. "We'll take them out in stages."

The hostile fire had died down considerably and what remained was carefully watched by the experienced Americans. As a puff of tell-tale smoke drifted up following a report, the forest-trained Virginians slammed rounds exactly in that direction, rarely hearing a cry of pain but at least forcing the enemy to keep his head down.

Slowly, agonizingly, the militia made its way back to the line of march with its broken, bleeding burdens on makeshift stretchers. The firing ceased and soon Virginians were primarily a hospital force with only a few pickets skirting along as a protective screen.

Over a small fire that evening, the gloomy troops ate a dismal meal, spiced with bitterness and recrimination. The moans of the wounded contrasted with the glum silence around most campfires, only occasionally interrupted by quiet conversation.

Chewing listlessly on a hard johnnycake, Drew said, "It's all over. We'll never take Duquesne again. The French will have the Ohio for as long as they want it."

"And mebbe the Delaware and the Potomac too, if they've a mind," another soldier added.

"Pity the poor frontier families," Paulie said, "they'll have no peace for years after this."

"'Washington will do something," Crispus said, clenching his fist. "He's an American and this is America. What have the British to do with us, anyway? They don't understand our ways."

The British did not understand the ways of North America, it was true, but they died trying to learn them. A thousand persons, including Braddock and most of the officers died or were wounded that day on the Monongahela, The enemy suffered hardly at all in comparison, with less than fifty casualties, dead and wounded.

xxxxx

As the weeks and months passed, the bitterness of defeat grew less painful. Crispus and Paulie continued in militia service for the rest of their terms of enlistment. Paulie's prediction of disaster along the frontier proved true. Pioneer families were burned out, considering themselves fortunate if they escaped with wounds and the loss of all they owned so long as they had their lives. The soldiers' task was to put out fires, escort refugee families, and track Indians, destroying them savagely and surely.

The conflict between French and British along the Monongahela spread to all of North America and even across the waters to Europe and Asia. Known in the colonies as the "French and Indian war," it was baptized the "Seven Years War" by Europeans. Indian massacres slaughtered hundreds of men, women, and children along the frontier as the French war against civilians was pressed to a bloody and atrocious climax. Some captives were boiled alive in large cauldrons, others were slowly roasted to death, while still others had their skin stripped off their bodies.

To stop the slaughter, frontiersmen built forts to which they could flee when word of an invasion was spread. From these, the colonists dealt powerful blows against larger attacking forces.

Crispus and Paulie saw action at some of these outposts as Rangers in the service of Colonel Washington, who had been given command of the Western portion of Virginia. Taking part in flying columns designed to strike back at Indian camps and French posts, the two friends learned how to track and scalp with expertise, once killing a French Lieutenant and a powerful Ottawa tribe chief in the same engagement. They earned their six dollars a month...when it was paid them.

After one foray against the enemy Crispus and Paulie sat with Drew in a tavern in Winchester, a large, ever growing refugee town on

Virginia's western border. Several years of fighting had made them lean, ruthless frontiersmen who could endure combat and hardship stoically. Hard-drinking and hard-bitten, they had seen life and its cruelties in the years since they had seen Boston last.

"What is there for me in Massachusetts?" Paulie asked in a voice part sad, part bitter. "You have Nora. But all I have is my sister and memories of the man I must call my father. My sister I love greatly, but she is married these many years now and no doubt with many children. My home is the sea, or right here in Virginia."

Drew chuckled and drawled: "You'll never be t' home in Virginney unless you drop that New England tongue ya brang with ya."

"I'm a Massachusetts man," Crispus said, "and I think I will always be."

The cruel war had dragged into its jaws all manner of people. Innocent and dutiful men such as Crispus and Paulie as well as the idler, the drunk, the sadistic killer, the felon. Although drafted into it by ill luck and the machinations of Tom Walter and Hugh White, they had made the best of it. Their terms of service up, they were discharged and told they were free to go.

Washington, nodding gravely at them, said, "You have served your countrymen with honor and great courage. Few men have sacrificed so much time and strength. Now that you are free to go, I have only one more request to make of you. My duties call me to Philadelphia and then to Boston. Will you do me the pleasure of accompanying me as honored veterans?"

Paulie nudged Crispus with his elbow and whispered. "Guess I will always be a Massachusetts' man, too."

Chapter 9

Early February rain fell icily on the little party of horsemen making their way over a frozen stream, their last crossing before reaching Philadelphia. For some miles now, the narrow pathways which passed for roads in America had begun to widen, sometimes to a width of sixteen or twenty feet, more than enough to allow two carts to pass each other without forcing one or both onto the perilous shoulder of the road. This spaciousness was a sign of what the party could expect when they arrived at the Quaker City. The good burghers and private citizens of the town went out of their way to invite travelers to enjoy their trade and hospitality.

The landscape was covered with late winter ice and snow. Trees gave no sign that spring was a mere seven weeks away. Their branches splintered by the weight of ice and the cruel winds of the last few months, they seemed more like dreary fossils than living organisms. Only the pines kept their verdure but their branches, too, had suffered severe buffeting from the harsh winter.

"How long will it take us to reach Philadelphia?" Paulie asked Drew, wiping water from his face with a soggy buckskin sleeve.

"Shouldn't be more 'n two miles now, I'd guess," Drew answered, letting fly a stream of tobacco juice. "It's on a hill so you'll be seein' it in a short while."

The party of a dozen riders plodded on, hooves churning the icy rain into mud, rain running down sodden cloaks and across soaked buckskin leggings.

"Not an inch of me is dry," Paulie said. "We might as well be on the sea again."

Crispus grinned and nodded, adding, "but at least there's no seasickness here."

"You always see the bright side, Crispus, " Drew said. "Don't you ever get down 'bout things?"

Crispus thought a bit and answered: "Sometimes. But not for long. My Mammey had a motto I try to keep: 'Nothin's gonna get me down.'"

"The Good Book don't teach us nothin' like that," Drew observed. "Only Mammies!"

"Oh, the Book teaches that, all right," Crispus said, "whole Book o' Job does. Job was a friend o' God who did nothin' to deserve any punishment but God gave it to him just the same to test his love. What we don't understand we must accept as God's will. Job said: 'I have dealt with great things that I do not understand; things too wonderful for me, which I cannot know.'"

Washington, leading the party, held his hand up, stopping the riders. "We camp here for the night. Enter the city early tomorrow," he ordered.

The men grumbled and shook their heads impatiently. Dismounting, they led their rain-soaked horses to a copse of trees which would provide some meager shelter from the rain. Saddles and packs were removed and riders stroked their mounts' backs with wire brushes, producing an ecstasy of trembling comfort from the animals.

"Half a day too early," Drew growled impatiently, checking his horse's shoes for loose nails and the hooves for stones or twigs which might cause laming. "I'm not so sure I agree with that Book o' yours when it forces travelers ta freeze and drown two miles away from a warm bed all because of a rule against travel on Sunday. If we lived by the Sabbath rule in fightin' with the redskins, you can be sure they'd be sleepin' in the mayor's bed in Philadelphia right this minute."

"Stop yer jabberin', Drew," a corporal ordered good-naturedly, "and start lookin' for dry wood for a fire."

Laughing, Crispus and Drew strode off to find a few pieces of firewood dry enough to burn. They were back in an hour with two armloads of reasonably dry wood which was soon kindled into a smoky blaze. A few lucky shots had meanwhile brought down two big rabbits. Lean in flesh from the harshness of winter, they were still good eating and a welcome relief from the customary diet of johnnycake and dried beef.

After the meager meal the party crawled into their two man canvas sleeping shelters, glad to be out of the pelting rain for a while. The first action taken was to peel off boots and massage life back to their feet. This was a universal ritual practiced by all soldiers in every army, at every time. Despite drenched clothing and limbs numbed from cold, they slept soundly, exhaustion proving stronger than any discomfort.

During the night, the rain stopped and warm air out of the west swept across eastern Pennsylvania. A brief warming trend turned February momentarily into late March, freshening the spirits of the troops as they rose from the still soaking ground.

A quick northward jog brought them to the outskirts of Philadelphia. The sun obliged them by warming their clothing and making their way easy.

The sprawling city was like a great hand fanning from the shores of the Schuylkill River. Houses, scores of them in every stage of construction, were being built in orderly rows along spacious streets fifty feet wide. The main road of Philadelphia, which Colonel

Washington led them down, was well-named Broad Street. At a width of one hundred feet, it was the widest street in North America.

Crispus had spent less than one week in any large American city in his entire life. That was ten years earlier in November 1750, when he made his ill-fated and brief sojourn to Boston. He had seen and learned much in that time, but years of sailing and soldiering had wiped out many memories. But nothing he had observed in Boston prepared him for such a sight as Philadelphia in 1760. With 25,000 people within its borders, the Quaker City was forty percent larger than Boston. And its 3,000 buildings - hundreds of them newly erected to accommodate the huge numbers flooding in - dwarfed Boston in number and quality. By contrast, Boston with all its charm and beauty, was a provincial capital while Philadelphia was a major world city.

The planned, orderly street layout of the larger city contrasted starkly with Boston's densely packed, crazy design. Houses were made of brick, rising two or three stories above well-swept streets. Sidewalks were smooth, clean and bordered by posts connected by chain to protect pedestrians from runaways. Streets were filled with shops of every description, dazzling the eyes. Fifty booksellers made Philadelphia their home and its citizens their customers. Butcher shops, printing firms, warehouses, millinery establishments, tailor shops, and taverns catered to every taste and pocketbook.

At eight o'clock in the morning, the party reached the Governor's palace on Front and Broad Streets where they dismounted to hear the final orders of Colonel Washington.

"I can not say how long my business will detain us here, but a few days or even weeks of idleness will do you no harm. You have all been paid wages up to date and you know where to stable your horses. Find a reputable ordinary and have regular meals." Washington's youthful face was lined with months of weary work and for him there would be little rest. Younger than most of his escort, they still deferred to him as if he were their elder in age as well as superior in rank.

"Avoid fighting," he went on, adding with a smile, "you've had enough of that, surely. And be careful to travel and lodge in pairs or trays. Corporal Eliott will report to me your addresses and will be responsible for you at all times. Good morning to you."

The men cheered and waved their hats, breaking up into small groups to attend to their horses' needs and then to their own. As soldiers, especially with black troops among them, they were automatically directed to "Hell-Town" for their lodgings. A squalid quarter of town, it welcomed any who came with ready money in their wallets and offered a supermarket of human vice as long as cash was paid. One piece of advice from Washington they did observe. They took advantage of the ordinary, a full meal offered at low price at the same time daily. This satisfied their food requirements and built up their strength. For three days, they rested and stayed out of trouble, their only fights being with the eternal bedbugs who attacked them in massed formations whenever they lay down on the cloth-covered straw that passed for mattresses in their cheap lodgings.

Their strength restored, some of the younger soldiers began to look for adventure and mischief. Fighting and wenching, they took up all the time and energy of Corporal Eliott. On the fourth morning, word came that Colonel Washington had completed his mission and they were to report to him by the stone bridge at the foot of North First Street.

"We're off to New York, lads," Eliott said, "as wide awake a town as in all the Colonies."

Blessed by more good days, the party made its way leisurely up the Jersey coast toward the city on the Hudson ninety-five miles away. Owing to heavy flooding caused by the sudden thaw, some of the too few bridges available were washed out and ferry service across swollen rivers and streams proved impossible. The journey therefore took eight days.

Ferry crossings were the principal reasons for the slowness of the travelers. Every ferry had its separate owner with peculiarities of scheduling, tolls and general rules. Some used poles to cross their rafts over, others oars, and still others used ropes strung across the water to pull the boat over. Horses were sometimes hitched to winches, rolling the lines attached to a ferry around a winch head. For longer crossings, such as over the Passaic or the Delaware Rivers, sails were used. Only by the use of sails could the rushing tides of these swift rivers be counterbalanced. The Delaware was a mile wide this part of the year, although during summer months it was at times too shallow for even the flat-bottomed ferries to scull across. Occasionally, the party reached a river, such as the Raritan, where the tidal water level rose and fell drastically throughout the day. Waiting for its twelve foot height to recede, they could cross free of charge when it fell to two feet.

A few times they stayed at inns but these were buggy and vermin-infested, with terrible food and filthy caretakers. It was preferable, then, to hunt the abundant game and eat fresh meat and sleep in tents under the stars.

On a frosty morning in Jersey, the riders spied a wild hog rooting on a sloping hill. Without orders, the entire party stopped and Washington motioned to Drew, the best shot among them, to try for it. The horses stood still, not even snorting, the frost coming from their nostrils like white smoke in the clear air.

The rifle shot felled the hog instantly, filling the woods with echoes. Spurring his horse, Crispus trotted up the slope. A small hole was visible in the animal's head. The bullet had gone cleanly through the brain. Nearby, a half-eaten rattlesnake attested to the hog's appetite.

"Eats snakes," Crispus said, as he threw the kill over his horse's withers.

"Good!" Drew said, "it will be sweet eatin'."

The other men nodded. Already they could taste the fresh pork they were going to have that night. Saliva began to flow at the inside corners of their mouths.

That night, after a day of hard riding, they cooked the hog over a roaring bonfire, Crispus having slaughtered it as he had learned to do on Brown's farm, splitting the best quarters for the evening meal. Crisp brown skin, the hair singed off by the fire and juicy chunks of well-cooked white flesh gave the party delights that took them back to their days growing up, mostly on farms or in small towns surrounded by heavily rural areas.

The days passed quickly; the miles slowly. Long waits, sometimes overnight, held them up if they arrived at rivers late in the afternoon with the ferry on the other side. Then it was either find refuge in a sleazy inn or camp out on high ground. Taking the high ground came

naturally to soldiers and as woodsmen they knew the dangers of flash
floods at any time.

On the seventh day they reached Elizabethtown, New Jersey, which
gave them a fine view of the vast harbor, the finest in North America,
and the busiest by far. Rather than take the ferry from there to Staten
Island or directly to New York, they stayed over in Elizabethtown and
the following morning set off for Newark, the last big town before the
Hudson crossing. Arriving in Newark, Crispus was struck by the broad
streets and pretty churches. While resting before the last leg of their
journey, he met a small boy and shared some of his johnnycake with
him.

"Where do you live?" he asked.

"Above that shop yonder," the boy answered.

"The cordwainer's shop?" Crispus asked.

"Yep," the boy said, "My father's a shoemaker."

A pang struck Crispus, nearly bringing tears to his eyes. A shop and
a small child, and Nora, that was all he longed for.

"Saddle up, you men," Corporal Eliott called. "We want to reach
New York before the east ferry departs."

Spurred by that hope, they trotted off. Crossing both the Passaic
and Hackensack Rivers posed no problems, since these were so heavily
traveled that boatmen had the trip down to a science. In less than ten
minutes, the Passaic ferry cable had drawn them over to the River's
eastern shore. A short ride brought them to the broad Hackensack,
which was crossed by sailboat in half an hour.

For the next two miles, they were slowed to a walking pace by the
marshy terrain. The road was almost invisible at this time of year and
the sudden thaw made a mockery of it. Horses stumbled in foot deep

cavities filled with icy water. By the time they reached the lordly Hudson, about four o'clock in the afternoon, the winter sun was fast seeking its nightly rest.

"Come on," Washington called, cantering forward, "let us catch that ferry before it strands us here."

The troopers raced after their reckless young Colonel, heedless of danger. Ahead a few hundred yards was the sail of the large North River ferry. As they came up to it, they reined in. Some looked glumly at it.

"There's a carriage and four horses already there," Drew said.

"And a dozen folks and their baggage," Paulie said. "There'll never be room for all of us."

"Let's try," Corporal Eliott said, spurring after Washington, who was almost at the ferry slip. The troops clattered after him.

"Come aboard, gentlemen," the ferry boatman said, rubbing his hands at the rich new source of fares. At eight pence a person and double that for horses, he stood to make a good few shillings on this last trip of the day, usually a lean one.

The boat laden with carriage, a dozen horses and two dozen passengers, pushed off from the western shore of the North River. With one man at the wheel and another at the sail, the bulky craft made its way into the rapid Hudson tides. The trip was not a pleasant one. Swells spanked spray over the square cut bow, drenching passengers and frightening the horses.

"Hold onto your horses!" was the boatman's cry.

Each man kept a tight hold on his horse's leather harness, stroking and soothing the animal to keep it calm.

A southeast wind fought against the boat, forcing the crew to tack several times. Large chunks of ice, lately broken up because of the thaw, thudded against the ferry's hull, doing no damage to the boat but frightening horses and passengers alike.

Across the swollen river Crispus could see the outline of three substantial islands: Manhattan, Long Island and Staten Island. Washing their shores were the waters of the majestic bay which swept down into the Atlantic ocean past two narrow straits on either side of Staten Island. Easy to defend, Crispus thought to himself, his years of observing the seaports of Africa and the Pacific giving him some familiarity with coast defenses.

It was dead of night by the time the ferry reached its slip on the southwestern tip of Manhattan, a few hundred yards from the Battery. Even at that, New York was aglow with light and its streets filled with people rushing to complete their daily errands before hurrying home.

The horses were led off the ferry, mounted, and guided eastward to Broadway, thence to the Wall Street for lodging and food. They found an inn, "The George," vacant enough to care for them all, then settled down for the night.

The next morning, Colonel Washington set off for City Hall on his business for Governor Dinwiddie while the party familiarized itself with the quaint Dutch settlement that had become the second largest city in British North America (18,000 population) and its leading trade center.

Walking north from Wall Street, they came to South Street and paused to watch the bustling stevedores wrestle diverse cargoes on and off the dozens of sailing vessels docked along the East River. Bales of fur skins bought from Indians near the upper portions of the Hudson

River Valley were stacked along with cargoes of mahogany from the West Indies waiting reshipment to London. Barrels and casks of flour, butter, meat and rum were being carried aboard vessels bound for the West Indies. Iron and timber and various other trade goods were stacked in neat piles, lining the wharves in expectation of ready carriers filling faraway orders.

All of New York was like its docksides, people and goods never resting, always on the move to the next destination. The citizenry moved rapidly along its littered streets, sticks flailing at all manner of stray dogs.

"These dogs be the worst I've seen in any town I been in," Drew said, pegging a stone at one aggressive hound.

Crispus and Paulie grinned at each other. Paulie said: "In China they have no problem with dogs. They could eat these four legged meals in one night."

"Oh, the Winnebagos, too," said Drew, "they like nothin' better than a boiled puppy to sup on. I've had it with 'em and if ye can forget the look on their little pinched faces as they goes into the pot, they make a tender tasty dish."

Extremes of wealth and poverty struck the newcomers with special meaning in New York. Ladies of great wealth were carried by on curtained litters by uniformed black slaves, while half-dressed immigrant children scurried through the crowds, seeking dockside spoils or even untended purses. Workmen in stained leather breeches with thin overcoats and ancient beaver hats plodded by in worn shoes, brass buckles hanging off. Some carried trays of tools, others had sacks with them, but all seemed to be clutching something.

The noises of wagon wheels, cursing draymen, horses hooves, and shouting children mingled with the hundred tongues of New York in 1760. In addition to English, the language of the conqueror, one could hear guttural Dutch spoken by a quarter of the population, a remembrance of the New Amsterdam days. But French and Spanish, German, Italian, Portuguese, and scores of other languages easily found place in New York.

"I have never seen a city like this," Paulie said with some awe, as they completed their tour late that afternoon.

"It is like no other," Crispus said in agreement.

"What gives it this quality?" Paulie wondered.

Crispus thought a moment, then answered: "It seems to reject nothing and no one. Everyone and everything is welcome."

Drew said, "You may be right, philosopher, but as for me, my stomach tells me it will reject nothing offered to it. Come, the ordinary at "The George" must be almost ready and if we don't get back soon our comrades will do our share of eating for us."

After dinner Colonel Washington called them together to announce his plans.

"My business will be completed by midday tomorrow. Corporal Eliott, in the morning you will take two men to arrange passage for us on the first suitable vessel bound for Boston. Private Drew, you will seek stabling for the horses for a month or more. Be sure you drive good bargains. These New Yorkers...." the Virginian's voice trailed off before the words were spoken. The troops grinned and nodded knowingly. Some had already bargained with the canny, outspoken business people of New York.

After the meeting, Drew suggested to Crispus and Paulie that they venture out to see New York at night.

"You and Paulie go," Crispus said, "I had better stay here."

"Ah." Drew said, "there's no laws 'gainst blacks goin' about at night-only slaves. If ye be with white men, it's all right. Come along, we'll only be in this strange town one more night."

Wearing a muffler around the lower part of his face, and pulling his coonskin cap down over his forehead, Crispus ventured out. He left gun and knives at "The George" and did not even carry flint and steel. So fearful were New Yorkers of fire that they forbade any person of color to carry torches. Less than twenty years before, the so-called "Negro Conspiracy" had occurred in the city. This "plot" had its origins in lies told about blacks robbing and burning in conspiratorial fashion under the influence of a white tavern-keeper. People had fled to remote farming areas such as Harlem to escape the expected violence. But the only violence was against blacks, a score of whom were hanged or burned alive and many others exiled.

The three friends swung up Wall Street and turned south on Broadway, headed for the open common by the Battery. Twilight had just come and street lights were being lit. These, coupled with porch lights of private residences and the glowing window lights of eating places, painted the drab streets with soft cheerful colors. All manner of persons were abroad: sailors off a king's ship, British soldiers, farmers heading back to Brooklyn after disposing of their produce in New York, butcher boys carrying tidy packages of meat to the homes of the affluent and a sprinkling of early evening drunks and prostitutes.

Ahead of them a group of soldiers and merchant seamen were closely congregated in a packed circle. Suddenly a club emerged above the heads and beat down. The circle weakened and widened, sailors and soldiers stepping back to square off against each other. Soon, a general melee was in progress, stones flying, sticks flailing, and even an occasional knife flashing. At half a block's distance Crispus, Drew, and Paulie watched the violent scene. One burly seaman seized a soldier, lifted him high above his head and sent him crashing through a chandlery shop window.

A shrill whistle, followed by running feet, brought the night watch to the fray. Eight husky men, the entire night force of the city, led by a guard captain, trotted in formation toward the rioters. "Cease! Disperse!" the Captain called. The watch fanned out to net the rioters, moving past the three comrades, who squeezed against a building wall. A few officers cast suspicious looks at them but left them alone.

The brawlers, seeing the orderly force they faced, melted away, except for three injured men who lay moaning on the filthy cobbles of the street, deserted by their comrades.

"Get these men to Bridewell!" the Captain ordered. Watchmen roughly raised the unfortunate fellows, all of whom were drunk, and bound them tightly. Half a mile up Broadway, where it intersected with Chatham Row, was the city's infamous prison, called Bridewell.

The commotion over, Paulie said to Drew: "Have you seen enough of New York?"

"For a lifetime," Drew answered, "let's get back to 'The George.'"

The following morning, Corporal Eliott set off with Crispus and Paulie in tow, seeking a Boston-bound ship. Along South Street's pier they found a number of seaworthy crafts, including the two-masted schooner *Sultana*, famed for her speed and beauty.

"Where bound?" Eliott called to the Master, who leaned against the railing sucking his pipe.

The Master, as vital to the ship's welfare as the rudder, removed his pipe, spat, and answered: "Bristol."

Eliott and the others looked crestfallen. It was not often one saw a ship of such grace and it was a shame to be denied the chance to travel on it.

"We be bound for Boston," Eliott said, "do ye know of any ships leaving soon so bound?"

"We be," the Master said, laconically, spitting again. His Scots accent marked him as a Lowlander.

"I thought you said Bristol?" Eliott said.

"That too," the Master said, "but Boston first."

"Have ye room for twelve, including accommodations for my Colonel?" Eliott asked.

"Forty shillings for the lot. Three each for the common 'uns and seven for the gentleman. We sail at the tide." The Master turned away to supervise a party looking for frayed lines and torn sails.

By four in the afternoon, the *Sultana* was tacking northeastward up the East River. Timing the tide to pass Hellgate's treacherous currents, which had been the death of three score ships over the years, the *Sultana* slid gracefully on light winds past Throgs Neck. Only the main sail was set, this being necessary to slow the eighty-five footer as she navigated the dangerous shoals around Execution Rock. Once past this point, there were no more obstacles and all sail was set for the bracing trip through Long Island Sound.

Only three more days, Crispus mused, four at the most, before I see Nora. Ten years without her, he thought, how had he borne it?

Sometimes it had nearly been too much for him. But now, only days away, he could wait.

Swiftly the *Sultana* ate the foamy miles, her light gray and cream hull cutting through the waves with all the familiarity of the ever present porpoises which accompanied them around Cape Cod.

Paulie joined Crispus at the rail. "This is the finest ship we've ever been aboard. It even smells sweet, " he said.

"It has never been slaving or whaling," Crispus remarked.

"One of the crew told me it carries important passengers, mail for the government, and such," Paulie said.

"No stench in that," Crispus added, commenting on the usual condition of ships of his day. Very few escaped ugly smells for the life of the vessel.

"Crispus," Paulie asked earnestly, "what will you do when we reach Boston?"

"Find Nora," Crispus said feelingly.

"And afterwards, for your life?"

"Open a shop, practice my trade, if I can."

"Crispus, we have been friends all our lives. Could I join you in your work?"

"You are white. You can be a gentleman. Why would you want to make shoes?"

Paulie could not speak. To him, Crispus was the finest man he ever knew. The ten years they had spent together were -- despite the dangers and hardships -- the happiest of his life. Now these were drawing to a close, and the day by day association they had enjoyed might be no more.

"Let us be partners, Crispus, partners in a clothing enterprise," Paulie said, for all his maturity, the words still taking on a boyish ring.

"I know little about an enterprise, Paulie, all I know is cordwainin'" Crispus, said wearily. At forty years of age what he sought was a few years of life with Nora, a snug home, and enough to live on.

"Oh, Crispus, you're smarter than all of us, even Hettie. You always were, Momma used to say," Paulie said enthusiastically.

"Let us wait 'till we be home before we make plans," Crispus said.

Through four beautiful days the *Sultana* sailed, meeting no heavy seas or wind. Late in the afternoon of the fourth day they reached Boston's approach channel, known as Nantasket Road, between Gallops and Hospital Island. Curving around Long Island, the *Sultana* raced and beat a deep sea fishing schooner into the Fairway and, with the wind at her back, was soon heading dead toward the Long Wharf.

A mile from the mainland, a cannon went off from a picket ship stationed near Bird Island. The picket, a small sloop, raised the quarantine signal and lowered a boat.

"What is it?" the Master called roughly down to the little row boat, bobbing alongside the *Sultana*'s hull.

"Smallpox," the bosun in charge of the boat answered, "think it came from down the coast, New York or Philadelphia way. Five days of quarantine, then we come aboard."

The *Sultana*'s master clamped his lips together and stamped away. No use to argue. Every port in America did this from time to time.

Five days, Crispus said to himself. After all these years. He saw Colonel Washington approaching.

"What is the delay, Mr. Attucks?" he asked, the form of address indicating his recognition of Crispus' civilian status.

"A quarantine, sir," Crispus answered, "the smallpox."

Washington touched his own pockmarked face, remembering the smallpox attack he had suffered in the West Indies a few years earlier.

"A good thing, too," he said, barely audible, as he strode away.

Each night, Crispus watched the twinkling lights of Boston, wondering which of these might illuminate Nora's home. Or...was she still in Boston? Perhaps she had moved. And Hettie Brown, no, Hettie Pyle, now. She married Richard Pyle, their near neighbor, that fateful day, Crispus recalled. Scenes from the wedding came to him, some of them too painful to remember.

The eternity of five days dragged to a finish and the *Sultana*, having passed Boston's health inspection, was allowed to tie up at the Long Wharf.

Bidding the Colonel, Corporal Eliott, Drew, and the others whom they had accompanied so far goodbye, Crispus and Paulie set out to find Hettie.

The streets they had run through that bleak night a decade earlier seemed cosier now and more sedate. Much had changed in ten years. The earthquake of '55 had done much damage. There were new buildings everywhere. Even the people seemed different - less prosperous. That would be wartime, they thought. Boston was crowded with refugees from the horrible massacres of Western Massachusetts. This was the fruit, they knew, of Braddock's defeat, something they had been fighting against in Virginia for three years.

Free, for the first time in forty years, no longer a fugitive from anything or anyone, Crispus stood on the Long Wharf heedless of the commotion which buzzed around him. No jostling by stevedores or bumping by wheel barrows could bring him back to his surroundings.

He relished the feeling of freedom as it swept over him. Edging away from the crowd, he found a quiet corner and dropped to his knees.

"Lord, I'm free and in Boston. I'll never leave freedom or Boston 'till I die. Thank you, Lord, for this gift."

The artless prayer flowed on to touch his loved ones and his future. Supplication mingled with Thanksgiving as he searched to find an appropriate gift for his Maker.

"I'll make Boston a better place, Lord, somehow I'll make it a better place."

Rising, he found Paulie and they set off through Boston's crooked streets.

"Where do we start looking?" Paulie asked.

"I don't know." Crispus replied. "Should we go to a government office or a magistrate?"

They both shrank from that idea and sought a nearby tavern to ask.

"Pyle?" the tavern owner repeated when asked the name, "Richard Pyle? Can't say I've ever heard of him. Try the Selectmen's Hall on Milk Street two blocks south of here."

They tried several more inns to avoid approaching a government office, but failing that went to Milk Street.

A thin gray-faced clerk on a high stool labored over a huge record book, scratching history across its pages with a goose-quill pen. He looked up furtively, then returned to his journal, his boney fingers working rapidly across the page.

Crispus and Paulie waited...waited... waited. They glanced at each other, grinning, then pushed through the knee high gate that separated office from waiting room. As one, they picked up the old clerk by the elbows, lifted him high and sat him on a batch of records.

"You... you can't do this. Put me down, put me down. If I fall I'll break a leg," he sputtered.

"First, tell us where to look to find the home of Richard Pyle," Paulie said good naturedly.

"Never, never. Help! Help! Murder!"

"Old man, if I climb up there, there will be murder," Crispus said, smiling. "Tell us what we want to know."

Fearing the menace in Crispus' scarred face, the ugly missing teeth, he gave in. "Over there, over there. Let me down and I'll do it."

They took him off his perch and soon had the address, taken from a tax record book.

As they left, Paulie said: "The next time a peaceful citizen asks what is his due, be sure you treat him kindly." He pointed a finger at the trembling clerk and added: "Or...We ... Will... Be ... Back."'

Laughing, they set off for an address on Hanover Street. "That is the way you deal with the government," Paulie said.

"Yes, we must remember that," Crispus answered with a smile.

From Milk Street it was less than a mile across the North End to Hanover. The streets still teemed with people from every country of Europe and Africa as well as from the Atlantic colonies and Canada. No snow covered the ground but the pale sun did little to lift the chill from the city's shady streets.

On the corner of Cold Lane and Hanover, they found Number 3, recorded to the name of Richard and Hettie Pyle.

"Why, it's a tavern," Paulie said, in surprise. "The Green Pine Inn."

"What a fine name," Crispus said. It would be like Hettie, he thought, to pick such a name.

The two men studied the neat, three gabled building. Of wood frame, its shingles were cedar and painted a rich green. White trim outlined the many windows. It was set back from the corner behind a well-kept lattice fence. Two large pines overshadowed the building, adding a sense of permanence to the property. The name was neatly painted on a sign post set in front of the property, a pine tree symbol also painted on it.

Crispus found himself trembling at the prospect of lifting the front door latch. He looked at Paulie, noting that he was pale with nervousness.

Pressing his lips together, he swung the door inward.

A plump woman bent over a basket of bedding, sorting it into piles to be stored in a linen closet along the hallway. She was gray but vigorous, her body obviously used to hard work. In a corner, a crib held a sleeping infant. A small boy knelt in the huge fireplace of the inn's dining room, sweeping ashes into a scuttle.

She looked up, straightened, and knit her brows together. Her eyes narrowed to make out the figures standing in the light of the open doorway, then widened in disbelief and joy.

"Crispus! Paulie!" She cried. "It's you, you're home! Oh, praise God! Praise God!"

Embracing them both, tears streaming down her cheeks, she found it impossible to speak. Tears flowed just as readily from the eyes of the two men, although more effort was made to conceal them.

"Crispus, Paulie, you're back, you're back." Turning to the boy at the fireplace, she called, "Richard, little Richard, come meet your uncle and our dearest friend, Crispus."

The boy put down his brush and came over, wiping his hands on his smudged apron. He gravely extended a hand and offered greetings.

"He is your child, Hettie," Paulie said. "There can be no doubt of that."

Hettie beamed and stroked the boy's hair. "Oh! Crispus, I am forgetting myself. Nora, you wish to see Nora."

"Is she here?" he asked eagerly.

"Yes, of course, she works with us here. I'll call her."

"Wait," Crispus said. "Let us be seated at a table first."

Backs to the kitchen, Paulie and Crispus sat themselves at a window table.

"Nora," Hettie called. "We have guests."

Through the swinging kitchen door came the slim form, the difference being a pronounced limp. Long sleeves upon her arms covered heavy scarring. And worst of all, her once beautiful face had a hideous angry fire scar running from her left ear to her collarbone.

As she approached the table she stopped, studying the broad-shouldered form of the black man seated by the window. Putting her left hand to her face, she fainted dead away.

Chapter 10

Beside the Green Pine Inn was a small wooden building long unused. Behind it was a one story house, snug and neat, with a well-kept roof and many windows.

"These are yours and Nora's, Crispus," Hettie said. "Richard and I decided long ago that if you ever returned to Boston we would share our property with you. Nora has lived in the house these many years."

"I can't take them, Hettie. I did nothing to deserve them," Crispus protested.

"Not so," Richard said. "Brown, God rest his soul, was a poor farmer. Nothing on his farm worked well except you. You earned the buildings, Crispus, and the acre that goes with them for your vegetables."

"And Paulie," Hettie said, turning to her brother, "half of the Green Pine Inn is yours, since we bought it with the money from the sale of the farm."

"Congratulations, Paulie, " Richard said, clapping him on the back. "You are now an innkeeper. That entitles you to rise early, retire late, and work your fingers to the bone in between times." He paused, adding, "and give half the fruits of your honest toil to king, colony, and town."

Nora on his arm, Crispus took a tour of his new estate. In the small building which fronted on Cold Lane, he found a bench with all his tools just as he had kept them when he was a slave on Brown's farm. Knives and awls gleamed brightly at him, wood handles immaculately clean, metal razor sharp and lightly oiled.

He took a skiving knife from its holder and tested it gingerly on his thumb.

"You kept my tools, Nora," he said gently.

Nora looked at him, love and tears glistening in her brown eyes. "I kept everything for you, Crispus, just as I knew you would want it."

The day was declared a holiday, all work ceasing and given over to celebration. They took themselves to the Green Dragon Tavern on Union Street to enjoy the hospitality of a friendly rival. The proprietor, a distant cousin of Richard's, welcomed them warmly and put out the red carpet for them. It was a day of remembering good things and laughing over some of the humorous adventures Crispus and Paulie could tell. Little Richard, his mouth wide with awe, listened raptly to the tales his uncle and his new friend told.

Visions of elephant hunts and whale chases, shipwrecks and pirate attacks filled his boyish soul with fire.

Late in the afternoon, Crispus and Paulie set out for Abel Hayrood's house to visit his widow, Martha. It was a fine day for March, cold and windy, but clear signs were around that winter's worst rigors were spent and better days were near. The black quarter seemed little changed from ten years before. Hole in the wall groggeries, a broken down smithy shop, crazy outbuildings held up by little more than the habit of leaning against each other. Streets, usually filthy in Boston, were unspeakably so in this neighborhood. Pigs and dogs roamed unchecked, rooting at refuse thrown in open sewage trenches and joining in the general raucous symphony of the streets.

The old house was still there, just as run-down as before.

"Crispus!" Martha cried, wiping her hands on her apron. "You're home safe, thank God. Come in, come in both. You are welcome here."

Noting that she did not look behind them, Crispus surmised she knew of Abel's death.

Martha, sensitive to their feelings, anticipated by saying: "My Abel will not be coming, I know. A kind gentleman named Carr told me so a few years ago."

It was the first Crispus and Paulie had heard of William Carr since the impressment at New Bedford.

They had last seen him pelting down the wharf, trying to escape the pursuing soldiers.

"Did, did he leave anything with you?" Paulie asked, hesitantly.

Martha responded guiltily. "I am so glad you are home. It has been a great weight on me. And I fear you will be angry with me for what I have done. I spent some of it."

Crispus and Paulie laughed. "It's yours, Martha, all yours," Crispus said.

"No, I could not keep it all. I did use a little of it. Some of what I thought might be Abel's share."

She raked her small fire to one side of the fireplace, then removed two stones far in the rear. Hooking a battered andiron onto the handle of a metal box, she dragged it out, unlocked it, and poured the gold and silver coins onto the table.

"I only used a few pieces. Just enough to keep them from taking the children and putting them in the Work House. And it's very dangerous to show money around here. There are people who would burn you alive for it."

"There's enough to keep you and the children all your lives," Paulie said. "You must leave here and find better quarters. And this money must be kept in a safe place."

"You mean it really is mine?" Martha asked, her eyes welling up with tears. "Oh bless you, bless you, for the good men you are. Now my children will have something to start life on. I can send them to school. That was always Abel's wish."

They sat at the rude table drinking weak tea while Martha wept uncontrollably, giving in to her grief after years of Stoic postponement.

"Forgive me," she said. "I just couldn't help it. Abel was so good."

"We know," Paulie said. "He was a fine comrade."

Later, exhausted and in better possession of herself, they talked of the week that had led to their exile ten years before.

"Do ye remember Phillis and Mark, Crispus?"

Crispus nodded, the cruel beauty of Martha's cousin recalled to memory.

"She's dead, you know. Her and him, that Mark. Good enough for them, too."

Crispus' eyes widened: "How did it happen?"

"They murdered old Captain Codman, their master. First they tried to kill him by burning the house down. Then they poisoned him, arsenic it was. That was five years ago."

"What happened to them?" Paulie asked.

"Phillis was roasted over a slow fire. It took nine hours for her to die. I took the children. I felt they needed to see what happens to those who do evil, even their own kin."

"And Mark?" Crispus asked, remembering the knave who had turned them over to the authorities that fateful night in the grog shop,

"Hanged 'm on the Common over Cambridge way. Left his body chained and hanging, a feast for crows and gulls," Martha said, bitterly. "T'was he brought my man to his death."

"Not Mark," Crispus said sadly. "I brought Abel to his death. The day I met him...."

"Oh no, Crispus," Martha interrupted, "not you, not you. I did not know you well before you were forced to flee but I knew enough. Abel told me you were the best friend he ever had, even only knowing you a few days."

The evening came and with it a brief humble meal. Before curfew the friends left for Cold Lane, promising to return soon.

"I would like to take her oldest boy to 'prentice," Crispus said to Paulie, "there might be enough work for him."

Paulie said: "Hettie hoped you would take little Richard as apprentice."

Crispus smiled: "I'll take 'em both. Then, I'll spend my time bossin' 'em and readin' my Bible."

The next few weeks were spent in bliss. Nora and Crispus came to know each other as never before. Their love deepened and the feelings they had stored up for ten years heightened and elevated their union spiritually and emotionally. Forgotten was the ugliness of their physical forms.

During the last week of winter, Bostonians began to hope for a balmy April to favor their gardens and their spirits and to reduce the high fuel costs which made winter such a dreadful siege for so many. But March continued cold, requiring still more wood for the stoves, braziers, and fireplaces.

After so many months of acquaintance with fire, some Bostonians grew careless, taking it for granted and ignoring its dangers. Chimneys grew clogged and leather fire buckets got misplaced. Rules requiring homeowners to keep ladders and hooks and dawbing poles to reach roof fires were laxly enforced. Boston's eight fire companies kept alert, however, drilling regularly with their pumpers and hooks.

On the eighteenth of March, Boston's slumber was shattered by an explosion at dock side. Military supplies had ignited and blown up, causing injuries but no fatalities. During the following day, five alarms were sounded and the engines were kept busy day and night.

None of the fires occurred near Hanover Street and Cold Lane. Nor did they require much assistance from the citizenry of Boston. But they put the town on edge.

On the nineteenth, Crispus returned from the Jackson tanning yard on Market Street, his barrow laden with cured hides. His two apprentices rushed to help unload. Young Richard and Abel were willing apprentices, their unskilled hands under Crispus' instruction becoming valuable tools to help them earn their way in life.

"Put those in the shed, hanging," Crispus told them. Wiping his hands, he went through the shop to the house. Nora was stirring a rich stew for the midday meal, which Crispus ate with huge hunks of fresh bread, washing it down with tea.

At night, disaster struck. Bells and cries summoned all to help as fire, started on the thatched roof of the Jackson Tannery, spread to other buildings nearby.

Crispus was aroused by the sharp knocking of the firewarden, commanding all men to report for duty. He strapped on a leather tool belt and put several knives and a hatchet in the loops.

"Bar the door," he cautioned Nora, conscious of the way looters and thugs operated in times of confusion.

As he left, he spied Richard and Paulie hastening out, heavy coats unbuttoned.

"Over there," Richard said, pointing to the yellow glowing sky. "Let us go."

At a quick trot, the men headed east on Hanover Street, cutting across a field along Wings Lane and passing a church on Brattle Square. By the time they reached Devonshire Street, they could feel the fire's heat and smell its noxious vapors.

Two armed fire wardens stopped them: "Halt, you men, where are ye bound?"

"To assist at the fire," Richard answered.

"We have greater need for you at the warehouses on King Street. The looting's started already. We'll join a guard party." the warden said.

Through the hazy darkness they ran, reaching King Street, the broadest street in the town, in a few moments. Handsome residences and business establishments with warehouses bursting with goods posed a ready invitation to Boston's riff-raff. Already, men could be seen coming out of the newly jimmied doors carrying off valuables.

"Stop! Stop!" the fire wardens ordered. The only result of this was to hurry the thieves.

"Come on, charge them!" the wardens ordered.

"Wait a bit, friend. There are a dozen or more of them and only five of us and only you two are armed," Richard said. "Should we not wait for reinforcements?"

"Yes, yes, you're right," the excited warden said.

As if in answer to his remark a ball from a musket whizzed by, striking the stock of his musket and whipping it out of his hands.

"Let us go, quickly," the warden ordered, "or they will be on us."

The party retreated up Shrimpton's Lane and did not pause until it reached Fanueil Hall on Dock Square. The great Hall, its gilded grasshopper weather vane gleaming in the light of the fire, became a rallying place for the citizenry.

Rounding up twenty more men, some with firearms, the wardens led them back to King Street to confront the looters. A fierce battle ensued, made the more horrible by the grotesque shadows of the combatants standing out against the flames. Crispus, Paulie and Richard stayed side by side, Crispus in the center. They had armed themselves with long poles and used these as bayonets against the assailants. As a result they cracked a few heads but suffered no injuries themselves.

No longer needed on King Street, they were sent to join the firefighters on Cornhill. Crispus and Paulie were put on the pumps, pumping water into leather buckets for the firefighters. It was exhausting work, but beer and hard spirits were available to slake their thirst and keep their morale up. As well, selectmen and other leading townspeople brought out food to maintain their strength.

"By God," one of the fire company's captains said, wiping his blackened face with a red handkerchief, "we've got her now. She's near under control."

"No!" a fireman cried, "she's starting up again! Confound that wind!"

A wind from the northwest swept over the dying fires, stroking them with powerful gusts and spreading them across town toward the Bay.

"Water! More water!" was the cry, forcing redoubled efforts from the men at the pumps. Despite the night cold, sweat streamed down grimy faces. The pumping figures, illuminated by the licking flames, created grotesque silhouettes against the buildings behind them.

"Tough work," Paulie grunted.

Crispus smiled, his ragged teeth the only white objects on his face. "Like the whaler, I'd say."

Remembering the years spent over the molten blubber cauldrons, Paulie could only smile. What a life we've had, he thought, not bitterly, but in wonder.

Through the night they worked, hour after exhausting hour, their work undone every minute by the strong winds which whipped the flames from roof to roof, driving families into the night air and making ashes of the treasures they had spent years accumulating. Clustered around the firefighters, the thinly clad victims, some barefoot, watched tearfully as the fire ate up their lives mercilessly. From block to block and home to home, businesses included, it was the same miserable holocaust. Bitterness was on every face, deepening the misery felt. How had it started? Whose act of carelessness or malice had plunged their comfortable lives into emptiness, destroying tools and clothing, furniture, books, and all those special things that humans save as remembrances of their lives.

Morning came, and with it more aid. People from nearby towns, seeing the glow against the sky, offered their engines and their backs to grapple with urban America's most bitter enemy.

Late that day, seated at the main table of the Green Pine Inn, the tired friends exchanged experiences and rested in each other's company.

Richard had gone back to the fire site to check on another building he owned. It was a total loss.

"We are alive, at least," Hettie said. "And no lives were lost in the fire. That much we must thank God for."

"True," Richard said, "but many lost their livelihoods and misery will be our fare for many years to come."

Paulie asked: "How much damage was there?"

"Some three hundred and fifty homes and businesses destroyed. Many others damaged. At least two hundred families burned out. Lost, everything lost," Richard said, wearily.

"Richard, you must not be so despairing," Hettie said. "The Lord will see Boston through and we will do what must be done to succor our neighbors. We must take in at least two families in our spare rooms."

Richard protested: "We have no spare rooms. Our rooms are our stock in trade. If we use them for charity, we lose them for our livelihood."

Hettie shook her head: "That may be, but God's will must be done." This ended Richard's argument. Hettie alone was formidable. Hettie and God were invincible.

In the next few weeks, all up and down the colonies, the news of Boston's distress spread. Boston's leading newspapers, the *Newsletter* and the *Gazette*, so widely read in other cities, satisfied the colonists' hunger for news of the disaster.

Fresh on the heels of this event came, in rapid succession, the loss of Fanueil Hall to fire and another bout with smallpox. Colonial legislatures in New York and other colonies voted assistance; the churches gave generously, as did private individuals. And even Britain's business sectors gave one of their best customers substantial gifts to help it recover.

These tangible symbols of friendship helped raise the spirits of Bostonians somewhat but the crushing blows hurt Boston greatly and it took years to recover.

Crispus' life returned to normal during the remainder of the year 1760, the only interruptions in the placid life being two, one joyful, one sad. In midsummer, Nora became pregnant, the child due the following spring. The last week of the year brought with it news of the death in October of old King George II. A jealous and petty man at times, he had for a third of a century ruled as a moderate and balanced sovereign. His subjects held against him his foreign birth, being one of the Hanover kings, more accustomed to the language and customs of Germany than of England.

Colonies buzzed with speculation about the new king, young George III, the old monarch's grandson. The Green Pine Inn was a political tavern, where ideologues met to test their theories over their tankards. Other public houses catered to rough and ready types, low women and vulgar men who would as soon fight as speak. But at the Green Pine, civility and heated disagreements were the bill-o'-fare.

Crispus enjoyed nothing more after a hard day's work than to sit with his friends at a corner table, nursing a tankard of ale through the evening while he listened to travelers, shipmen, craftsmen and townsmen declaim about the political questions of the day. He wondered as he read the *Gazette*, who a man named Sam Adams might be and what kinship, if any, he might bear to the Adams' family he had met ten years before. He noted, too, the arrival of John Adams, Esq., of Braintree, to Boston to practice law. Other names kept popping up during the '60's: James Otis, John Hancock, Thomas Hutchinson. Slowly, Crispus sorted out their ideas and either rejected them or incorporated them into his philosophy.

Several travelers arrived from London in 1762, stopping at the Inn. They were merchants but well-connected and had much gossip to pass on, chiefly about the new king.

"What sort of man is our young king?" Richard asked, serving the men their tankards while Hettie loaded their plates with roast meats and beans.

The merchants, flattered by good food and pleasant service, loosened their tongues: "He's a queer one, he is," one said, "very fussy and precise."

"Yes," the other agreed, folding a piece of beef over with his knife to spear it with his two-tined fork, "he's fussy, he does not only put date and year on his letters but adds the hour and minute as well." He took the wad of meat and packed his mouth with it, like a charge of powder shoved into a cannon.

"And he likes to be agreed to," the first one said.

"And not interrupted," said the other through his manful chewing. "For a boy of four and twenty, he's mighty set in his ways."

"There's somethin' about him," the first merchant said, trailing off, "can't say what 'tis."

"But 'tis not right," the other said bluntly. "Or *he's* not right."

Seeing the puzzled looks on the faces of his listeners, he pointed his index finger to his head and made a quick circular motion. The others drew back in astonishment.

Richard was quickest to react. As the innkeeper, he was in charge of the place and responsible for its good order. Sharply, he said, "Sir, there'll be none of that here. I presume you speak in jest."

Realizing he had gone too far, and that treason or anti-sedition laws could be invoked against him, the merchant took the cue. "Only in jest, good innkeeper, only in jest."

But the damage was done and all Boston would soon be talking about young George III, who was a little queer or "tetched." These judgements would be based on scores of stories circulated by travelers of all kinds throughout the colonies.

Crispus was interested in the new king as in all political events, even though he hung back in discussions as ill-equipped to comment. He was now a man of business, with two apprentices kept busy all the days. He himself worked far into the night to provide for Nora and the welfare of the child. Money became more important to him than ever before and with it a keen interest in where it went. In the 1760's, England, Massachusetts, and Boston began to lay claim to a greater share of their subjects' and citizens' wealth than ever before. Taxes were high, hateful, and unfairly administered. Time after time, Crispus saw neighbors prosecuted for tax delinquency, some going to jail for it.

Bostonians grew suspicious of any action by any government, local, provincial, or imperial. The war, which still dragged on and would not end until 1763, contributed to the city's woes. High taxes to pay for it, the human sacrifices of their young men, and runaway wartime inflation created misery which no amount of loyalty or patriotism could balance. Crispus found that leather, fuel and metal costs rose far faster than the price of his finished leather products. And taxes, assessed at wartime rates, took a great share of his substance annually.

"How do we deal with this?" he asked Richard one evening while relaxing at the Green Pine.

Richard pulled at his pipe, the white smoke rising slowly to the timbered ceiling where it joined the myriad smells so familiar to tavern frequenters. "You are new to business, Crispus, so what I may say may shock you. We deal with a government that cheats us, lies to us, and conspires against us. How else can we deal with them save in kind? We can not do otherwise and still support our families."

He gestured with his pipe toward his small bar, with its well-stocked bottles and jugs shelved neatly behind it. "Without cheating, that rum and all the other potables would cost five times what they do. I'm glad I'm not in it, but if I was in the rum importing or distilling business instead of the rum-dispensing business, I would surely cheat and bribe and forge the way my friends in it do."

"And," he added, looking slyly at Hettie, busy at the other end of the tavern, "I'd have no Bible scruples about it. An eye for an eye is what I call it, or a shilling for a shilling, if you like."

Paulie joined the table, bringing three tankards of ale.

"Mind, I'm not a rabble rouser, and I wouldn't welcome rebels in my home or tavern," Richard said. "Most of them are just troublemakers."

"But they get results," Paulie argued, "nothing convinces our leaders more than a visit from some of Ebenezer Machintosh's followers, tearing up their potatoes and cabbages."

"Paulie, you are becoming a radical," Hettie said, joining the group at that moment and smiling as she said it.

Crispus said quietly: "I don't hold for Machintosh's violence, but that may be what we all need to do."

"Crispus!" Hettie said in mock astonishment. "Of all people, you advocating mob violence!"

"Sometimes that is the only way justice can be done," Crispus answered.

Steaming plates of food came from the kitchen, carried by Nora and Emily Seiden. Nora was heavy with child while Emily's two year old son Christopher trailed by his mother's side.

Crispus and Paulie rose quickly, taking the heavy bowls from their hands. They brought chairs and all joined in a family feast.

Conversation ranged away from politics and taxes with the coming of the women and touched on crops, local gossip, and childbirth.

Emily Seiden had little to say at table. Dressed simply in a home-made lindsey-woolsey gown with a short light flannel frock over it, Emily sat with her large eyes cast down, concentrating on her little boy, seated quietly on her lap. A German immigrant, Emily was a new widow, her American-born husband, Roger, having been killed in an attack on an Indian camp in Western Massachusetts a few months earlier. The Seidens had been fellow church parishioners with Richard and Hettie so it was natural for them to invite her to live with them as their friend and employee. Not that Emily did not have other offers. Several bachelors and one widower had asked for her hand within a week of Roger Seiden's death, her light blonde hair, large blue eyes, and lissome figure, added to her capacity for hard work, being strong inducements.

Emily chose life with Hettie and Richard because, as Godly people, they could be relied on not to abuse her. She needed time to think, to choose from among few options available to eighteenth century women.

"You're quiet tonight, Emily," Richard said, teasingly.

Blushing, Emily smiled at her friends and answered in a heavy but charming Rhenish accent: "You all know so much...and speak so good."

"If we spoke as well as you look," Paulie said gallantly, "we'd all be poets!"

"Ah ha!" Richard said, winking at Hettie, "our Paulie can turn an elegant phrase to a handsome face."

Hettie added: "A pity he can't go further than that." The group laughed goodnaturedly.

Now it was Paulie's turn to blush. At his age, bachelorhood was very rare in America. He had never felt drawn to anyone before he had met Emily and now he felt himself too late. No, by God, not too late. Roger Seiden was a good man. And the child was honorably come by. He could raise it as his own.

Paulie awoke from his reverie to find everyone staring at him, eyes glistening with laughter.

"Paulie," his sister cried with glee, "we've been talking to you! Where have you been?"

Paulie sat upright and grinned sheepishly. Glancing directly at Emily he said with feeling: "somewhere else...with someone."

"Take care, Paulie," Nora said, "that could be an engagement."

"Yes," Hettie added, "and we're all witnesses."

Paulie faced Emily: "will you...will you become my wife?" he stammered.

Emily's soft eyes disappeared under long lashes. She had made her mind up as soon as she saw him a few months earlier. And this one was *her* choice. After all, she thought, she had known Paulie for months. Her husband Roger she had first met on board the *Bremen* when she had arrived as an indentured servant. He had been one of the many men to swarm aboard holding items of clothing. She had not known what was happening. When he threw the garment on her shoulder, she later learned, he was claiming her as his prize. She went home with him as his servant but in weeks Roger had made her his wife, freeing her from her indentures. He had been kind to her because he was a Godly man, but she had no choice over whether she would work for him as his servant or his wife. And, with Paulie, her baby would now have a father.

She saw Paulie's face in an agony of expectation and smiled: "Yah, Paulie, yah. I vill marry you!"

The tavern exploded into applause and laughter. Richard rushed to the bar, taking down his best brandy while Hettie brought her mother's most treasured glasses to toast the happy occasion.

xxxxxx

Years flew by and families grew. Both Crispus and Paulie settled into their new lives enthusiastically, learning their crafts and accepting the challenges of supporting families in the perilous 1760's. War ended, and peace, which for French and English could never be very long, returned to the colonies.

But peace was expensive, almost as expensive as war. This was especially true after the Treaty of Paris of 1763, which ceded Canada to England, virtually marking France's exit from colonial affairs in North America. Half a continent had been added to Britain's holdings - enough to dazzle any imperialist.

But Bostonians were not imperialists; they were mostly simple folk who wished to live in tranquility and comfort, although the city had its share of firebrands. The events of the last five years of the sixties gave them neither comfort nor peace.

First came the taxes. One of the most hated was the Stamp Tax of 1765, a tax on all kinds of papers and documents. What especially incensed Bostonians was that the tax applied to newspapers, too, interfering with their sacred right to say what they wished in print, however outrageous it might be.

Reaction to the Stamp Act was swift and violent. Even before the act went into effect, Bostonians, among them Ebenezer Machintosh and his supporters, burned down the homes of two officials they believed to be connected with the tax. The tax was repealed.

But Britain had not built its empire by retreating. A few years later came more taxes, this time adding paint and glass to paper and culminating in a tax on tea. The money raised was to be used to support the officials and troops needed to collect it, a sort of welfare fund for government agents, Bostonians believed.

Bostonians boiled over at this, demanding repeal and urging boycott if the laws remained in effect.

Crispus, whose loyalty to Boston was as strong as that of any native born citizen, joined in the opposition when time permitted him to be away from his bench. But this was rare, because, blessed with a son and two twin daughters, he and Nora had little time for leisure. What time they had was spent with Paulie and Emily and their son Christopher Seiden, as well as with Hettie, Richard and their family.

Crispus was a magnet for all the children, attracting to his shop little Christopher, his own son John, and a regular clientele of neighborhood boys, including Samuel Maverick, who desperately wished to join the bigger boys, Richard and Abel, now becoming shoemakers in their own right.

Normally a quiet man, Crispus enjoyed having the boys near and rewarded them with glimpses of some of his adventures. In the brightly lit shop, with sun streaming through small-paned windows and doors, they sat open-mouthed on overturned wooden buckets and heavy fire logs. The rich smells of leather and dyes mingled with odors of clothing and sweat and dead ashes, giving the boys a memory they would never forget. Crispus transported them away to Africa or 'round the Horn. Sometimes he took them to Bible lands where his deep knowledge of Scripture made it possible for him to weave breathless tales of adventure mixed with moral touches deftly applied.

When he made deliveries of his work, Crispus often took the boys along to show them the wider world and familiarize them with Boston's maze of streets. They never stopped asking questions. Late one June day in 1768 they passed the Common, on the way to deliver a pair of boots to a customer at his warehouse on the Long Wharf. On the way a crowd had gathered.

"Crispus," Christopher Seiden asked, "please can we see what they're doing?"

"All right, but we won't go too close," Crispus said, leading the boys to a hilly promontory from which they could overlook the action.

"What are they doing, Father?" John Attucks asked.

"Burning a boat, it seems," Crispus answered.

A mob of sailors and working men had built a great bonfire, the key fuel of which was a sleek little sloop.

Crispus saw his friend William Carr on the outskirts of the crowd. He waved and Carr trotted over, a smile on his face.

"Are these all yours, Crispus?" he said in his soft brogue, gesturing to the half dozen boys. "If so, you've been a busy man since last I saw ye."

Crispus grinned and answered: "Only one of these is mine, and fine twin girls at home."

"And how is your Nora?" Carr asked, and nodded his head in satisfaction when Crispus told him.

"Some things God puts right," Carr observed. "You waited a long time for this."

Crispus, embarrassed by his friend's rare sentimentality, changed the subject, asking the reason for the burning boat.

"'Tis a protest," Carr answered. "John Hancock's sloop *Liberty* was seized by the customs down on his wharf this midday. The seaman were so angry at losing their places they made a great row. They even snatched yonder sloop from the customs men, conveyed it here and have set it on fire, little good though it may do."

"When will all this stop?" Crispus asked.

"When we be free, Crispus," Carr answered vehemently. "We must shake the British off or we'll never taste liberty, nor prosperity neither. Their taxes and policies are drivin' us to ruin. But, you're a readin' man, Crispus, you know that better than I do."

Carr turned back to the fire, now blazing brightly in the gathering dusk. "Ah," he said, "here comes brother Patrick." A slight man left the edges of the crowd and walked toward them.

"Your brother?" Crispus asked William Carr. "I did not know you had one in this country."

"I did not, 'till two years ago when my gentle Patrick joined me." He beckoned to the younger man and called affectionately: "Come over here, Paddy Bawn, and join us."

As Crispus and Patrick shook hands, William said: "These be the two persons in all the world I most regard. The most peaceful men I know yet fiercest in anger."

"We share that thought, too," Patrick said gently, as Crispus nodded his agreement.

Crispus added: "But about the peaceful, William, in your case, we're not sure," as they all laughed.

The youngsters, attracted to the fire, were playing games. Running about the Common, they picked up twigs and sticks and threw them into the fire. Some threw stones at the burning boat's grotesque skeleton.

"I'll be getting these lads home," Crispus said, "or their mothers will be sending search parties for them."

William Carr said: "Let them play a while, Crispus, I have news you should know." Lowering his voice he said: "Your brother is with the garrison here."

Crispus looked surprised: "Tom Walter here?"

"Down from Halifax he is, and saucy as ever. Broke up a tavern over the Neck way last week with some of his rascally friends."

"He'll stay away from the Green Pine," Crispus said, jaws set.

As he shepherded the children home, Crispus reflected on his brother, the plague of his life. Every time he had come close to achieving or holding to something good in his life, Tom had turned up. No, he thought there was no connection. It was not Tom who shaped his life but the will of God. And if it was hard, it was no harder than God served Job.

Still, he thought, as he lifted the latch to enter his front yard, Tom was a bad penny who always turned up at the first sign of trouble. What would it be this time? He felt a chill creep across his back.

xxxxxx

The burning of the customs boat showed how little control British authorities had over the colonists. Every day, one incident or another divided the city. Young children were part of it, too. While adults complained and plotted in taverns and kitchens, their children threw mud and rocks at the hated "lobsterbacks," as British soldiers were called.

Poorly led by junior officers with no experience, many barely more than sixteen year olds whose parents had purchased their officer's commissions, British troops were badly disciplined and trained and often out of control. The troops lacked decent food and lodging and in winter suffered terribly in cold and leaky tents.

Most inhabitants of the city refused to supply or to help prepare meals. Worse than all this discomfort, which, after all, as soldiers they had endured before was the outwardly displayed contempt of the Bostonians. How they hated the Redcoats! "Lobsterback! Lobsterback!" was the cry which followed the troops as they walked the streets and rang through their ears as they sought sleep on ill-smelling and moldy bedding.

For the troops, everyday life was normally dismal but what they suffered from the most were the boys of Boston. Never noted for their discipline and always in motion, these denizens of the streets were the missilemen of the day, flinging anything they could lift at anything in sight. No window was safe within fifty feet of a small boy. Dogs, raccoons, squirrels, cats, and birds were their natural enemies. But soldiers became the newest targets of opportunity. Dangerous enough to be exciting, the troops were still under terrific restraints by their superiors and this made them perfect objects for youngsters.

Harsh punishment awaited any soldier who used excessive force against a youngster in Boston. Adults who saw the heavy troop concentrations in Boston as Parliamentary bullying could not fail to communicate this to their children. Curses muttered against Commodore Samuel Hood's *Romney*, sitting at anchor in Boston Harbor, were translated by children into snowballs thrown at miserable soldiers seeking a little warmth or friendship in Boston.

"Our children are being used by the hotheads," Hettie said, at a meeting one evening in the inn. "They are looking for fun and a little mischief and the rabblerousers use them against the customs men and the soldiers."

"Vat can ve do?" Emily asked, ringing her hands. "Christopher must go play. But it is so dancherous."

"We can't lock them up," Richard said, "though I'd like to 'till this is all over."

"All we can do is warn them to stay away from mobs," Paulie said. "But I doubt t'will do much good."

But Christopher Seiden, Paulie and Abel, and even young John Attucks could not be held back. Their animal spirits drove them into the streets, linking them with older boys and naturally inducing them to their games. Loudest and fiercest of all was young Samuel Maverick, a firebrand in his late teens. Unable to apprentice with Crispus, Maverick alternated between odd jobs in his mother's boardinghouse and occasional work for an ivory carver. Maverick, in-law to the fiery radical Machintosh, was well-known to Boston radicals.

Most of their games were innocent enough, being rough and tumble stuff. But now and then they joined the fringes of the patriot conspirators and the hubbub took on more serious meaning. By the beginning of 1770, the patience of Bostonians was stretched to the breaking point. Unable to attack troops or customs, for fear of reprisals, they turned their attention to their fellow-citizens who consorted with the enemy. One of the worst of these was Albion Robertson. An informer, Robertson was hated for his temper, his vicious tongue, and his outspoken Tory views.

On a cold late February day in 1770 young John Attucks went out to play with Christopher Seiden and some of their friends. They took the wooden sledge Crispus had made for them and went to the Common for sleigh-riding.

The last injunction they had heard was from Nora and Emily, cautioning them to remain away from soldiers and unruly crowds. Obedient children but still boys, they resisted the temptation right up to the moment it arose.

"Remember what they said," John Attucks said to Christopher, before pushing him off for a ride down one of the Common's slopes.

"I'll remember, I'll remember," Christopher said and raced down the hill. All around him on this February 22nd were other children, sleigh-riding, snowballing and frolicking innocently. It was a cold winter day but the bright sunshine dispelled some winter gloom. Only the dreary tents of the troops preserved their drabness.

After an hour's play, the boys stretched out on the snow or perched on rocks to eat their lunch. A few apples appeared and vanished almost immediately, along with bread and meat and some johnnycake.

Across the Common was the great house of John Hancock, one of the most respected men in the Colonies and one of the few wealthy Patriots. His windows overlooked the tent village, their cheery glowing lights at night giving cold comfort to the occupying troops.

Lunch was interrupted by a distant whistle. The boys perked up and scanned the Common for a glimpse of its origin. More whistling and some of the groups began to move off in the direction of the noise. As they started off, John and Christopher looked at each other, remembering their orders but too curious to obey them.

"We'll just go look," Christopher said. John nodded to the older boy, his friend for all his life. Grabbing the sleigh rope, they joined dozens of other youngsters on their way to the commotion on the North End. A dark gray windless sky overhung the city. Snow lay all about and more was expected. Smoke from a thousand fires drifted upward almost vertically and, without a breeze to dissipate it, painted the clouds with its soot. All Boston appeared gray in the late winter dullness.

Passing some shops, they noted where tar had been smeared over windows and coated with feathers, grim reminders by the Patriots that dealing with the British could only result in one thing: violence from the aroused citizenry. Nothing was done to discourage boys from breaking signs and windows or frightening customers away by their antics.

When Christopher and John reached the street where the commotion had started they saw a crowd of several hundred young persons, chiefly boys, ringing a hard core of adults. "Look, there's Samuel Maverick." said John Attucks. "Sam! Sam!"

Slightly built but strong, young Maverick snaked his way to the outskirts of the crowd.

"What is it, Sam?" John asked. "What's goin' on?"

The crowd was a jolly one, just enjoying an altercation between Albion Robertson and one or two Patriot leaders. Robertson was the only person in a temper as he shook a stick at some boys who came too close to the front of his house.

"See that crab yonder," Samuel said, pointing to Albion Robertson. "He's charged with watching his own home and the shop of his friend next door. As a few of us were puttin' little reminders on the shop's windows, he came by to drive us off."

Maverick laughed, gesturing to the crowd which grew by a dozen or two every few minutes. "As you can see, he did not succeed."

In front of Robertson's house, scuffling broke out and soon missiles were sailing through the air. Glass splintered and flew into the interior of the lower floors.

"Hello," Maverick said, squinting to see, "look's like it's gettin' ugly. You two stay here. Your Maws will turn your backsides to lobster red if they ketch you in this crowd."

All gaiety had left the crowd by now as it concentrated its efforts on Albion Robertson's house. Robertson's flinty features glowered from an upper floor and his rasping voice showered them with invective. Bricks and eggs forced him to pull his head in hastily but he soon reappeared with an ugly looking musket.

Far from being intimidated, the crowd laughed at this dramatic turn.

"He's bluffing!" someone called.

"That's Robertson, always half-cocked." another voice called.

"Boom!" the charge went off and the crowd surged backward, a few younger boys giving out panicky screams.

"He shot over our heads," one bystander explained.

"No," another said, "Old Robertson was just bein' himself - all powder and no ball." The crowd enjoyed the joke and flowed back to the house.

By this time, the Robertson house was a splintered wreck. The door had been battered in, all windows smashed, siding cracked and hanging crazily.

John Attucks knew they should not be there, even on the fringes of the crowd as they were. "Please Christopher, let us go! We have to go."

Robertson came to the second floor window and slowly raised the musket to his shoulder. He was speaking but was too far away to be heard.

Christopher looked up to the window, turned to John and said: "You're right. We should go." He turned back, bent over to pick up the sleigh rope.

A thunderous report erupted, echoing through the narrow street. Christopher rose up almost on his toes and bent awkwardly backward, stiff and ungainly. A dozen red spots burst through the white play frock he wore. Christopher had taken the brunt of Robertson's pea shot charge, although some of the shot caused slight and scattered injuries among the crowd.

John rushed to his friend's side and gently eased him down to the snow covered street. "Help us!" he cried, "someone help us!" Tears nearly blinded him, running freely down nose and cheek. The blank curious faces of the mob somehow enraged him. Why did it have to be Christopher? Why his best friend? Why not me? John thought.

Christopher tried to speak, a blood-dyed bubble building on his lips. "Maw," he said. "Maw, I'm sorry." His eyes swung to John and a weak smile etched on his face. With his little remaining strength, he grasped John's hand and held it, squeezing it for comfort.

A few hands lifted him and carried him around the corner to Dr. Kirk's office on Bartly Street. John Attucks refused to part from his best friend's side and the kindly doctor allowed it.

Stripping off the boy's clothing, he examined the wounds. Every shot had accurately and remorselessly torn into Christopher's lungs or stomach. A thin stream of blood coursed out of both sides of his mouth, sure sign that the boy was drowning in his own rising blood. Several more physicians arrived but could do nothing except shake their heads sadly.

Outside the house, the sounds of hell resounded as the large crowd swelled to double and triple its former size. Screams and curses rent the cold air. John asked Dr. Kirk to send for the family and soon Paulie and Emily were at Christopher's bedside. Hettie and Richard were there, too, as were Crispus and Nora. The boy's breathing thickened and labored. For an hour or more, nothing could be heard in the room but the heavy breathing. A knock on the door brought Crispus outside, confronting four Committee men.

"We want to see the boy," one said. "He can tell us that it was Robertson who did it. Then we'll hang him for sure."

Crispus said quietly: "Leave him alone. He has little time left."

"Let us in," the man said. "We want to know his last words. We can use them for the Cause."

Crispus measured the exact distance to the man, then swung his powerful fist once. The fellow sank against his comrades, his shattered jaw sagging weirdly down from his face. The others saw the flame in Crispus' eyes.

"Leave them alone in there," one said. "They've had enough grief for one day."

Christopher died that night, in his mother's arms, but grasping John Attucks' hand. There was no way, in spite of their wishes, that the Patriots would allow them a quiet funeral. It must be a circus, a liturgy, a parade for liberty.

Christopher Seiden had the funeral of a potentate; his burial in Old Granary cemetery on Monday, February 26, 1770, was witnessed by thousands of well-wishers who had never heard of him but viewed him as a victim of British oppression. Afterward, at the Green Pine, which was shuttered for the day, the families gathered to console each other.

Paulie, who had come to love his stepson as his own, was bitter in his grief. "Those Patriot beasts are using my son as if he were a penny broadside for their cause."

Shifting on his bench and bringing his fist down on the table he added: "I hold to the Patriot cause myself but 'twas a rancorous man and a surly mob killed my son and not the British government."

The others nodded, not looking at him to spare him their stares. They sat a while in silence, until Crispus arose. "When will it end?" he sighed, and left the inn.

Boston's British garrison continued to shiver during the last week of February, 1770. They were as sullen and resentful as they were uncomfortable and cold. While the Bostonians felt themselves hemmed in by the troops, it was really the reverse, since five or six hundred widely scattered soldiers could do little to cow a population of Boston's size. To make ends meet between paydays, the troops were reduced to seek work at odd jobs, When they were not met with abuse they usually got curt refusals. At Thomas Symmond's Inn, a few regulars of the Twenty-Ninth were drowning their sorrows. Frustration ate at their spirits, like an acid that burned through all vessels holding it. It painted their hearts with bitterness and their faces with a sour dye. Eager to strike out, yet lacking a target, they sought to console each other with invective and obscenity.

"The boys is the worst," a Welshman complained. "They never stop the stones and ice and curses."

"But it's the elders egg 'em on," a grenadier said. "They teach 'em to hate us and praise 'em for doin' us damage."

"The next 'un crosses me on guard gets the butt o' my rifle across his mouth." This was said fiercely by Private Hugh White.

"Good for you, Hugh!" Tom Walter boomed. "Clap 'em against the brains. That's what teaches 'em best."

Bringing his fist down on the table with a force that made the mugs jump, he added: "God, how I hate these Boston swine.'"

"Why you old black rascal," the Welshman joshed, "you're a Boston man yourself, are ye not?"

"Not me! Not never! I first come from Framingham way," Walter said, adding, "and I don't care much for the west country neither. All o' this New England is rotten and cold to me."

"Ain't you got family here?" the grenadier asked. "I once't heard in Pennsylvania ... "

"A brother, half-brother is better. Cheated me o' my freedom. Hated me. Hates me. Lied to my Commanding Officer and had me broken at the Monongahela. He lives here now, he does, the dog."

The others perked up. Here was a flesh and blood villain they could deal with.

"Lives here in Boston, ye say?" one asked.

"Yes, with his Indian wife and children. He's a cordwainer." A cloud of hatred spread over Walter's face as he muttered: "I shoulda been the cordwainer. Brown promised me. But that wife o' his treated Crispus as a pet, she did."

"Why, let's get the bastard," the Welshman said. "Here's 'un deserves our tender care."

"How?" Walter said. "He's got friends. I know. I watched his house many times. Always boys hangin' 'round his shop. Friends are inn keepers. I hate them too - Hettie and Paulie Brown. Think they're better than other people." Walker's bloodshot eyes swiveled around to scan them all. As if imparting a confidence, he added: "No chance o' settin' fires. There's always someone around."

"I remember those two," White said, rubbing his shoulder, " that coward Brown did for me when we were with Braddock in the fifties. I don't want fires. Who cares for fires, you scoundrelly rascal? It's blood we want, not flames. I know Brown, too, and I've a score to settle with him."

"One villain at a time," the Welshman warned. "First Attucks, then Brown."

White said: "If it's up to me, 'twill be t'other way 'round.'

The dim inn, filled with sweating soldiers and their gaudily painted doxies, grew fetid as smoke and body heat joined cooking odors. Serving women weaved their ways through crowds of soldiers, dodging pinches and balancing heavy trays with metal plates overloaded with plain, ill-prepared food.

Ignoring White, the Welshman asked Tom Walter: "Have you any ideas, Tom? What's his weakness? Drink? Women?

"Brats," Walter answered automatically. "He loves the scum. Always lettin' 'em hang 'round his shop. 'Specially the boys. Never minds when they kick up."

"Can't hate a man fer that," the Welshman observed.

"I could," Hugh White said gruffly. "Brats set me crazy with their snotty noses and snivellin' ways. That's why I left the old lady and joined the corps. Couldn't stand 'em pukin' and cryin'.."

"Luck for the youngsters, I'd say," the grenadier said, causing the group to break into laughter. He returned White's surly stare with one just as insolent.

The Welshman held up his hand. "All right. Enough o' that. How do we give this brother o' yours what he deserves? What's his name?"

Walter told him and the Welshman said: "Fine, we know this Attucks takes kindly ta lads. One of them was buried just a few days ago. That was Christopher somethin' or other."

"Snyder or somethin' like that." White answered.

The Welshman went on: "Maybe he knew the boy, who knows?"

"I know," Walter boomed. "He was Paulie Brown's son, or stepson, I'm not sure."

"And this Attucks is a friend o' Paulie Brown?" the Welshman asked. When Walter nodded, he slapped the table with the flat of his hand. "That's how we get 'im!"

"How?" several voices asked.

"Tell 'im we know who killed his friend's son."

"Everybody knows that. It was Albion Robertson. He's under lock and key fer it, 'waitin' trial," the grenadier said.

"That's what everybody thinks," the Welshman said vehemently. "We'll tell 'im we know otherwise, invite 'im to Symmond's place here and do 'im in. You say he's got children? A son? Good, we'll say his boy's life's in danger."

The grenadier asked: "But what do we do once we get 'im here? Beatin' doesn't seem worth while."

"Press him," the Welshman said flatly.

Broad grins lit up every face, especially Walter's. "Better than beatin', better even than death. Send him to a king's ship forever."

"The townspeople 'ill never stand for it," the grenadier said, "there's strict orders."

"Not against roundin' up deserters," the Welshman said. "Look you there's an amnesty in effect now. Light punishment to all who surrender or are rounded up with no resistance. We'll make up our own detail same night the sailors go and just take him for one of the black deserters and turn 'im over to the Navy. The next sweep is fer Monday, fifth o' March. Some of you come on the detail, too, if you're off duty."

"I'm off duty," the grenadier said.

Walter nodded: "I am, too."

"I'm on watch at the Customs House." White said.

"It's agreed then," the Welshman said, "we'll get Attucks fer a deserter. They'll tickle his back for a bit and treat him to a nice sea breeze. That enough fer ye, old Tom?"

Walter beamed and nodded eagerly.

xxxxxx

A foot of snow, hard packed and dirty, lay over Boston, kept there by frigid days and nights. Occasionally, a fresh layer was piled by nature, adding a temporary and false coat of whiteness which soon succumbed to soot and took on the normal gloomy veneer of colonial winter. No snow or sleet could keep Boston's young indoors, though. They must be out at all hours, ranging through slippery streets, running their ever present sticks along fences or rapping them on walls.

Crispus' shop and the Green Pine were a bit out of town and rarely experienced visits from the youths. Besides, they stood in well with the Patriots now that Christopher had become a martyr. Crispus sat in his shop, puzzling over a letter he held in his hand. By hard work he slowly began to decipher the nearly illegible scrawl. It read:

Crispus Atiks
You have a son. He will die as Christopher Syden done. We know who kilt him. To save your son comme to Symonds eating House on Royal Exchang lain. Tell the inn keeper you are Michael Johnson. He will come get me. Come March 5. 7 in the evening. Come alone.

Signed, Tom Walter, your brother.

A wave of fear crept over Crispus. Anger rose up and nearly overmastered him. A plot to kill young Christopher! But why? What had the lad done? Everyone knew who had killed him. It was Albion Robertson. Or was it? Crispus read the letter again. His brother could never have written this or any other letter, since he was illiterate. That meant that at least one other person was in on whatever Tom was planning. Should he go? He knew he had to if it would help solve Christopher's murder and possibly save John's life.

Crispus sought out Richard Pyle and explained some of the background between himself and Tom Walter.

"I could not go to Paulie," he said. "It's best he be kept out of it. But I want someone to know."

"I agree," Richard said. "I'd like to go with you.."

"No, that might make them suspicious. I must go alone."

On the evening of March 5, Crispus sat at a rough-hewn corner table in Symmond's seedy eating house on Royal Exchange Lane. Feeling out of place among the soldiers, he picked over a plain meal he had ordered for appearance sake and waited for the ancient clock on the sooty mantelpiece to sound seven. He had announced himself to the proprietor as Michael Johnson and had watched while a boy had been dispatched on an errand.

Crispus' journey to the inn, less than a mile from his home, had been the strangest he had ever experienced. Boston seemed to glow with an atmosphere of pent-up tension. At one moment filled with ugly throngs, its streets the next would be eerily and unaccountably empty.

At ten past seven the front door swung open and Tom Walter strode in, his eyes searching every corner for his brother. Crispus lifted his head and stared at the big soldier. Taller than most, he was a powerful man, despite signs of dissipation on his face. Ignoring several troopers who waved at him from their tables, he beckoned Crispus to follow him outside. Crispus left his meal with no regret and joined Tom on the slippery walk in front of Symmond's place. Before his eyes could adjust to the darkness of the narrow lane, Crispus felt himself drawn along a wall and into a quiet back alley.

As his vision adapted to the darkness, he saw two soldiers flanking Tom, both armed with fixed bayonets.

"Are you named Michael Johnson?" a Welsh accent asked. Crispus looked at Tom, who nodded reassuringly.

That was the code. Was this a trap or would he learn Christopher's true murderer and perhaps prevent harm from coming to John?

"I am Michael Johnson," he said quietly, slipping his hand unobtrusively beneath his coat. "What information do you have for me?"

"Only this," the Welshman said: "I arrest you in the name of the King, for desertion from His Majesty's ship *Romney*, now in Boston Harbor!"

Almost before the words were out, Crispus had a razor sharp skiving knife out and deftly swept it across the Welshman's forehead, a fraction of an inch below his pulled down beaver hat and just above his eyebrows. The razor sharp knife cut so cleanly that the sundered skin seemed untouched. Then a sheet of blood burst from the wound.

"I'm blind! I'm blind!" the Welshman cried, clutching at his face, his rifle tumbling to the street.

Crispus brought his hand back to slash at Tom but the third soldier struck him from behind with the butt of his musket, the blow glancing off his shoulder but still powerful enough to drive him to his knees. Tom jabbed at Crispus with his bayonet but Crispus grabbed the weapon and pulled the heavier man off balance. Again, another blow from the grenadier's musket felled Crispus, sending him sprawling on his stomach in the gutter. His knife had slipped away and Crispus only had time to see the two soldiers above him, their musket butts raised. Down these came, bruising Crispus' legs.

The soldiers were so eager to harm their victim, they failed to see a stealthy figure behind them. A pole several inches thick knocked the grenadier senseless.

Tom Walter turned in fear: "Paulie! Don't!"

Paulie drove his staff into Tom's stomach, doubling him over. He dropped it and knelt by Crispus.

"Are you all right, friend?"

"Just bruises," Crispus said. "Why did you come? I asked Richard..."

"He was worried, we told me."

A figure loomed above them, bayonet in hand.

"Paulie! Watch out!" Crispus cried, as Tom lunged. With all his strength, Crispus pushed Paulie out of the way and struck out with both feet, deflecting the musket and tripping Tom at the same time.

Both men pinned Tom to the slushy ground.

"What you gonna do, Crispus? I'm your brother! Can't kill a brother!"

Recovering his knife, Crispus placed the point on Tom's neck. "One shout from you and I'll slit your throat. Tell us who murdered the boy and who's threatenin' my son."

When Tom hesitated, Crispus pricked him lightly, a thin trickle of blood streaming down Tom's neck.

"I'll tell! I'll tell! It was White, Hugh White. He done it. He planned it."

Crispus dug the knife deeper. "Why? Why?"

Thinking fast, Tom said: "He hates Paulie and he wants Paulie's woman, the yellow haired one. That's why."

Crispus and Paulie exchanged glances. "Where is White now?" Paulie demanded.

"On...on guard duty on King Street. The Custom's house."

Quickly, they trussed up the three soldiers, gagged them and hid them in the dark alley.

"Hurry," Paulie urged.

"Wait, Paulie, my brother is a terrible liar. We don't know White, do we?"

"We've got to find out. It's too late to save my son but it might not be too late to save yours."

As they reached King Street, they found a huge crowd surrounding the Custom's House entrance. Half a dozen soldiers and officers were there, threatened by an ugly mob. Ice and snowballs whizzed through the air and curses beat at the ears of the restless troops.

Crispus and Paulie edged through the crowd, shouldering and pushing to the front. Crispus spotted Samuel Maverick.

"Which one is White, Hugh White?"

Maverick pointed to a big soldier standing in front of him.

"There's the bloody lobsterback," Maverick said, spitting in the snow in front of White. "He's scared out of his wits now we're all here. Not like he was an hour ago when he was beatin' an innocent boy."

"That's right," another voice said, "could've killed the boy, too."

The officer in charge of the detail fingered his sword nervously while he talked to several well-dressed Bostonians.

Paulie pushed toward White: "What do you know about my son's murder?"

White brought his bayonet down to the level of Paulie's chest. "Push off, you scum, or I'll put some light through ya."

"No! You tell me what you know about my son!"

Crispus pulled at his elbow. "We'll learn nothin' here. We'll get White another day."

"But the soldiers we beat and tied up," Paulie argued. "We'll be arrested."

"No," Crispus said, "it was a private grudge they were tryin' to settle with me. We'll hear no more of it."

"I know my brother. He's too cowardly to try more now."

A great shout went up and both men spun around. The crowd shrank back as the troops presented their muskets to the firing position. Crispus watched as White swung his piece directly at Paulie.

The look in White's eyes as he sighted Brown Bess along its smooth muzzle was cruel and sure. There seemed no doubt in that unwavering glint of the man's intent. His finger squeezed evenly, waiting for the order.

Paulie's skin prickled, his blood running cold.

He and Crispus had faced guns many times before but never had they seemed so close nor made them feel so vulnerable.

With the other guards, Pvt. White had formally presented his piece on Captain Preston's order, dipping his knee and shoving the full-cocked weapon toward the King Street throng. The drill was an awkward message.

The ugly mob, far from being intimidated, grew more furious.

"Cutthroats!" came the cry.

"Bloody lobsterbacks!" rang up and down the line.

More strident voices shouted: "Fire! You bloodthirsty hyenas!"

Except for the human tumult, the night was calm. Soft snowflakes fell through the windless night, randomly spreading a coat of clean cold whiteness on the drab ice-encrusted streets. It was a clear cold evening, typical of March in Boston. Spring was almost at hand, yet winter would not let go. Lights from the windows of homes and shops painted golden patterns in the snow.

The quiet night served as a passive backdrop to the human drama then unfolding in the street before the Customs House. The soldiers stood, like red-uniformed toys, their muskets presented. Captain Preston, the hapless officer in charge, looked distraught. Nerves stretched to the limit, he seemed about to disintegrate. Ice chunks and snowballs flew from the crowd, a few finding their mark upon bright red tunics.

The order to fire and the trigger movement occurred simultaneously. In that second Crispus jostled Paulie off balance, his own husky frame interposing itself between his friend and the murderous ball.

A pain --- like an enormous leaden fist --- crushed into his chest, the slug flying true to its mark. It parted two ribs and grazed a lung, plowing straightway through the aorta. No reflection, no memory came to Crispus' mind. Just the final message to his brain. Only a feeling, a glow of tranquility, came to him as he sank down to the icy base of King Street.

"Crispus!" The word came from miles away, echoing down the chambers of time. From another world. The last sensation was of damp warmth inside his winter shirt. And he was gone.

After earning his Ph.D in History from Columbia University, Dr. Arthur J. Hughes became a professor at St. Francis College, where he has taught for many years. He is the author of four other works on historical and political subjects. He and his wife Irene have six children and live in Queens, New York.

Printed in the United States
36976LVS00005B/235-285

9 780967 828664